GO, *Lovely Rose*

GO, *Lovely Rose*

BY JEAN POTTS

Charles Scribner's Sons New York **1954**

TO: *My Favorite Sister*

GO, *Lovely Rose*

I

"Dead as they come," said the old doctor zestfully. "Don't know as I ever saw a deader woman. That's the only kind of patients I get any more, is the dead ones. Now that I'm retired, they don't trust me with anybody's still kicking." He cackled at his own joke.

"Who?" repeated young Dr. Craig. "You haven't told me who yet." He didn't like to push the old man (nearly eighty, and spry as a cricket, though names were apt to slip his mind) but at the same time, he felt, it would be nice to know the essential facts. He had come back from a confinement case in the country to find the old doctor waiting for him, all agog with his news. It had clearly been an exciting afternoon; as the old man said, he was seldom called out any more, except in emergencies.

"I haven't? Why yes, it was—" The quavery voice faltered to a stop. "Oh rats. Right on the tip of my tongue. Know it as well as I know my own. Why, yes, Mrs.—you know, she's been keeping house for the Buckmasters for years—"

"Oh," said Dr. Craig. "Mrs. Henshaw."

They smiled at each other in relief.

"Henshaw. Of course. There she was, at the foot of the cellar stairs, where they'd found her, with her neck broken. When they couldn't get you they called me. Yes sir, the old back number comes in handy once in a while. Plain case of accident, but I told them to get the sheriff up there, and the coroner. Make it official. They agreed with me." The old doctor clasped his hands in front of his round little stomach and nodded with satisfaction.

"It's all settled, then," said Dr. Craig. "Fine." He stretched out his long legs and prepared, good-humoredly, to listen to the story all over again. Tough luck for Mrs. Henshaw. But one thing about it, it had brightened the old doctor's afternoon; it would keep him in conversation for weeks to come.

II

"She's dead, Rachel. Dead as a mackerel. Fell down the cellar steps and broke her neck."

The words seemed to leap at her out of the telephone. Her brother's voice—blurred at first on account of the poor connection; the long-distance operator couldn't understand it—was all at once abnormally loud and clear.

"Dead, Hartley? Dead?" Rachel latched on to the word as if it were a brand-new one, never heard before. It would be a good idea, she decided, to sit down.

She didn't ask who. No need to. Mrs. Henshaw, she thought. Mrs. Henshaw. Dead as a mackerel. How many times, throughout their blighted childhood, had she and Hartley prayed for this? Please, God, make Mrs. Henshaw die. Make Papa get a new housekeeper. Please, God.

It had come true at last. Rachel's mind sped off like an arrow released. She and Hartley could sell the house in Coreyville now; it would pay for Hartley's college; and with her share she could— In a split-second vision she saw herself in mink, or maybe sables, in something filmy and impossibly expensive, floating down a staircase on the arm of Greg Larrimore, while an audience composed exclusively of glossy blondes watched and yearned. . . .

Childish. But she couldn't help it; it was so dismal to feel out-classed the way she did at the parties Greg sometimes took her to, and it distorted her judgment about Greg himself, and—

"It was an accident. That's what they decided. An accident," Hartley was saying, and the old taint of frightened stealth in his voice did something queer to Rachel. It jerked her back to another place, another self. For a moment she stopped being the independent young secretary with an apartment of her own in Chicago and became instead that other Rachel, that long-legged, wistful-eyed child who hadn't escaped from Mrs. Henshaw.

Nonsense. There was her own pleasant living room right in front of her, real as anything. Certainly she had escaped. So had Papa, by his own death. Hartley—But even Hartley was free now, with Mrs. Henshaw dead.

"When did it happen, Hartley? How did it happen?"

The line went blurry again. Hartley's voice took on the forlorn quality of a scratchy phonograph record. He was singing: " 'Who knows how or when?' "

Hartley," said Rachel sharply. She remembered what Myra Graves had written in her faithful Christmas letter: You might as well know it. I'm worried about that boy, the way he's been drinking lately. "Hartley, are you drunk?"

"Not me. Never more sober in my life."

"Well, then, tell me what happened."

"I don't know. That's just it, Rachel. I can't remember—" He broke off, and the pause seemed endless. Then he went on quite matter-of-factly. "Myra Graves and I found her. At the bottom of the cellar steps. She'd been there quite a while, I guess. Myra wanted to borrow a cup of sugar. That's why she came over."

"I see," said Rachel. She felt curiously out of breath. "Look, Hartley, why don't I hop on a train and come down tomorrow—"

"Don't be silly. Why should you? Don't be silly. You weren't even here when it happened. You couldn't—" Again the breaking off, the endless pause. "That's not why I called you. There's nothing you can do. It's all been done. No reason for you to get mixed up in it."

"What do you mean, mixed up in it? Hartley—" She couldn't seem to get *hold* of anything. "Hartley, is something wrong?"

"Not a thing. What could be righter? She's dead at last, all's right with the world. Remember how we used to pray? Remember—" There was such a long silence, this time, that Rachel thought the line must have gone completely dead. But Hartley's voice wavered across the miles to her once more. "I can't remember. Isn't that funny? I can't remember." Then came a click and a hum. He had hung up.

She sat still, in obscure alarm. And urgency: she ought to be doing something. Like what? Call Hartley back, insist on extracting some sense out of him? No use. There must be someone (not Greg Larrimore; oh, most definitely not Greg) she could turn to for advice. Nobody in Chicago could be expected to understand. It had to be somebody in Coreyville.

She hesitated between the two possibilities—Hugh Bovard and Myra Graves. Both of them would know what, if anything, was wrong; for that matter, everybody in Coreyville would know. But these were the two she could trust. Hugh had been Papa's best friend; for Rachel the atmosphere of warmth and reassurance that had surrounded Papa still clung to Hugh. He would tell her the truth. If it was something serious he would know what to do. If it wasn't serious (and mightn't it, after all, be just her imagination working overtime?) Hugh would—well, he might laugh at her. Not Myra, who had lived next-door for as far back as Rachel could remember. Myra would say, in her comfortable, cheery voice, I don't blame you a bit, I know exactly how you feel. . . .

Myra's first words, after she had recovered from the fluster of a long-distance call, made Rachel's heart sink. "Rachel honey, I was just debating if I'd ought to call you or not. Hartley told you, I guess? About Mrs. Henshaw?"

"Yes." The question burst out of her. "Myra, what's wrong? Tell me what's wrong."

Immediately Myra's tone became guarded, and Rachel remembered about the party line. "Nothing particular wrong that I know of. It was an accident. Hartley told you that, didn't he? It was an accident."

"But he sounded so—"

"He's a little upset," said Myra quickly. "Only natural, finding her the way we did, and all. You know Hartley. Kind of high-strung."

"He kept saying he can't remember. What did he mean, he can't remember?"

"Oh, that." There was an uneasy silence. "Well. Well, you know how Coreyville is. The least little thing, and people start talking. . . ."

The telephone in Rachel's hand felt slippery. People were talking. It was an accident, but people were talking. "Myra. Tell me straight out. Should I come home?"

Myra's answer came in a rush, and to Rachel nothing could have been a more powerful endorsement of her own rising panic. "Yes. Yes, I think maybe you better come."

III

She had told Myra she would catch the afternoon train. Instead, she made the morning one, so of course no one met her. She was the only passenger for Coreyville, and as she stepped off the train and saw the platform deserted in the failing light of winter afternoon, a wave of lonesomeness washed over her. Al-

ready the train was moving off, whistling around the bend in forlorn dignity. Across the tracks Coreyville's Main Street, wider,
emptier than she remembered from seven years ago, straggled off
up the hill, with the court house at the top.

She picked up her bag, and a voice behind her said, "Was you
expecting to be met? There's a phone inside, if you wanted to
call."

The depot agent, Mr. Garrett, was standing there, peering at
her from under his green eyeshade. His alert, wrinkled little face
brightened. "Now wait a minute, I ought to know you, don't tell
me. . . . Why sure. You're Doc Buckmaster's girl. Rachel Buckmaster. Sure. Know you any place." He shook her hand with a
triumphant flourish. "Yessir. Why, you was nothing but a kid
when you left. Fleshed up a little since then, ain't you? I was
just saying to the wife the other day, says, 'Wonder whatever
became of Rachel Buckmaster?' What put me in mind of it, was
Old Lady Henshaw passing on."

Was there more than just friendly curiosity in his manner?
A kind of avid speculation, perhaps? Rachel shifted from one
foot to the other.

"A terrible thing, to go like that." Mr. Garrett shook his head
with mournful relish. "All alone in the house when it happened,
far as anybody knows. Laid there quite a spell, I guess, before
they found her. Yes. Well, it comes to us all. Let's see, you ain't
been back to Coreyville since your Papa passed away, I guess,
and that's been—"

"Three years," said Rachel, "and I didn't come back then."
(It had been the summer of her Canadian vacation; the message
hadn't reached her in time. Which, perhaps, was just as well. It
would have seemed too strange to see Papa no longer in a hurry,
minus his big booming laugh and genial doctor's manner.)

"That's right," said Mr. Garrett, "you didn't get back then,
did you? Slipped my mind there for a minute." She could see

the wheels going round in his head: Seems funny, she couldn't make it for her Papa's funeral, but here she is for Old Lady Henshaw's. Right johnny on the spot. Can't tell me there was any love lost between them, either, even if the old lady was all the mother Rachel can remember. Hated each other like poison. Yet here she is. Seems funny. Seems funny.

"Too bad Hartley ain't here to meet you," Mr. Garrett was beginning; then, as his attention focused on something behind Rachel, his voice rose to a holler. "Hey, Doc! Hey! Hold on a minute! There's Doc Craig," he explained, indicating a rather battered coupe that was bumping its way across the tracks toward Main Street. "He'll give you a ride home. It'll beat walking."

Rachel's protests got lost in the shuffle. Dr. Craig—a stranger to her; he had taken over Papa's practice three years ago—turned out to be youngish and on the homely side. He said he was pleased to meet her, and hop right in, he'd be glad to give her a lift.

He wasn't like Mr. Garrett. He didn't chatter. By the time they were past Main Street Rachel was beginning to develop forebodings about his very lack of conversation. Might Dr. Craig's silence be as significant, in its way, as Mr. Garrett's talkativeness? She stole a glance at him, and found that he was giving her a pretty thorough inspection. He grinned, cool as you please.

"How does the old home town look to you?" He tossed it out with an air of mock-politeness, as though, having sized her up as the prim type, he had no objection to playing along with the small talk she probably expected. During the remaining three blocks they agreed on the weather (raw, even for February) and Chicago (Dr. Craig had taken his training there; he liked it too). Rachel relaxed. He might be a cool customer, this Dr. Craig, but even Rachel's hyper-sensitive imagination could find no cause for alarm in his manner. Then they stopped in front of the house, and his face (he had a long, humorous upper lip) grew suddenly serious.

"Let me know if there's anything I can do for you," he said, and she knew that he felt sorry for her, he thought she was going to need help.

"Thank you very much." She whisked out of the car before he could help her. "Don't bother, please. I can manage. My bag isn't heavy." She slammed the car door shut and faced the house.

It was just the same. Tall and gray, with an angular bay window and two separate front porches, neither of them big enough for the rocking chair comfort of other Coreyville porches. A short distance from it, set back in the yard, and half-hidden by the trees, sat the little square box of a building that had been Papa's office. The name must still be there, in flowery letters on the dust-thick window. G. F. Buckmaster, M.D. And here was the front door, with its frosted glass picture of something like a crane, standing on one reedy leg. And the door bell, which, under her hand, gave off a husky wheeze, like an old man's voice. What if Hartley was too drunk to hear, or not there at all? What if the door was locked and she couldn't get in?

Quick steps in the hall; the red glass chandelier bloomed into light; the something-like-a-crane quaked on his one leg as the door was pulled open.

"Myra!" Rachel reached for the solid comfort of Myra Graves —the round face framed in frizzy graying hair, the plump shoulder, the cheerful voice exclaiming that for goodness' sake, we didn't expect you *yet*, here child, you must be half-froze, come on in out of the cold. Myra was here, just as she had always been, in Rachel's moments of extremity. Everything was going to be all right: Hartley would be sober, the abject child that had been Rachel would dwindle and vanish into the past, Mrs. Henshaw's spell was broken forever. . . .

Myra's lively chatter, as she bustled down the hall, seemed indeed to place a check mark beside each item in Rachel's mind. "Now you mustn't worry about Hartley, it was the shock, finding her the way we did, that's all, just the shock. . . . Rachel honey, you do look elegant! I always knew you'd turn out good looking, once you got past the gawky stage, and all I wish is *she* could see you in that outfit. . . . Not very nice to say, I guess, but you know I never had much use for her alive, and no sense changing my tune now she's gone. Funeral's all set for tomorrow. Well, no use dragging it out, she hadn't any folks except the one sister, and she's not coming—at least we didn't get any answer to the wire we sent her. . . ."

The reassuring tide of monologue swept Rachel into the library on a wave of confidence.

She didn't see Hartley right away. The library, the room itself, overwhelmed her. Nothing was changed, it seemed, since the days when Mrs. Henshaw used to shut Hartley and her up here with what she called their traps. The carpet still blossomed with its pattern of unlikely, faded roses; the jolly little fire (that was different; Mrs. Henshaw never would have permitted that) flickered over the heavy chairs and the black leather couch with its green "throw" that was always slipping off. Papa's traps had been consigned to the library too, and here they still were—his medical books jammed into the book cases all along one wall, and on the mantel piece his pipes and the cribbage board inlaid with mother-of-pearl.

All familiar, so familiar that Rachel half-expected Mrs. Henshaw to thrust her ill-tempered fox-face, with its wonderful crown of red hair, in at the door and scold: "How many times do I have to tell you young ones you're not to make such a mess? There, Hartley, you've got those dratted paints all over the rug! I told the Doctor that's what would happen! Rachel—Rachel, you hear me?—you pick up those doll clothes, every scrap, this minute!"

What happened instead was that Hartley—with Queenie, his old brown water spaniel, lumbering along behind—got out of his chair by the fire and crossed the room to meet her. It was three years since they had seen each other, three years since Hartley came to Chicago, right after Papa died, and Rachel had been so sure he was going to make good his escape from Mrs. Henshaw and stay. Why hadn't he listened to her arguments? Why, after that telephone call, had he insisted on coming back here?

How tall he looked! Well, he was nineteen years old, grown up. But he still moved in the uncertain, almost apologetic way that never failed to fill Rachel with a kind of angry sorrow.

"Hey there, Rachel," he said, and it was plain that he was occupied with the embarrassing question of whether or not he was expected to kiss her. They ended by shaking hands awkwardly.

The disconcerting thing about Hartley's face, Rachel found, was that it was a good deal like her own. Here were the large hazel eyes, the high forehead, the cleft chin—and yet all subtly distorted, so that Rachel felt as if she were looking at her own reflection in a pool of not quite still water.

A nightmare reflection, really, for Hartley's eyes held an expression shocking in its intensity. Rachel had no word for it. She saw it. And knew at once that everything was not going to be all right, that the assurance she had drawn from Myra's chatter was hollow, her own confidence fatuous.

To hide her panic, she turned to Queenie, who was thumping her tail in sedate welcome. "Queenie, you fat old frump," she cried—too gaily, perhaps—"What have you got to say for yourself?"

It seemed, indeed, that Queenie might be on the point of speech. Her faithful golden eyes gazed into Rachel's earnestly; the tight brown curls on her sides heaved a little. In a way, Queenie was a symbol, living proof of the fact that on one occasion Papa had defied Mrs. Henshaw. Hartley's going to have a dog, Papa had said; that's all there is to it. No boy of mine is going to be raised without a dog. And who, thought Rachel, would know more about Hartley than Queenie, with her lifetime of pattering at his heels in single-minded devotion? Tell me what's wrong, Rachel wanted to say, tell me. . . .

But Queenie did not talk. She did not quite talk.

Myra did. And Hartley ground out a disconnected assortment of pleasantries in the nervous style of a schoolboy reciting. There was much flurry over hanging up Rachel's coat, settling her beside the fire. Silence, apparently, must not be permitted to fall, not for a moment. Rachel found herself chattering too.

And just when it looked as though, in spite of all their efforts, there was going to be a lull in the conversation, they were saved by Bix Bovard.

Bix didn't bother with the doorbell. She just came bursting in, breathless, as wispy as ever, and looking somehow pathetic in a scuffed leather jacket that Rachel recognized as having once belonged to Hartley. (So teen-agers still did that, thought Rachel, feeling very old indeed. It was still considered the height of something or other to get yourself up in your boy friend's clothes, and the nearer the shoulder seams came to your elbows the more real class.)

"Hey there, Gruesome," said Hartley.

"Hi." For a moment a radiance, almost a blush, suffused Bix's face. It made her nearly pretty. Her eyes were, in fact, beautiful, and always had been. Luminous, gray eyes. But her lipstick was smeared on with a fine disregard for the natural boundaries of her mouth. And her hair! It was straight, light-brown in color, and Bix had apparently cut it herself. In a poor light. With a dull pair of scissors.

"Gee, Rachel, you look stunning!" She thrust out a rather grubby hand. "I'd never have known you. I mean—"

"Oh, brother," said Hartley. "The original good will ambassador!"

Everybody laughed, and Rachel said Bix had changed too, quite grown up.

"Just as skinny, though, isn't she?" Myra Graves ran her hand affectionately over Bix's butchered hair. "I declare, doesn't your mother ever give you a square meal?"

"Of course she doesn't. My mother wouldn't give me the time of day." Bix tossed off this bleak bit of truth nonchalantly, as if she couldn't possibly care less. She lit a cigarette and grinned at Myra. "For God's sake don't look so wounded, Myra. Lots of mothers and daughters are—incompactible. I mean incompatible."

"I guess I'm old-fashioned." Myra sighed as she picked up her coat and started buttoning herself into it. But it was impossible for her to stay gloomy for more than a minute. "Now Rachel, anything I can do, you let me know. I've got the church supper on my hands tonight, or I'd have you over. But I brought Hartley some ham and baked beans, so you won't have to worry about cooking. And I'll run over, first thing in the morning."

Rachel snatched the chance and saw her to the door. "What's it all about, Myra?" she whispered. "What's the matter with Hartley?"

"Well." Myra fiddled with her coat collar. "I don't like to say anything, till you've had a chance to talk to Hartley alone—Oh, pshaw! I'll tell you what I know, and all I hope is you can straighten him out and get him to keep his mouth shut."

"Keep his mouth shut! So far that's all he's done, with me."

"Not with other people," said Myra darkly. "He's been talking foolish all over town—that's what started all the gossip. I vow, I could switch him good, the way he's been acting. Nobody saw a thing out of the way at first. We found her, Hartley and me, plain case of accident, she'd fallen and broken her neck. But then he got this notion. Can't remember, he claims, where he was or what he was doing that afternoon—"

They stared at each other helplessly.

"And the trouble is," Myra went on, "seems like nobody else knows, either. He wasn't at Business College—not that that's anything unusual, he don't go to his classes but about half the time. He wasn't at the pool hall or any of the other places where he hangs out, down town. Nobody saw hide nor hair of him, all that afternoon."

"But that's ridiculous." Rachel grasped at a straw that she would ordinarily have closed her eyes to. "He was just out drinking some place. Got tight and blanked out. It happens all the time."

"He didn't act drunk," said Myra slowly. "When I ran over to borrow a cup of sugar and we found her, I mean. He seemed all right. It was the shock, that's what I think. The shock. Oh Rachel, she was an awful sight! Her neck all out of kilter. . . ." Myra's voice sank to a haunted whisper. Then she took a deep breath and went on. "Well, anyway. He's been asking all over town, trying to figure out where he was, and naturally it's caused a little talk. You know how Coreyville is."

Yes, Rachel knew. She had already had a sample of the talk, from Mr. Garrett. She recognized it now: "All alone in the house when it happened, *far as anybody knows*."

"Mrs. Lang got ahold of it," Myra was continuing, "and you can imagine what a story *she's* been making of it. Especially after the fuss between Hartley and Mrs. Henshaw last week."

Rachel swallowed. "Fuss? They had a fuss?"

"A humdinger," said Myra with rueful relish. "Seems she burnt up all his pictures. You know what a great hand Hartley's always been for painting and drawing. Still is. More than ever. I've always thought the boy was pretty good at it. Not that I'm any judge of art. Well, what does Mrs. Henshaw do but burn up the whole works, all the sketches and pictures he's been working on for I don't know how long. Claimed it was by mistake, she thought it was trash."

"Trash," echoed Rachel.

"Oh, he was wild when he found it out, just wild. Hartley don't get mad very often, but when he does, watch out. He hot-footed it right down town—Mrs. Henshaw was in at Lang's Store, doing the marketing—and he sailed right into her. Mrs. Lang said she thought he was going to—" Just in time, Myra caught herself.

"Everybody heard that too, I suppose," said Rachel hope-lessly. "And now everybody knows he can't remember where he was when it happened. Myra, what shall I do?"

For once, Myra's stock of comforting words failed her. She just put her arms around Rachel and held her tight. "If anybody can straighten him out," she said finally, "it's you, Rachel. That's why I thought you'd ought to be here. He'll open up to you. It'll come to him, he'll remember when the shock wears off. It's just the shock." Before she hurried off into the gathering darkness, she added one thing more. "He was always good to her, Hartley was. Real good. Better than she deserved."

A feeling of unreality crept over Rachel; none of this could possibly be happening. Mrs. Henshaw was very likely not dead at all, but still lurking somewhere close at hand, ready to pounce. It was a ghostly feeling, and yet strong enough so that, as she started back to the library, Rachel caught herself moving in the old, self-effacing way, as if she should apologize for taking up space. To snap herself out of it, she shut the door behind her with an unnecessary clatter.

Hartley and Bix—and the pint of whiskey—froze into instant immobility. He had the bottle tilted up to his mouth; Bix stood close to him, waiting her turn. Their heads were turned halfway toward Rachel, and something in their attitudes made her think of derelicts, the bums on Skid Row huddling in gritty doorways, gulping down their joyless drinks. She was suddenly angry, and Bix didn't help a bit.

"Oh, oh," said Bix. Quiet and resigned. The culprit caught red-handed and facing some familiar, tiresome punishment at the hands of the righteous.

You brat, thought Rachel. You insufferable little brat. How dare you make me feel like a social worker!

"If you've going to have a drink," she said evenly, "why not have a civilized one? I could use one myself. Only—I'm sorry to be so stuffy—I think a glass and some ice would be sort of nice. If it's not too much trouble, Hartley."

"Sure. Well, sure," said Hartley, and scurried off to the kitchen, still clutching the bottle.

Rachel sat down in the Morris chair and lit a cigarette. She hoped she looked relaxed.

Bix turned to face her. "I can't help it if you think I'm an indesirable influence," she began belligerently.

"Undesirable," said Rachel. "And I can't help it either. There's just one thing, Bix. I don't see why you had to call him up three years ago, when he came to Chicago after Papa died. It *was* you, wasn't it? I don't see why you had to drag him back here. He should have gotten away from Mrs. Henshaw right then. Then none of this would have happened—"

"What do you mean, none of this?" said Bix very quickly. "I can't see that anything so terrible has happened. Au contrary. So she falls down stairs and breaks her neck. Good for her. That's what I say. Good for her. Everything's fine and dandy now." Tears sprang to her eyes; she blinked disdainfully. "Just fine and dandy."

"Here we are," said Hartley, coming in with the tray. The phrase, for Rachel, carried a wistful echo of Papa's jovial voice. "Here we are, m'boy." That was what Papa used to say, when, after a day's hunting, he and Hugh Bovard—Bix's father—used to settle down in this room for a convivial evening. Occasionally there were other cronies, but more often it was just the two of them. The editor and the doctor. Hughie and Doc. The mellow, masculine rumble of their voices, the aroma of their tobacco, the slap of the cards as they played cribbage, used to give Rachel a wonderful sense of warmth and comfort. Hughie and Doc. They had been lifelong friends, closer than brothers.

"How's your father, Bix?" she asked, and got an aridly polite "Very well, thank you," for a reply.

You couldn't call it, really, a successful social gathering. Bix, balancing herself on the slippery couch, assumed a formidably correct manner that nipped in the bud the feeble conversational shoots Rachel put out. Hartley just sank back in his chair, withdrawn and silent.

At last the tall old clock in the corner pulled itself together with an alarming series of clicks and whirs and struck six. Hollow and deliberate, the voice of doom.

"I must be going," said Bix, springing up in relief. "Thank you for the drink. It was so nice and civilized."

IV

Now, thought Rachel. I must straighten Hartley out, I must get him to open up. When he came back from seeing Bix to the door, she produced a shaky smile and a shakier attempt at normalcy. "We've got so much to catch up on, Hartley, we won't know where to start."

"Yes," he said. Nothing more.

Silence again. Were they going to sit in this room all night long without uttering a word? At least, when they were children, they had whispered their guilty little secrets to each other, shuddered in unison at the possibility of discovery, reached for each other's hands when all hope of escape was gone.

But now it was as if Hartley and she were no longer inhabitants of the same world. She sat down on the hassock at his feet and put her hand over his, and still the distance stretched between them.

"Tell me," she said. "Tell me what happened."

Beneath her fingers Hartley's strong, nervous hand went suddenly tenser than ever. His nightmare eyes stared past her.

"There's nothing to tell. We found her at the bottom of the cellar stairs. That's all."

"But didn't you hear her fall?"

"I wasn't here. I got here just as Myra did. I was—I don't know where I was."

"Those steps always were treacherous," said Rachel a little breathlessly. "And she was always in such a sweat, to get whatever it was done. Couldn't hurry fast enough."

"I can't remember," Hartley said. "I can't remember where I was."

The fire made a sad puffing sound and flickered briefly on his rapt face. His eyes, though they were still fixed on Rachel's, were not seeing her. And for a moment Rachel no longer saw him. An ugly, an impossible little picture flashed between his face and hers—a picture of an old woman at the top of a murky, steep flight of stairs, bending forward (what a little push it would take); and there was the hand, crafty and powerful, reaching toward her shoulder. . . .

It couldn't be true. It was a lie, that little picture, a lie twisted out of Rachel's own overwrought nerves. There had been no hand. There had been only Mrs. Henshaw losing her balance and plunging down the stairs, probably with one last bitter squawk against the world and all its exasperations.

Except that Hartley was seeing the picture too.

Her brother; her shy, funny, sensitive little brother. He was always good to her, Myra had said; and in a way it was true. Hartley had been less rebellious than she. He hadn't run away. But he must have wanted to. He must have longed for escape from that annihilating tongue, from those eyes that could at one glance lay waste your confidence, wither the very core of yourself. He had not escaped. Not even now.

When the doorbell wheezed they both stiffened, leaning toward each other beside the dying fire. Queenie began a growl, and stifled it, at Hartley's warning gesture.

"Don't answer it," they whispered to each other, unnecessarily. Whoever it was rang again, waited, rang again.

Rachel's heart sank at the next sound. It was unmistakable. The front door was undoubtedly opening; their caller was walking in, heading of course for the line of light under the library door.

It was the footsteps that transfixed them. Rapid, peremptory, and purposeful, those footsteps touched off in Rachel the old panicky dread; she reached for the thin comfort of Hartley's hand. Together they faced the library door, and as it opened Rachel felt the last barrier between herself and Hartley's nightmare dissolve.

Mrs. Henshaw was standing in the doorway.

V

She wore a black coat, decent rather than fashionable. Her hat had a flashing silver buckle in front, and she carried a shabby suitcase.

"Well," she said, and her edged voice attacked them, her reddish-brown eyes accused them. "It does seem like you'd let a person in."

Her hair, thought Rachel, her beautiful red hair. It's turned all white. She's dead, of course, she's lying down there at the funeral parlor; and yet here she is and we're in for another tongue-lashing.

"I'm sorry, we didn't hear the bell." It was Hartley speaking, and he was getting to his feet, crossing the room with his hand outstretched. He must be in a trance, thought Rachel. "Won't you come in?"

The voice pounced on him. "I suppose you're Hartley."

He admitted it. "This is my sister Rachel," he added, and Rachel nodded like a puppet responding to a tug on the strings. Not a trance, she decided. Insanity. They had all suddenly lost their minds.

"We didn't expect you," Hartley said.

"I'm sure I don't know why not. You wired me, didn't you? Well, then. Granted we weren't as close as some sisters, I've still got enough family feeling to come to Rose's funeral, I hope." The piercing glance switched to Rachel. It was unnerving. Even though she understood now that the eyes that were impaling her were not Mrs. Henshaw's, it was still unnerving. "I must say," commented Mrs. Henshaw's sister, "I didn't expect to see *you* here. Didn't think you and Rose got along."

"Let me take your wraps, Mrs. Pierce," said Hartley, and as she whisked out of her coat he added, half to himself, "You look so much like her—"

"I don't know about now. We used to favor each other, as girls. Or so people said. I haven't seen Rose in more than fifteen years. To hear her tell it, she never could get away for a visit. Why not, I'd like to know—*I* wasn't going to pick up and come visit *her*. Just as busy as she was. Busier. And with my own family, not somebody else's."

A variation on Mrs. Henshaw's favorite theme: "I don't know why I should be expected to worry my head like this. Over somebody else's young ones. Anybody else would let you go to the orphanage, where you belong. You wouldn't have things all your own way there, I can tell you."

It was like hearing double. All through supper Rachel struggled against sinking back into the old paralyzed silence. But the nervous little stabs at conversation that she made sounded extraordinarily inane to her the moment they were uttered; she felt that they deserved the treatment Mrs. Pierce-Henshaw gave them—terse slaps of answers that disposed of them on the spot. It was no use. The layers of Rachel's poise seemed to fall away, exposing the wretch, the hopeless incompetent that Mrs. Henshaw had always said was there.

But I did run away, she reminded herself. I did scrape up enough courage for that. Courage? Or just a weakling's desperation? When it came to that, Hartley may have found his way of running away, too. . . .

She looked across at her brother's haggard face. It revealed nothing. That careful blankness had always been Hartley's defense. I don't know, Mrs. Henshaw. I don't know anything about anything.

"Well!" Mrs. Pierce's voice cracked at them like a whip. "It's a funny thing to me that I have to bring the subject up, but it doesn't look like you're going to do it, either one of you. A person would think I didn't have the right to know. What happened to Rose?"

"I'm sorry," Rachel stammered. "We—I thought you knew—"

"How, I'd like to know? Mental telepathy?"

"It was an accident," Rachel was beginning, when Hartley spoke.

"She fell down the cellar stairs," he said dreamily, "and broke her neck."

Mrs. Pierce caught her breath. Her round, red-brown eyes,

like the eyes of some fierce bird, blinked once or twice. She did not speak.

Her silence seemed to Rachel more ominous than any words could have been. Was the terrible machinery starting up, at this very moment, in Mrs. Pierce's mind? "Something funny about it, from the beginning," Mrs. Pierce might report—tomorrow, next day, maybe even tonight—to the sheriff. "Something funny about both of them. And then the way he came out with it at the supper table. . . ."

To her own astonishment, Rachel rose to the occasion. "It happened while she was alone in the house," she began; and her voice was just right—matter-of-fact, seasoned with sympathy, sure of itself. She could see, from Mrs. Pierce's face, that it was right, it was convincing. As she went on talking she felt almost giddy with her own strength, as if she were telling Mrs. Henshaw herself that she had died in this way and no other. Not only telling her, but convincing her of it. Standing up to Mrs. Henshaw for once.

It was a small, private triumph, and it turned out to be only a stop-gap. Hartley soon had them right back where they had started.

Rachel saw the terror flare in his eyes as soon as Mrs. Pierce mentioned, with genteel delicacy, "the remains." Had Rachel viewed them yet? Well then, they could all go down to the funeral parlor this evening; Mrs. Pierce wanted to make sure, anyway, that the arrangements were in order.

"No. No!" With a violent gesture Hartley pushed back his chair and stumbled to his feet. "I can't! Rachel, you know I can't!"

Again the glint appeared in Mrs. Pierce's eyes. Her mouth straightened out, just the way Mrs. Henshaw's used to when she was dealing with a tantrum.

"All right then, don't. But I must say, young man, it seems mighty funny to me, the way you're behaving. Seems to me the least you could do—"

"It's just that Hartley's upset." (I sound too nervous, Rachel thought. I mustn't sound so nervous.) "It's all been a shock to him, and he's upset."

"I guess he is," said Mrs. Pierce drily. She too rose, smoothing down the lap of her black crepe, straightening belt and cameo brooch. "Well. I'm sure it doesn't matter whether anybody goes with me. I wouldn't want to put you to any trouble. I wouldn't want to upset anybody."

"I'll go with you," Rachel hurried to assure her. "Of course I'll go with you. Hartley—"

"All right. I'll drive you down. But I'm not going in there. I won't do it. You can't make me."

The kitchen door slammed behind him, and in a moment they heard the roar of the car backing out of the driveway.

They drove the three blocks to Manning's Funeral Parlor in silence. Rachel could see Hartley's profile, stubbornly turned toward the street light, as she and Mrs. Pierce got out. He would get cold, waiting there without his overcoat. He looked cold already. And very lonely.

Mr. Manning, dealer in Dignified Services At Prices That Are Right, greeted them at the door, his voice so hushed as to be almost soundless, his manner fantastically polite. How good it was to see Rachel again, yes indeed, even under such sad circumstances. And of course this must be Mrs. Henshaw's sister; a remarkable resemblance to the departed, yes indeed, remarkable. Bowing and scraping, he ushered them into a chilly room, arranged them beside the coffin, adjusted the light, and stepped back, poised to receive the praise due him.

Mrs. Henshaw lay still at last, her thin little hands folded, as she would never have folded them, at her waist. Her hair had turned white, almost as white as Mrs. Pierce's, and again Rachel felt a queer pang of sorrow for that wonderful red hair. But even death, even Mr. Manning's art, could not keep Mrs. Henshaw from looking cross. Her brows drew together, flaring in annoyance above the sharp, haughty thrust of nose; she seemed on the point of springing up and giving Mr. Manning—or somebody—a piece of her mind.

From beside Rachel came on indignant-sounding gulp; she was startled to see tears squeezing out of Mrs. Pierce's fierce red-brown eyes.

"I just—Poor Rose, what an awful way to die—"

An awful way to die. Yes. Rachel saw again Hartley's bemused eyes, heard again his whisper: "I was—I don't know where I was."

Mr. Manning glided forward to take charge of the bereaved sister and was promptly brushed aside. All Mrs. Pierce asked, she said, was that Rose be given a decent, respectable funeral tomorrow. Exactly what Mr. Manning was prepared to provide, yes indeed. Abstractedly Rachel listened to his smooth, hushed preview of the services.

She did not look at Mrs. Henshaw again.

And when they came out Hartley was gone. No sign of him, or of the car. Rachel steadied herself against the porch rail. Bix, of course. Hartley and Bix were no doubt tearing along some country road, or parked somewhere, huddled over another bottle of cheap whiskey.

"What's happened to your brother? Gone off and left us, has he?" Mrs. Pierce's tone implied that she was not in the least surprised; that, in fact, Hartley's disappearance was somehow gratifying to her.

"He may have gone home to get his coat. I expect it was chilly, waiting. Maybe we'll meet him on the way."

They did not meet him on the way, of course. The house was

empty except for Queenie, who clicked anxiously down the hall
when she heard them and did not bother to hide her disappoint-
ment that they were not Hartley.

"I'm sure he'll be along soon," Rachel said several times, and
Mrs. Pierce let this feeble statement lie where it fell. Perhaps
out of pity. Perhaps it was pity too that prompted her to retire
to the spare room as soon as Rachel got the bed made up. Now
at least Rachel could suffer without an audience.

She went back to the library; there was more wood in the
box, and she took quite a little while building another fire. Then
she sat and looked at it. "I don't know what to do," she said to
Queenie. "I wonder what I should do."

But Queenie did not know what to do either. She padded
around uneasily, ears alerted, eyes questioning.

"There's no cause for alarm," Rachel explained to Queenie.
"He and Bix have simply gone off somewhere, he should have
told me, but kids are like that, thoughtless, he's upset, only
natural, the shock. . . . I can call Myra if it gets really late. Or
Hugh Bovard. There is absolutely no cause for alarm."

Queenie was polite about it. She sat down and put her head
on Rachel's knee. She went through all the motions of relaxing.
But they were just the motions. Rachel hadn't convinced either
of them.

VI

"That does it." Fritz, foreman of the *Coreyville Tribune,*
switched off the big press in the back room, pushed back his
green eyeshade (leaving a smear of ink on his knobby forehead),
and made his standard press-day quip: "One more week's work
for Jesus. The *Tribune* rides again." The other members of the
Tribune staff—Hugh Bovard, who was the boss, and Gloria John-

son, who never missed an opportunity to refer to herself as Mr. Bovard's Girl Friday—obliged with their standard responses. Which, in Hugh's case, was no response at all. He had heard the quip too many times. Gloria, who had heard it a good many times herself, still produced her tireless smile. She just loved her job.

Sometimes Hugh wished she didn't. God knew what he'd do without her, of course. But there was something slightly alarming about all this devotion to duty, this unflagging co-operation, this willingness to serve. In any capacity. That was the thing. Any capacity. Every once in a while the idea—sly, humiliating— flitted across Hugh's mind. He spread a fresh copy of the *Tribune* out on the big table, pretending to study The Stylette display ad, secretly watching Gloria as she cheerfully, nimbly, wrapped the singles into tight gray sticks ready for the mail bags. There was a smear of ink on her forehead, too. Gloria's complexion was inclined to be spotty, and she seemed to have more than her share of teeth. But below the complexion and the teeth was this rich geography of shapely legs, trim little waist, tenderly swelling bosom. Tenderly swelling, eagerly trembling with each of Gloria's movements. The Promised Land. Wrapping the singles was another piece of dog work that had been turned over to Gloria. Would you mind if I left the bill collecting to you this month, Gloria? Would you mind if I asked you to stay overtime and help Fritz with the telephone directories? Would you mind, Gloria, if I ripped off that oh-so-proper blouse of yours, and that skirt that switches around all day long, and. . . .

Good Lord, thought Hugh, at my age. At a time like this. Althea's birthday, and here he was ogling a kid, only half a dozen years older than Bix.

He folded up the paper and reached for his jacket. "Good layout on The Stylette, Fritz. Matter of fact, the whole paper looks pretty good this week. Thank you, ladies and gentlemen, thank you." (That was *his* standard press-day quip, to which Fritz paid no attention. Trust Gloria, though. All the teeth showed in appreciation, the Promised Land swelled and trembled.)

"We're early, too. It's only six o'clock." He had rushed things this week, on account of Althea's birthday. There was plenty of time, now, to pick up the steak he had ordered, plenty of time for the special dinner and the present and the evening at home that this time—oh surely, surely this time—would go right.

"Why shouldn't we be early?" commented Fritz. "Pretty poor pickings on the news this week. If Mrs. Henshaw hadn't busted her neck we'd be running personals on the front page."

There it was, under Hugh's hand. Mrs. Rose Henshaw Killed In Tragic Accident. (Rose, he thought; of all inappropriate names for a woman like Mrs. Henshaw. A rose by any other name. Last rose of summer. Go, lovely rose. It intrigued him, that last one. Go, lovely rose. She had gone, all right. For good and all.) Fifty-six years of age. . . . For nineteen years housekeeper in the home of the late Dr. G. F. Buckmaster. . . . Discovered by Hartley Buckmaster and Mrs. Myra Graves. . . . Survived by. . . .

That had been a problem, that "Survived by." There was the sister, of course, but what about old Francie Henshaw? Should he be mentioned? Technically he was still Mrs. Henshaw's husband, though they hadn't spoken to each other for thirty years, and Francie had been known to go to fantastic lengths to avoid meeting her on the street.

They had never even been able to agree on a divorce. Francie frequently declaimed on the subject to Hugh, whom he considered the only person in town worthy of his friendship. "An abomination," Francie would thunder, in revivalist accents, "the woman is an abomination upon the face of the earth."

In the end Francie himself had set the course of etiquette for the *Tribune*. So there it was: "Survived by her sister, Mrs. Viola

Pierce of Westburg, and her estranged husband, Francis L. Henshaw."

"You're right, Fritz." Hugh smiled. "May Mrs. Henshaw rest in peace. She picked the right week to break her neck. There's Bix," he added, as the front door slammed and a rush of footsteps sounded through the front office and on, past linotype, cabinets and hand presses.

"Hi! News, Daddy, news. Rachel Buckmaster's back for the funeral. Got here on the four thirty train."

"So what do we do, get out an extra?" said Fritz, grinning. "You've missed the boat, kid. We'll feature it next week."

Bix made a face at him. "She looks like a million dollars, Daddy. A simply stunning black suit, and she's got long hair, done up in a, what-do-you-call-it, a—"

"A chignon?" offered Gloria, who could always supply the word you were groping for.

"Yes. A chignon. She made me feel like an absolute flump."

"So Rachel's back, is she?" Hugh took a thoughtful drag on his cigarette. "Somehow I didn't think she'd come. Though I suppose she and Hartley will want to settle things up. Well. Well, it'll be good to see Rachel again. I always liked her. Plenty of spunk."

Though, to tell the truth, he hadn't been aware of Rachel's spunk until she picked up and ran away. Maybe it had surprised her too, poor, scared-looking little thing that she had been, to find herself escaping from the Henshaw blight. Doc's daughter, he thought, and he felt the familiar pang, like homesickness. Damn, he missed Doc. If it weren't for Althea's birthday, he'd call Rachel right now.

"Okay, Miss Flump," he said, smiling at his own daughter, "do me a favor, will you? Run over to Havelka's and pick up the steak for dinner."

"On condition," said Bix. "For a price. The condition being that you buy me a black suit. Will you, Daddy? Please?"

"We'll see about that." But of course it was settled. He always bought Bix everything she wanted. And it didn't do a bit of good, it didn't make up for Althea at all.

"Oh Daddy, you've got to! There's something so civilized about a black suit," Bix cried before she dashed off.

"She's so cute," said Gloria. "No wonder you spoil her, Mr. Bovard. She's so cute. I'll help Fritz finish up here, Mr. Bovard. I'll be glad to. Why don't you go on home? You've been looking awfully tired lately."

"Spare me the details of how I look, will you?" he said curtly. "If I'm tired it's my own business." The end of Gloria's nose quivered, as it always did when he snapped at her. Which, he supposed, was far too often. It occurred to him that he probably had a reputation for cussedness to match his father's. The Terrible-Tempered Mr. Bang, they used to call the old man, half-affectionately; maybe they were already doing the same with him.

He felt ashamed of himself. "Here," he said, "I've got another batch of passes to the movies. Why don't you and Fritz blow yourselves to a show tonight?"

Out of the corner of his eye he saw Fritz' face flush up dully, and he thought, ah ha, so Fritz has been peering at the Promised Land too, through his thick glasses. Well, more power to him.

Gloria's thanks trailed after him effusively as he headed for the front office.

He took the present for Althea out of his desk drawer and once more studied the card he had written this morning. "With all my love. Hugh." There it was. All his love, and it wasn't enough, it wasn't what she wanted. Only he couldn't stop hoping. He went on and on. Stubbornly, monotonously hoping, like a bird that knows only the one call.

"What did you get her?" Bix, with the package of meat under her arm, was looking at him with the hostile, contemptuous expression he knew so well. He ignored it. Tonight was going to be a success, come hell or high water. He was going to *make* things go right.

"You'll see. All in good time." But his joviality suddenly cracked. "Bix. Bix, did you get her something?"

"Of course I didn't. Why should I?" Her eyes met his, cruelly honest, and Hugh felt a swift throb of envy. Bix was free, she had long ago stopped hoping for anything from Althea. He envied her.

"Oh *hell*, Daddy. I'll go get her something now, if you feel that way about it."

"Skip it," he said huskily. "Come on, let's go cook the steak."

The Bovard house was on the same street as the Buckmaster's. Brick, another one of Coreyville's old-fashioned houses, set far back from the street. It was a pretty place in summer, with its tapestry of ivy on the north side, its bridal wreath bushes banking the front porch, and the cool, deep shade of its box elders and elms. But winter gave it the sad, ruined look of a decayed gentlewoman dressed in tatters. It didn't seem to Hugh that it had looked that way when he was a boy, even in the bleakest February. Yet actually there had been few changes, either inside or out, since the days when Hugh's mother and father were alive. They were still using quite a lot of the old folks' furniture. From time to time Hugh went on a buying binge, but he was apt to be carried away by grand-scale gadgets, like the electric dishwasher and the glass-enclosed shower for the bathroom. The living room, he felt, probably needed something done to it. He wasn't sure just what, and Althea didn't seem to take much interest. Even when she did, her projects were likely to wind up unfinished, abandoned after the first spurt. It was as though something had been left out of Althea, that happy ingredient that made it possible for other women to busy themselves contentedly with the details of their daily lives. She tried; time after time Hugh had seen her try, and time after time he had seen the desolation sweeping over her face: Oh, what difference does it make? What does it matter, whether the drapes are blue or green, whether there are any drapes at all. . . .

At least there was a light on in the living room, Hugh noted as he and Bix got out of the car and crunched their way across the patches of stale snow in the yard. That was a good omen. On the really bad days Althea did not bother with the light—perhaps she did not even notice when darkness fell—and Hugh would find her sitting there, staring empty-eyed into the shadows.

"Hello, there!" she called, quite gaily, when they came in the door, and Hugh felt the lift of hope, incurable, unreasonable. Althea was curled up in a corner of the couch, a magazine in her lap. She wore a pale blue dress—she seldom wore anything but pale blue or gray—but this dress had a perky, jolly-looking little white collar.

"Happy birthday, darling," he said, and kissed her, neatly. Althea hated long, plastery kisses. "Bix and I are all set to produce the best dinner you ever sat down to." He would save the present until afterwards, he decided. Maybe he could talk Althea into having a drink with him. Maybe tonight she wouldn't draw away from him, aloof and weary, making him feel like some damn animal.

Why yes, Althea said, a drink would be nice. One of those fizzy pink drinks. "Your hands, Beatrix!" she added, in her faint, sweet voice. "Really!"

"What—" Startled, Bix looked down at her hands. "Oh. You mean the dirt. That's from Gym. I'll wash them. In fact—" Her face flashed into a smile, and it occurred to Hugh that here was Bix's birthday present, the best she could muster up. "—I intend to take an entire, guaranteed anaesthetic shower while you and Daddy get drunk."

She clattered cheerfully up the stairs, and Hugh went out to the kitchen to make the drinks. The sink was full of dirty dishes. (The electric dishwasher hadn't made any difference; it frightened her, Althea said, all that whirring, efficient machinery.) He whistled while he got out the ice and shaker.

"You don't look a day over seventy," he told Althea jovially when he brought in the tray. "Remarkably well preserved, Mrs. Bovard."

There was, to Hugh, something heart-breaking about the remnants of his wife's prettiness. She had been an extremely pretty girl—ash-blonde, fragile as a spun-glass figure. The fragility was still there, and though the ash-blonde hair was turning white it kept its gentle, youthful curl. But grief had cut gullies in Althea's delicate face; only at rare moments—like this one—did her eyes lose their empty look. My poor darling, thought Hugh, my poor ghostly girl.

"I went to club this afternoon," she was saying now, with the bright air of a child reporting her own good conduct. For Hugh was always pleased when she went to club or anywhere else; it wasn't good for her, he said, to spend so much time alone.

"And what was cooking at club?"

"Why, let me see—Oh, Mrs. Henshaw, of course. Nobody talked about anything else. Hugh, have you heard all this gossip about Hartley?" Althea's face took on a look of gentle puzzlement. "You should have heard Mrs. Lang! She all but accused Hartley of murdering Mrs. Henshaw. In fact, she said the sheriff ought to investigate all over again—"

"Oh, my Lord!" Hugh burst out. "Somebody ought to buy that woman a muzzle. Of all the crazy, malicious gossip! It was an accident, I don't care how many quarrels Hartley had with the old witch, or where he was when it happened, it was an accident. The sheriff and everybody else is satisfied, whether Mrs. Bloodhound Lang is or not."

"An accident. Yes. Of course it was an accident." For a moment it seemed to Hugh that Althea's voice throbbed with a queer kind of excitement. It made him feel not quite comfortable; after all, no use dwelling on it. "It couldn't be anything else. She was all alone in the house, so how could it be anything else?"

She saw him watching her, and lifted her glass for another dainty sip. Her voice got back to normal. "They all seemed to think Hartley and Rachel will sell the house. No reason why they shouldn't, now that she's dead."

That was the way Doc Buckmaster had left things, in his will. The house (which was about all Doc had left) went to Hartley and Rachel. But with the provision that Mrs. Henshaw could live in it as long as she chose to. She had so chosen. Naturally nobody was going to buy the house as long as Mrs. Henshaw went with it.

"No reason at all," said Hugh. There, Althea was all right again. She wasn't going into one of those unhealthy brooding spells of hers, after all. "It's high time Hartley got out of Coreyville. He's just wasting his time, hanging around here, pretending to go to Business College. I don't know why he didn't leave when Doc died." (As a matter of fact, Hugh had a strong suspicion that Bix was the reason. Anyway, part of the reason. They had always stuck to each other, the two lost kids.) "Rachel's back, by the way. Bix said she came on the four thirty train."

"Really? I'll bet she's not going into mourning over Mrs. Henshaw."

"Well, she turned up in a black suit that certainly caught Bix's eye. Simply stunning. End quote. But I doubt if it's out of reverence for the dear departed." A pleasant glow was beginning to spread through Hugh. Here they were, he and Althea, having a sociable drink together, gossiping like any ordinary husband and wife. He moved a little closer to her on the sofa; if only, tonight, he could go slow enough, not try to rush her. . . .

"Let's see, Rachel's—Yes. Twenty-four. Just a month to the day older than Ronnie. Ronnie'd be twenty-four, Hugh, if we hadn't lost him—"

Hugh stiffened. "Now Althea, darling," he began uneasily. Oh God, wasn't she ever going to get over it? How could she go on like this, tearing herself to pieces over a son like Ronnie? Doc Buckmaster had told her bluntly, from the very beginning, that Ronnie wasn't ever going to be right. He had explained to both of them about Mongolism: it was one of those tragedies that happened with perfectly normal parents, nobody was sure why; there was no reason in the world why they shouldn't have other children; Ronnie would probably not live beyond the age of twelve in any case; the most sensible solution was to put him in an institution. Althea had not believed a word of it. Through the eight terrible years of Ronnie's life she had poured out every drop of her strength, every minute of every day and night, in blind, monstrous love. In a way she was still doing it. Hugh knew how she hugged her pillow at night, pretending it was Ronnie; he knew what she saw when she sat staring into the shadows on her bad days.

Ronnie at twenty-four. He shuddered involuntarily.

"That's right, Rachel's twenty-four," he said, snatching forlornly at the coziness of a moment ago. It didn't do any good to try to reason with Althea. He had tried it. He had tried everything. The only hope was to distract her. "Maybe we could drop in and see her, later on, after dinner. Or ask her over here. I'd like to see her again. Wouldn't you?"

Althea pressed her fingers against her temples and closed her eyes. "I'm so tired, Hugh. I don't know why I should be so tired."

"When do we eat?" asked Bix, plunging down the staircase

and into the living room. "I'm starved." She had on a terry cloth robe and scuffs, and the wet ends of her hair stuck out in little spikes.

"Those slippers, Beatrix," said Althea. "The eternal slap, slap of those slippers. Can't you *do* something about them?" Bix raised her eyes heavenward in an elaborate appeal for patience and fortitude. Then she kicked the scuffs off viciously. But Hugh drew a relieved sigh as he followed her out to the kitchen. At least they had gotten Althea's mind off Ronnie.

VII

The steak was, as Mr. Havelka had promised Hugh when he ordered it, tender as a virgin's—Well, anyway, tender. Even Althea's portion, which Hugh had been careful to make well done, because she couldn't stand the sight of blood. Bix's salad, too, turned out a success; for once she had exercised reasonable restraint with the hot stuff. Poor kid, she was doing her best. She dug out candles and stuck them in the center of each of the cup cakes they had for dessert, and when she and Hugh carried them in, with the tiny candle flames trembling bravely, they both sang Happy Birthday to You.

"How festive!" cried Althea, and she turned her face up gladly for Hugh's kiss.

Now was the moment for the birthday present. With a ceremonial flourish he brought out the package. (Gloria had gift-wrapped it for him; the silver rosettes were her idea.) He kept his eyes fixed, hungry with anticipation, on Althea's face as she slipped off the wrappings and opened the box.

"What—" A second's blank silence—she likes it, she doesn't like it, she does, she—and then, with a shriek of undisguised horror, Althea slammed the lid back on the box and covered her eyes with her hands. The cup cake in front of her toppled over with the violence of her recoil; the candle flame winked and died against the table cloth. "Oh Hugh, how could you! It's simply—"

"What's the matter? What is it?" Bix raced around the table to her mother's place and opened the box again, exposing the handbag which, the salesgirl had assured Hugh, was exquisite, the dream handbag of every woman in the world. Genuine alligator, with a miniature alligator decorating the front, complete down to the last wrinkled leg and crafty eye.

"You don't like it," said Hugh heavily. His face, he felt, was still frozen in the silly half-smile of expectant delight. He tried to rub it away with his hand. "Never mind. I can exchange it. The girl said I could exchange it."

"It's the chickest bag I ever saw," said Bix in a loud voice.

"I just—It looks so *real*," said Althea faintly. "Those awful little fat legs, and the tail. It switched. I swear it switched."

"I wasn't too sure about it myself, but you know how it is. Highly recommended by the salesman." Hugh forced a laugh. "I can exchange it. It doesn't matter."

"It does too matter!" Suddenly Bix's face was fierce red; she crouched over her mother, her shoulders hunched in an angry-cat attitude. "I think you're horrible. You've always got to spoil everything for everybody. You can't stand it to have Daddy feel good, even for a minute. Can you? Can you? I think you're horrible. A horrible, horrible woman—"

"Bix, for God's sake, stop it."

"I do. I hate you." Bix's voice cracked exultantly.

"Bix—" Hugh got out of his chair and took a threatening step toward her. Then he saw Althea's face, and stopped. It was turned up to Bix, and it too was exultant. Her eyes glittered, her whole face was pinched with a cold, bitter triumph.

"You hate me." Althea caught her breath. "How do you think I feel about you? Don't you *know* what you did to me? Don't you know that he'd be alive, Ronnie'd be alive today if it hadn't been for you?"

"Althea, what are you—"

"And you!" She flashed the word at him venomously. "Your doing, too. You and Doc Buckmaster. That brilliant family doctor, that true, true friend of yours. I can just hear him telling you, I can just imagine it. Another baby. Oh my yes indeedy. She'll get interested in another baby. . . . Couldn't you see that Ronnie was all I ever *wanted?*" Her voice rose, out of control, anguished. Sank again, almost to a whisper. "And while I was having this wonderful, therapeutic other baby, he lay there and died. Died because I couldn't take care of him. Died because—"

"It was flu," said Hugh hoarsely. "You know it was—"

"Flu! I could have saved him! He died because I wasn't there! I was the only one who understood what he wanted, what he needed. . . . And I wasn't there. I failed him. He knew, he always knew when I wasn't there. He died because—"

It was fantastic. Hugh couldn't have struck her. But his hand seemed to have been busy at something, because here it was out in front of him, tingling slightly, and there were the dull red marks on Althea's thin-skinned cheek. Dumbfounded, he stared at his own hand. Except for the shaking, it looked as usual—loose-knuckled, moderately hairy, with the worn gold signet ring. It was shaking like a Model T about to take off.

"My God, Althea." He sat down abruptly.

She was gazing, empty-eyed, at a point beyond his shoulder. After a moment she gave a long, sobbing sigh. Then she got up and walked out of the room. He heard her footsteps whispering, dragging a little, as she went upstairs.

"You're supposed to slap the patient when they get hysterical," said Bix nervously. "Standard treatment. We had it in First Aid."

"I'm glad to hear it. It's always nice to know you've done

the right thing." The candle in his cup cake was still burning, and he pinched it out. Bix watched him with big, scared eyes.

"Would you care to join me in a drink?" he asked.

She looked startled, not quite approving. "Well. All right. After I do the dishes. I guess I better do the dishes first."

There was a bottle of Bourbon, half-full, in the kitchen. Hugh carried it and a glass into the living room, sat down, and poured himself a drink. Standard treatment, he thought. Get drunk. The classic reaction; the one more mistake that didn't matter because all the other mistakes had already been made. He was really gifted that way. A genius at making mistakes. They passed before his mind's eye, like a parade of cripples and freaks. The times when he had been clumsy with Althea, or selfish, or just plain unperceptive. (He always saw afterwards, when it was too late.) The things he shouldn't have done, the words he should have said—all the trifling mistakes, right up to the final blundering climax.

He sipped slowly, listening to Bix, still barefooted, padding from dining room to kitchen, and then the hiss and whir of the dishwasher. Maybe she was crying out there; maybe he should go out and. . . . What was there to do for Bix? What was there to say? She was better off than he was, at that. She hated Althea, and said so. He loved Althea, and slapped her. And nothing was changed: Althea still loved neither of them, only Ronnie. Business as usual.

Not quite as usual, for Hugh. Because he would surely stop hoping now, wouldn't he? With that slap he had written finis to his flimsy chances; had, in a way, liberated himself. He didn't need to envy Bix any more. He could be hopeless too.

There was no sound at all from upstairs. How many evenings had he sat here alone, listening to the upstairs silence, knowing that the door to her room was locked? Knowing, too, that in spite of all he could do he was going to try that locked door, very gently, very quietly, when he went upstairs. Then there were the other evenings, when he hadn't sat here alone. . . .

He thought, fleetingly, of Gloria and the Promised Land. He might call her up, invent some forgotten chore at the office. He might just do that. Except that he had given her those movie tickets. She and Fritz and the Promised Land were no doubt installed at this moment in the stale dimness of the Elite Theater. Palpitating, one and all.

Oh, well. Even if he hadn't abdicated in favor of Fritz, it would have been the same old story. Like all the others—not any real good. Why was that? Why did he have to be the original accept-no-substitute boy?

Bix came in. Very matter-of-fact. It was quite possible she hadn't been crying out there, after all. She had a glass in her hand.

"I was just kidding," he said. "I don't really think you're old enough to drink. At least I don't think I should encourage you."

"It's unmaterial to me," said Bix loftily. She sat down on the couch and wiggled her toes. "Indian giver."

"Where's Old Faithful Hartley tonight? Way past time for him to show up, isn't it?"

"He's not coming. I told you, Rachel's here. Naturally he's not going to leave her alone, her first night here."

"That's right. I'd forgotten about Rachel. I ought to call her." But he did not move. His drink stood, neglected, on the table beside him. Inert, sunk in a haphazard reverie, he simply sat. Nothing seemed very real. Nothing except the recurrent thought, sharp as a flash of lightning: I slapped her. I *slapped* her.

The telephone split the silence. He leaped out of his chair, ridiculously alarmed. Evidently he looked ridiculous too: Bix was giggling a little. "It's one of them new-fangled contraptions, Pappy," she said. "You've heard tell of it. The telephone, they call it."

"Okay, wise guy." He settled his tie and went out to the telephone in the hall.

"Hello," said the voice, and he got an immediate impression of tension. "Oh Hugh, is that you? Hugh, this is Rachel."

"Hey there, Rachel!" He put a good deal of effort into the heartiness. "How's the big city girl?"

"Fine, just fine. I was just wondering if you'd like to run over and have a drink, for old times sake. . . ." Again Hugh felt the flicker of panic. "Hartley seems to have absconded with your young daughter for the evening, and I thought—"

"What's that? Hartley's not with Bix. She's right here."

There was a blank silence. "She is? You're sure?" Rachel sounded very far away. "But then—Then where is he?"

Not here. Not at home. . . . Hugh discovered that he was sweating slightly. He glanced at his watch. Only ten, not really late. No cause for alarm. "Why, I expect he's—Look, Rachel, why don't I hop in the car and take a quick cruise around? He's probably got involved in a red-hot game of pool or something. Did he take the car?"

"Yes. Oh yes, he's got the car. I hate to put you to all this trouble—"

"No trouble at all." Suddenly he had a vivid little picture of her, sitting there alone, waiting, scared out of her wits. Yes; for some reason she was scared out of her wits. But he didn't want to take her with him, in case—Just in case. "And look, Rachel, meantime why don't I drop Bix off at your place to keep you company? Okay? Fine. Don't worry about a thing. We'll be right over."

He didn't have to explain to Bix; she had heard, and was already flying up the stairs to get dressed. Hugh paused in the hallway. There were the stairs, and at the top of them the locked door, and behind it Althea.

Bix could tell her mother where they were going. Bix could explain that they wouldn't be late.

But perhaps. . . . Perhaps if he apologized (as of course he must, sooner or later), perhaps if he could get her to open the door, just for a minute; if he could put his arms around her, kiss her poor ravaged face and tell her. . . .

He couldn't help himself. It was still there, the indestructible, humiliating, idiot hope.

Fool, he told himself, you damn fool. But his feet paid no attention. They went right ahead, carrying him up the stairs.

VIII

Rachel couldn't make up her mind. Was she going to burst into tears or—there were moments when it seemed much more likely—into whoops of laughter?

Because there was something about Bix's face (deadpan from the moment she walked in the door) that made Rachel feel exactly like a fractious child consigned to a baby sitter who obviously had no intention of putting up with any nonsense.

"I brought my knitting," said Bix, and unfurled a complicated chunk of needles and yarn. "I'm making Hartley an Argyle sock for his birthday."

"Just one?" quavered Rachel.

"I gave him the other one for Christmas." Bix settled herself, more or less on her shoulder blades, and set the needles to plunging and flashing recklessly. Rachel and Queenie watched, fascinated.

After a while Rachel got up and made another of her excursions to the window. There was nothing to see, nothing but the bare winter trees shivering, and the street light on the corner swinging in the wind, and a crumpled newspaper skittering along the sidewalk.

"Haven't you any idea of where he might have gone?" she asked.

Bix shrugged. "Maybe he's eloped with that fat Lang dame. She's been trying to get her hooks into him all winter."

"Bix, this is serious! Don't you see—"

Bix gave her a long, steady, inscrutable look, and she swallowed the rest of the sentence. Whatever it might have been.

"Excuse me," said Bix. "I have to go to the bathroom."

Okay, Madame Defarge, thought Rachel bitterly, staring at the Argyle sock and listening to the thud of Bix's feet on the stairs. Then, as a freshly alarming idea struck her, she leaped out of her chair and across the room to the little marble-topped table. The gun, Papa's gun. It was always kept loaded because, according to Papa, the only safe gun was a loaded one, and if it was gone, if Hartley had taken it—She gave a gasp of relief. It was still there.

She jerked the drawer shut, at the sounds from upstairs. A muted shriek, feet running fast. When she got out into the hall, here was Bix, galloping wild-eyed down the stairs.

"There's somebody *up* there! In the spare room! Thrashing around, kind of muttering. I opened that door by mistake. . . ."

Rachel collapsed against the newel post, laughing feebly. "I'm sorry, Bix. I forgot to tell you. Mrs. Pierce. She got here just after you left this afternoon. Came down on the bus."

"Mrs. Pierce! Who's she?"

"For the funeral. You know. The sister." They were both whispering. Hissing away like a couple of ham actors cast as spies.

"You might have mentioned it," said Bix. "What's she like? I mean, is she—"

"Like as two peas. I thought it was her, at first."

"No wonder Hartley took a powder. And you forgot to tell anybody. Just a little matter you overlooked. The negligence! The incredulous negligence!"

"Incredible," said Rachel, stung. "And I can't see that it's any dumber than opening the spare room when you're looking for the bathroom." She paused, suddenly struck with the real incredibility, the downright impossibility, of Bix's making such a mistake. She must know this house almost as well as she knew her own. The bathroom was at one end of the hall, and the spare room at the other, next to Mrs. Henshaw's room. Rachel opened her mouth and then closed it again. Next to Mrs. Henshaw's room. Was that what Bix had been doing, at the wrong end of the hall? But what earthly reason could she have for prowling around Mrs. Henshaw's room? Rachel stared into the limpid gray eyes. They stared back unwaveringly.

"Anybody can make a mistake," said Bix haughtily as she turned and started back up the stairs.

This time she really went to the bathroom. Rachel, feeling like a sneak, listened to make sure. Though of course it stood to reason. Bix, knowing that the spare room was occupied, wouldn't be foolhardy enough to make another try. If indeed she had made one to begin with.

It might be pure curiosity, the irresistible lure of forbidden territory. For no one was allowed in Mrs. Henshaw's room. As children, Rachel and Hartley had worked out elaborate plots for getting past that door, simply because it was against the rules. One plot actually worked. Rachel still remembered how disappointed she had been. Because Mrs. Henshaw's room turned out to be just a room, after all. No hair-raising secrets. No witch's paraphernalia, no evil-looking concoctions. Just a room with old-fashioned furniture, like that in the rest of the house—marble tops on chest of drawers and table, candlewick spread on the bed, a fancily-carved desk, a pretty little sewing chair by the window.

Bix was still mostly child, after all. She might easily have been drawn to that room just as Rachel had been, years ago. And, if Mrs. Pierce's thrashings and mutterings hadn't interrupted her, she would have been just as disappointed, for just the same reason.

Rachel scurried back to her chair in the library and arranged, for Bix's benefit, a face of innocence. Bix did the same for her. Queenie looked puzzled by the whole performance. The old clock shuddered and whanged out the time. A quarter of eleven.

"He wouldn't go up to the Business College for any reason, would he?" asked Rachel. Bix didn't even bother to answer that one.

Out of nervousness, Rachel went on, rather tartly. "I can't see why he ever enrolled there, anyway. The Coreyville Business College. It's not even accredited. And if there's anybody in the world more un-fascinated by business than Hartley I don't know who it would be. Does he actually go to classes?"

"Oh yes. I mean, every now and then he does. He thinks the adding machine is a remarkable invention."

"I bet he does."

"Well, so do I," said Bix reasonably. "I guess he figured he might as well be doing something, as long as he was going to stick around here."

"But he didn't have to stick around here! That's just the point. He could have stayed with me and gone on to school. They have adding machines in Chicago, too. Not to mention art schools. That's what Hartley ought to be doing. It's the only thing he's ever been interested in, the only thing he's any good at. No wonder he drinks too much! He must be bored to distraction."

(She was saying too much, too many tactless things. She was jittering herself into alienating her best possible ally. Bix might be misguided, but she was still devoted to Hartley. They were both on Hartley's side, and Rachel was somehow treating Bix as if they weren't.)

But Bix was listening to something else, anyway. The knitting needles stopped flashing. "That's Daddy's car," she said, matter-of-factly. She got up and went out into the hall, with Queenie at her heels.

Rachel sprang up too, and then stopped in the middle of the room, her hands pressed tight together. Were there two sets of footsteps, or only one? Hugh must have found him; he surely wouldn't have given up the search yet. Maybe Hartley had drunk himself into immobility. Or maybe he had—done something rash. No no, he wouldn't do that, it mustn't be that. If the doorbell rang it would mean only that Hartley wasn't sober enough to navigate.

She heard Queenie's tail thumping on the hall floor (Queenie, whose ears were sharper than hers) and she gave a sob of relief. The doorbell did not ring. He was home, then. Home, and navigating. She took a few steps on her trembling legs.

Hugh Bovard came in the library door, holding out his hand and smiling. "The lost is found," he said cheerfully. (How different he looked, thought Rachel. How much older, how terribly tired.) "Safe and sound. I had a hunch he might be out at Louie's. Sure enough, there he was."

"Is he—all right?"

"Why, he's got himself sort of worked up about something. I don't know if he told you or not. Seems he blanked out, the other afternoon—" There was a mixture of caution and casualness in Hugh's voice. He ran his hands through his thick, graying hair—it had been sandy, like Bix's, last time Rachel saw him —and hunched his shoulder, in a gesture that she remembered. "He was talking a good deal, down at Louie's. Sort of wild talk. Not that anybody's going to take that kind of talk seriously."

"I'm sorry, Rachel." Hartley was standing in the doorway,

very pale, with Bix behind him. "Don't cry, please don't cry, Rachel."

"I *have* to," she blurted against his shoulder. "You weren't there when we came out of Manning's, and I didn't know where you were, and—"

"I drove around. I thought maybe if I drove around a while I'd remember. I can't. It's just a blank. I asked everybody I could think of that might have seen me, and nobody did."

She must not protest. To protest would be to admit that she too had seen the ugly little picture that obsessed him. She must stop crying and help him.

"It'll come to you, Hartley. Those things always do." (Unfortunately, perhaps.) "Does anybody besides me want a drink?"

"I'll fix them," said Bix promptly. "Come on, Daddy, you can help."

"Where is she?" asked Hartley. "Mrs. Pierce?"

"Gone to bed. Hours ago."

He glanced toward the door. "She's just like her. Remember how Mrs. Henshaw used to look at us, just stand and look at us for a minute, before she pounced?"

Unwillingly, Rachel remembered.

"She makes me feel like that. As if she's going to pounce. 'Don't try to lie to me, young man. I know what you've been up to. I've got eyes in the back of my head.'"

A gust of ghostly laughter swept them. Hartley had always had a gift for mimicking Mrs. Henshaw; he used to send Rachel, and himself too, off into gales of perilous merriment. What a funny, high-spirited creature he might have been! It wasn't fair, thought Rachel. It was wrong that he should have turned into this guilt-haunted wreck.

"She's going to pounce," he repeated. "She's just like Mrs. Henshaw. Maybe she is Mrs. Henshaw, come back to get even."

"Take it easy, Hartley," said Hugh, handing around the

drinks. "She'd come back if she could, all right. But she can't. So here's to her. Go, lovely rose. Bon voyage." He lifted his glass, smiling, looking a good deal more like himself than he had at first. Of course he was older. But he still had the high-spirited, confident air that Rachel had always found so reassuring.

Only Hartley was not reassured. "I've got to know for sure," he whispered. "Somehow I've got to remember."

For the first time Rachel faced the truth. Hartley did have to remember. He would never be free of Mrs. Henshaw until he knew for sure. Well, then. . . . How did you help someone else remember? Did you ask questions, hoping by chance to hit upon the one magic point that would turn the key? Did you talk irrelevancies, tricking the unconscious into doing its work while no one was looking? Or was it best not to talk at all—

"Well," said Mrs. Pierce from the doorway. "So you got back. High time, I must say." She wore felt house slippers—that was the reason she had taken them all by surprise—and a flannel wrapper, the color of dust. Her hair was covered by an incongruously dainty little cap. A boudoir cap. That was what Mrs. Henshaw used to call the ones she wore.

"I'm sorry if we disturbed you, Mrs. Pierce." Rachel, who, along with Hartley, had sprung up in nervous haste, collected her wits enough to introduce the Bovards. "We were just having a nightcap. Won't you come in and have one with us?"

Mrs. Pierce snorted. It appeared that she disapproved of nightcaps and of everybody who drank them. "Where were you?" she shot at Hartley, exactly as if it were her business.

Hugh rose to the occasion smoothly. "Hartley remembered an errand he'd promised to do for me. I'm afraid I'm to blame for the whole thing, and I hereby apologize. Not only for inconveniencing you and Rachel, but for disturbing your sleep."

"Sleep. I can't sleep." Mrs. Pierce sounded indignant about

it, but her voice quavered ever so slightly. "I keep thinking. Poor Rose. I don't see how it could have happened."

"We don't know for sure, of course," said Rachel. "The steps are pretty steep and narrow."

"I'd like to take a look at them," said Mrs. Pierce.

Here it was, the pounce they had been waiting for. Rachel waited for someone to protest. But no one did, and as they trooped out to the kitchen a secret excitement began to take hold of her.

How did you help someone remember? If you could lay the scene, the little replica scene that would set the mind on the track that it had followed (perhaps) before. . . . The pattern would repeat itself, wouldn't it? Automatically the mind, the nerves and muscles, would slip back into grooves that had been worn before.

Why not? Why not? Anything was better than not knowing for sure.

Here indeed was the little replica scene. The door, the musty smell that rose from the cellar, the light bulb, dim with dust, throwing tricky shadows across the steps. And Mrs. Pierce craning her neck like an inquisitive hen. Did she know how familiar that attitude of hers was, how many times Hartley had mimicked it? ("Hartley, what have you got there in that box? Don't tell me you're trying to sneak another puppy in here behind my back!") Did she know what a perfect replica she was?

Rachel stepped back, out of the scene. Beside her Bix was watching round-eyed, her mouth slightly ajar. Hugh leaned against the kitchen table, his drink still in his hand. The murky light fell on Hartley's face: the hollow cheeks, the eyes with their widened pupils fixed, trance-like, on Mrs. Pierce.

"She was cleaning house," he said softly. "I remember that. She was charging around like crazy, cleaning house."

It was beginning. The mind that had to remember had been

set on the track; the pattern—if there was one—must repeat itself. Nothing could stop it now.

"Pretty steep, you said." Mrs. Pierce threw an accusing glance
at Rachel. "Why, they're straight up and down." Her eye fell
on Hartley. "What are you muttering about?"

"Nothing. I just—"

"Straight up and down. A public menace." Clutching the
splintery hand rail, she leaned farther forward to peer. "And one
of them's broken."

"It wasn't before," said Hartley. He took a step forward, and
his hand, his long, strong hand, reached toward the defenseless
shoulder poised there over the darkness below.

Rachel watched. She could not stop watching. A paralyzing
chill crept through her; she could not even close her eyes.

"Be careful," Hartley said. "You might lose your balance."
And he drew Mrs. Pierce back, turned the light switch, and shut
the cellar door. His movements were quick and sure. Then, just
as quickly, just as surely, he turned and went out the back door.

"*Now* where's he going?" Mrs. Pierce wanted to know. "I
vow, I never saw the like!"

But Rachel and Bix (who must have caught a glimpse of his
eyes too) were already brushing past her, on their way to the
back porch. They stopped there. Hartley was a shadow streak-
ing across the bare yard toward Papa's old office. In a minute
a light bloomed inside the square little building.

"He pulled her back!" whispered Rachel. "He pulled her
back!"

"It worked," said Bix. "He's remembered." They waited,
shivering, while Hartley's shadow streaked back toward them.
He had a sheet of white paper in his hand.

"I remembered!" His voice was breathless but triumphant.
"She's just like her, and all at once it hit me—I always high-
tailed it for Papa's office when she got to cleaning house, and

that's where I was—I was doing a sketch of her—it's even got the date on it—"

He put one arm around Rachel and the other around Bix, pulling them into a tight little circle. United and jubilant they stood, and for the moment Mrs. Pierce's voice was of no more importance than a gnat buzzing in the background.

"I'll thank somebody to tell me what's going on here." Mrs. Pierce was sputtering away like a wet hen. "All at once *what* hit him? That's what I want to know. There's plenty more I want to know, too. Where was he when Rose fell down those stairs? Why's he acting so peculiar? I don't mind telling you, the whole thing's struck me as mighty peculiar, from the very beginning. . . . Where *was* he? What's he got in his hand?"

Eager-eyed, Hartley thrust the sketch toward her. "I know where I was. That's what hit me all at once!" he cried. "I remember it now. I was over in Papa's office the whole afternoon, I've even got this sketch to prove it, and so I couldn't possibly have—I mean—" Too late, he faltered into silence.

"Young man, do you know what you're saying? Have you any idea of what you're admitting? Well, I have, and—"

"He's admitting that he blanked out," said Hugh firmly. "The rest of us already knew that. He blanked out for a while, and now he's remembered where he was. That's no crime, Mrs. Pierce, and you know it as well as I do."

"I don't know anything of the kind! Don't try to tell me what I know! Here, let me see that." She snatched the sketch from Hartley's hand and turned toward the light streaming out from the kitchen door to inspect it.

Rachel's heart sank like a stone. Hartley had a caustic gift for caricature when he chose to use it, and he had chosen to use it on Mrs. Henshaw. There she was, a witch with a wart on her chin, gleefully tending a fire, her face the face of a fanatic, at once ridiculous and terrifying. No one could fail to recognize her. And no one, seeing the sketch, could doubt for a moment that Hartley hated her.

"Good God," said Hugh sorrowfully.

"What's this? What's this?" Mrs. Pierce clamped on to the sketch, eyes and hands.

"It doesn't mean anything," said Hartley. Too fast. "I was just mad at her because she burnt up all my sketches and stuff last week, and this is the way I worked it off. That's all."

Mrs. Pierce let the silence stretch out unbearably. Then she took a long breath. "That's all. Doesn't mean anything. No crime. Well, we'll just see about that. You may be satisfied there's been no crime, but I'm not, and I'm going to call the sheriff and tell him so."

IX

(Lois Dobbs, the night operator at the telephone office, said afterwards that she wasn't the least bit surprised when the call came in for the sheriff. She and her boy friend had been out at Louie's having a beer before she went on duty, and with her own ears she'd heard Hartley Buckmaster asking everybody in sight where he was the afternoon Mrs. Henshaw fell down the stairs and broke her neck. If that didn't sound suspicious, then Lois didn't know what did. She'd said to her boy friend at the time, she'd said. . . . Well, anyway, she wasn't the least bit surprised. The sheriff was, though. Lois thought he never was going to catch on. Of course he'd been wakened up out of a sound sleep. "But Ma'am, the case is closed," he kept saying. "I know they had a quarrel last week, I've heard the talk that's been going round. But the case is closed. Death by accident. The case is closed." "Then you march right over here and re-open it," this Mrs. Pierce, this sister of Mrs. Henshaw's, snapped at him, and before he knew it he'd said "Yes, Ma'am." It gave Lois the creeps, the way the sister sounded like Mrs. Henshaw.)

It was true that Sheriff Charlie Jeffreys had been wakened out of a sound sleep. But he was new at his job—his war record, with the Marines in the Pacific, had won him the election—and therefore extra-alert when it came to performing his duties as officer of the law. It didn't take him long to pull on his pants, grab his badge and gun, jump into his Chevvie and head for the Buckmaster residence.

So little time, in fact, that they were still out on the back porch when they heard him rattling up the street.

"Here he comes," said Hugh. "Now keep your head, Hartley. Charlie's a good guy, and he's going to see how ridiculous this whole thing is. You haven't got a thing to worry about."

"We'll see about that," said Mrs. Pierce with satisfaction. "We'll see what he's got to worry about."

Maybe it was the satisfaction in her voice that did it. She did sound extraordinarily like Mrs. Henshaw, and it may have been a sort of reflex action that hurled Hartley into unreasoning panic. Anyway, he bolted. Just as Sheriff Jeffreys got out of the Chevvie, Hartley lunged down the porch steps, zigzagged for a minute across the yard, and headed finally for Myra Graves' lilac hedge.

Hugh lunged after him, seconds too late. "Don't be a fool, Hartley! Hartley, you damn fool—"

"That's him, Sheriff!" shrieked Mrs. Pierce. "Don't let him get away! There he is!"

Fifteen years ago Sheriff Jeffreys had been the fastest quarterback Coreyville High School ever produced. Thanks perhaps to the Marines, he had not lost his speed. He sprinted for the lilac hedge as if he had been shot out of a cannon.

Scrambling sounds, grunts, a thud. "Don't let him shoot him," somebody kept sobbing. "Don't let him shoot him." It turned out that it was Rachel herself.

On the other side of the lilac hedge a car stopped briefly, voices called cheery good nights, footsteps tapped up the sidewalk, and then Myra Graves' voice rang out in open astonishment. "What in the world—Why, Charlie Jeffreys, what are you doing under there? Hartley! Charlie, you've hit him! Why, you ought to be ashamed—Hartley, you come right in with me, I'll fix you up in a jiffy—"

There was a good deal of confused muttering and a little more scrambling, before the three of them emerged from the hedge and crossed to the back porch. Hartley was stumbling, half-dragged, half-supported by Charlie, who was doing his best to look resolute instead of shame-faced. Myra trotted along behind, still exclaiming about band-aids and Well, she never and What in the world!

"Arrest him," screeched Mrs. Pierce. "Sheriff, I want him arrested this minute. There's something wrong or he wouldn't have run. It's plain as the nose on your face."

"Yes, Ma'—" Charlie was beginning automatically, when Hugh shouldered Mrs. Pierce aside and interrupted.

"Now look here, Charlie, what are you going to arrest him *for*? There hasn't been any crime. Death by accident—that's what the doctor said and that's what the coroner decided. You've got to prove there was a crime before you go around arresting anybody. And you can't, because there wasn't. This is the craziest damn thing I ever heard of!"

"I know, Mr. Bovard, but—" Charlie's round red face got redder than ever. He remembered to keep a tight, though probably unnecessary, grip on Hartley, whose head was hanging down like a groggy fighter's. With his free hand Charlie scratched his ear. He shifted from one foot to the other. "I know, but—"

"Crazy, is it! I don't care what the doctor said or what the coroner decided. There's something wrong, and if this isn't proof enough to suit you, then I'll get more proof. I'll get to the bottom of this if it's the last—" Mrs. Pierce's red-brown eyes (they looked ready to burst into blaze) switched suddenly to Myra. "You were here. You found Rose, so I gather. Now I want the straight of it. What did you do?"

"Do? What did I do? Why, I—" Myra got a grip on herself by switching her own gaze to Charlie. She squared her shoulders and began bravely enough. "You've heard all this before, Charlie, but if certain people aren't satisfied, why I'm perfectly willing to tell it again. I've got nothing to hide, and neither has Hartley. Like I told you, I ran over to borrow a cup of sugar. Nobody answered when I knocked, so I opened the door and hollered. Still no answer. Well, anybody else, I would have just walked in and helped myself, but you know how she—So I started back home. I'd got to the hedge when I heard Hartley call out my name, so I—"

"Where was he?" demanded Mrs. Pierce. "Where'd he come from?"

Myra kept her eyes fixed desperately on Charlie. "He was there. Right there by the porch steps. I don't know where he came from. I told him how I couldn't raise anybody, so we went in and got the sugar, and then we noticed the cellar door was open, and we—we found her. Well, of course, the first thing we thought of was a doctor. Only Dr. Craig was out in the country, confinement case, so then there wasn't anything to do but call old Doc Fulbright, he don't very often take a case any more, but—" She made the mistake of pausing, and Mrs. Pierce pounced.

"Why doesn't he? What's the matter with him?"

Myra was jarred. But still game. "Nothing's the matter with him. He's retired, gave up his practice years ago. But he still knows his business, old Doc Fulbright does, and don't let anybody tell you different. He said right off she was dead, and for us to call the sheriff. Gave it as his opinion it was an accident, but said we'd ought to call Charlie anyway."

"That's right. That's the whole story, Mrs. Pierce," Charlie confirmed—being as careful as Myra, however, to avoid getting himself impaled on those red-brown eyes. "I came over, me and Mr. Manning, he's the coroner, and we all agreed it was a clear case of accident. So Doc signed the death certificate, accidental death, due to a broken neck and a what-do-you-call-it where she'd hit the back of her head on the cabinet down at the bottom of the steps. That's it, and I don't see how anybody would have done any different."

"Well, I do," snapped Mrs. Pierce. "In the first place, they got a doctor that isn't even in practice any more. She said so. In the second place, did anybody ask where Hartley popped up from? No. Anybody think it was the least bit out of the way, him not remembering where he was till just a little while ago? Oh my, no. Not for a minute. Not even though they'd had a big quarrel—he's admitted it—just the week before. Third place, why did he run, if he's not guilty? I'd just like to have somebody explain that, if they can." She folded her arms and glared.

"That's so," said Charlie. He scratched his ear again. "You did run, Hartley. You—you resisted me."

Mrs. Pierce saw her advantage, and pressed it. "I'm glad to hear you admit it. If you can't arrest him for murder, you can arrest him for resisting an officer of the law, and after you've done that you can call in a doctor that at least claims to be in practice and find out what really happened to Rose. And I'll tell you this much, young man. If you don't do it I'll report you to the authorities and see that they do it. I want this case re-opened, and I want something more than a half-baked investigation, and I'm going to get it."

"Well, I guess I—" began Charlie.

Unexpectedly, Hartley lifted his head; he was still swaying slightly and now Rachel could see the lump on the side of his jaw, but he spoke with deadly distinctness. "Go ahead. Arrest me. Arrest me for murder. What's the difference whether I really did it or not? I wish to God I had. That's all. I wish to God I had."

Hugh Bovard threw up his hands in a gesture of surrender, and faithful old Queenie gave a whine of distress.

(Lois Dobbs said afterwards that she wasn't the least bit surprised when the call came through for Dr. Craig, either. But it was funny, what popped into her head. *Murder. Somebody's been murdered.* It wasn't anything that Charlie Jeffreys said. He just told Doc to get over to Buckmaster's right away, so it wasn't anything he said. A premonition, you might call it, woman's intuition. Because that was just exactly what Lois thought. *Murder.* She remembered the way Hartley had been talking out at Louie's, and she thought, *Murder. Somebody's been murdered.*)

The waiting, it seemed to Rachel, was harder to take than Mrs. Pierce at her most waspish. First there was the short wait for Dr. Craig. Charlie Jeffreys met him out in the hall and explained what had to be explained, and the doctor left without coming into the library. Then came the long wait, for Dr. Craig's return and his report. (How long did it take, for a doctor to find out whether somebody had been pushed down a flight of steps or had simply, accidentally fallen? How could he tell?)

They sat in the library, though the fire had long since died and it didn't occur to anybody to build a new one. Charlie Jeffreys, looking ill-at-ease but conscientious, sat close to Hartley. The rest of them, except for Mrs. Pierce, huddled together like cattle waiting for a storm, their faces blank with strain. Mrs. Pierce sat bolt upright in a straight chair beside the door, the image of suspicious vigilance. All right, ostracize me, she seemed to be saying. I'm ostracizing you, too. And what's more, I'm right. You'll see. I'm right.

Rachel kept thinking—of all things—of Mr. Manning, and how upset he must be, at having his careful handiwork on Mrs.

Henshaw disturbed. Every time she tried to collect her wits and figure out something constructive, her mind played the same irresponsible trick, producing only the crestfallen face of poor Mr. Manning. . . .

"There he is. That's Doc," said Charlie Jeffreys. He sounded scared to death, but he got up and went out to the hall—maybe out of an obscure feeling for the proprieties, maybe just to get away from the silence. It was twenty minutes of two, and Rachel was suddenly convinced that she could not possibly sit here and listen to the clock whang out another doom-voiced quarter hour. Voices murmured in the hall. At eighteen minutes of two she followed Charlie.

They were standing under the red-glass chandelier, Charlie and Dr. Craig. Rachel had seen him only sitting in the car this afternoon and now, distraught as she was, she caught the sleek tom-cat look of Dr. Craig's back. Her irresponsible mind again. ". . . administered after death," he was saying. "The fall apparently broke her neck, but her skull was fractured afterwards. And not by anything she hit on the way down, either. Something sharper. It would have killed her, if the fall hadn't. No slur on Dr. Fulbright, you understand. Anybody would have thought what he did, that she got the skull injury in the course of the fall. I would have, myself. Only there's no doubt about it, that's not what happened."

"Holy smoke!" said Charlie. "You mean somebody followed her down the steps and beat in the back of her head after she'd already broke her—" His eye fell on Rachel, and he gulped. "Holy smoke!"

"That's it," said Dr. Craig cheerfully. His back was still turned to Rachel. "If you can prove somebody pushed her in the first place you've got a nice, fat, juicy murder on your hands. All yours, kid."

Rachel gave an unobtrusive little gasp and fainted, neatly

enough, against the mahogany hall piece. When she opened her eyes again, Dr. Craig was bending over her. His face simply didn't match the sleek tom-cat back. Such a plain, even homely, face, with that long upper lip and stiff, spiky-looking black hair.

"Excuse me," she said. Then she remembered. A nice, fat, juicy murder. "Hartley didn't do it," she told Dr. Craig earnestly. "He hated her, but so did somebody else. Because Hartley didn't do it. We proved it."

"Good for you," said Dr. Craig.

After that Sheriff Jeffreys took Hartley off to jail.

X

Dr. Craig slept in the back room of his office, which was up above the drug store, and ate all his meals out. This arrangement, which wrung the hearts of Coreyville's female population, suited Dr. Craig fine. Having grown up with seven brothers and sisters, he had never before had the luxury of a room all to himself. He ate at odd hours, often hurriedly, and the meals he got out at Louie's or down at the Square Deal Cafe tasted good to him. So did the home-cooked dinners to which the Coreyville ladies sometimes invited him on account of their tender hearts (not to mention their eligible daughters). Food was food, as far as he was concerned. There was a tentative quality about the dinner invitations, because after all, Dr. Craig *did* have a wife when he first came, and though she hadn't stayed in Coreyville more than a couple of weeks, nobody was quite sure of his marital status.

This also suited him fine. For the nonce, anyway. For the nonce.

The morning after Hartley's arrest Dr. Craig woke up late, realized it was Sunday, and lay for a few minutes contentedly surveying his cluttered little back room and his own large feet, which stuck out beyond the end of the studio couch. He had forgotten to pull the shades again, and the winter sunshine lay in lemon-colored wafers on the dusty congoleum rug. Simultaneously the Methodist and Presbyterian church bells began ringing, loud and bossy-sounding, as if they were quarrelling over the souls of Coreyville. They had something to quarrel about all right, thought Dr. Craig affably. A real prize package: the soul of a murderer.

He couldn't quite see Hartley Buckmaster plumping for either the Methodists or the Presbyterians. But when it came to that, he couldn't quite see Hartley murdering anybody, either. Not even Mrs. Henshaw? Why not? Any logical reason?

Well, there was that sister of Hartley's. Rachel. Rachel Buckmaster.

All at once Dr. Craig found that he was no longer feeling so affable and contented. His feet were cold, for one thing. And he wished to God he'd remembered to get somebody in to clean this place up. Squalid, that's what it was. Squalid. With the obscure conviction that he was being persecuted—or anyway heckled—he stalked into the bathroom and stared moodily at his face in the mirror. What a pan. What a personality. What a life.

Daddy, what is logic? Very simple, Junior, it goes like this. Hartley has a sister, and the sister has a cleft chin. Ergo Hartley is not a murderer.

But somebody was. That was the hell of it. Somebody was, and Dr. Craig had lifted up his clarion voice and proclaimed the truth. Well, what else could he have done? Even if he had kept his mouth shut, the Pierce female would have dug up another doctor to prove her point. She might not have. Of course she would have. The woman was a steamroller. Besides, there was the matter of his conscience. A small matter. Granted. And Mrs. Henshaw deserved what she got. Granted. But wouldn't his conscience have given him a slight twinge, if he hadn't told the truth?

Very slight, he decided. Very, very slight.

It was deplorable, what a good-looking babe like Hartley's sister could do to a man's principles. And what she could do to his sense of logic was downright alarming. The realistic approach was needed, and Dr. Craig gave himself the full treatment while he shaved. Good-looking babes were fine. In their place. Which was—well, call it the field of indoor sports. Keep them there. That was the trick. Because the minute you put them on any other plane they stopped being fun and turned into trouble. You got involved, and you got hurt, and nobody knew this better than Dr. Craig.

Well, then. As long as his intentions remained strictly dishonorable, he was safe. He fought his way into his last clean white shirt and went down to the Square Deal for some coffee.

The waitress was a hefty girl named Erma, whose feet were always killing her. She and the only other customer—the kid from the filling station—were avidly discussing just exactly what you would expect. Yak yak yak, thought Dr. Craig. With callous lack of consideration for Erma's feet, he settled himself at the other end of the counter and propped the Chicago paper up against the sugar bowl beside him to show how he felt about conversation. Erma and the filling station kid ignored this signal.

"Hey Doc, what's the lowdown? Did Hartley really—"

Dr. Craig gave them a cold, forbidding, professional-ethics stare. "I made my report last night to the authorities, and when they see fit to release it you'll know all I do. In the meantime, Erma, what do I have to do to get a cup of coffee around here? Make it myself?"

Erma, who was accustomed to sociable little chats with Dr. Craig about her feet and last night's movie and her boy friend in the Navy, looked surprised and hurt. Which was just too damn bad, thought Dr. Craig. He fastened his eyes on the Chicago headlines, sipped his coffee, and listened for all he was worth to the conversation at the other end of the counter. Hartley had confessed. No he hadn't, he just said he was glad she was dead. ... Well, why would he say that if he hadn't... ? Charlie Jeffreys had called in the state authorities; a detective was coming tomorrow to take everybody's fingerprints. Hugh Bovard was getting a Chicago lawyer for Hartley, and somebody said that proved that Bix was mixed up in it too. Somebody else said Rachel Buckmaster was the one that was mixed up in it; she'd planned the whole thing because she and Hartley wanted to sell the house—

Dr. Craig slammed some money down on the counter and walked out.

"What's eating on Doc?" asked the filling station kid.

"Nothing except he's tired," said Erma loyally. "You'd be tired too if you'd been up all night, messing around with Mrs. Henshaw."

Main Street was deserted. Hardly a sign of life except for Havelka's calico cat, who was taking a fastidious stroll around the butcher shop window in search of the warmest patch of sunshine. The drug store sign creaked in the raw wind, and some busybody hens a couple of blocks away started cackling. Flawless Sunday peace. It occurred to Dr. Craig that he had nothing whatever to do. He walked up the block to where his coupe was parked and got in.

The chances were that Rachel Buckmaster was not at home. She was probably over at the Bovards', or at Myra Graves'. He thought of what he would say, if by any chance she was at home. Hello, there. I was just driving past, and thought I'd drop in and see if there's anything I can do. ... It sounded too officious. Making like the old friend of the family, when he hadn't even seen her until yesterday. Okay, then, too officious. Hello, there.

I was just driving past, and thought I'd drop in and see if you're feeling all right this morning. That might pass; after all, she had fainted last night. A semi-professional call, in a way.

There was a long silence after he turned the doorbell. So long that he was about to take his semi-professional call (what a pity, after all that brainwork) and depart. Then the door opened, and there she was, cleft chin and all. She had on an apron, and her hands were dusty.

He wasted his brainwork, after all, by blurting out, "Did you get over your swoon?"

"My what? Oh. Very well, thank you. Look, I don't know what to think, I've found something funny, I mean I haven't found it—" She stopped helplessly. "Won't you come in?"

He was already in. "What's the matter?"

"I can't find the candlestick," she explained. Something in her manner gave him the feeling that they were resuming a conversation instead of beginning one. It was such an oddly pleasant feeling that he got right into the spirit of the thing and followed her down the hall and out into the kitchen as if he knew exactly where she was leading him, and why. The door to the cellar stairs stood open, and they paused there, peering down at the broken step. In the murky light it looked ugly and jagged, like a fresh cut.

"Morbid curiosity, I guess," said Rachel. "That's what Myra said. She stayed overnight with me. She wouldn't even let me open the door. So I waited till after she went to church."

"Naturally," said Dr. Craig wisely. "And the—er—candlestick?"

"It isn't there. Come on down, I'll show you. I was going to open the cellar window because it's always so stuffy down there, so of course I reached for the candlestick to prop it up with, and it wasn't there. It isn't anywhere. I've looked all over."

They were at the foot of the steps now. Gingerly, Dr. Craig

raised the dusty little window. It needed something to prop it open, all right; the minute he let go it slammed shut.

"We always kept it right here," said Rachel. "On the floor beside the window."

"What kind of a candlestick was it?"

"Brass. Old-fashioned. It had square corners. One of a pair that belonged to Mrs. Henshaw. She once told me somebody gave them to her for a wedding present. She just had the one, though. Francie kept the other one when they separated. Kept it out of spite, according to her. She said one candlestick wasn't any good to anybody. So we always used it to prop up the window. It was just the right size."

Yes. Dr. Craig thought about the back of Mrs. Henshaw's head. From Rachel's description, the candlestick would be just the right size. And the right shape. And the right weight.

"I can't imagine," began Rachel, "why anybody would move it—" Her eyes got big.

The hell you can't, thought Dr. Craig. He cleared his throat. "This is ticklish. If it's been hidden some place where your brother might have put it, it's not going to be anything to cheer about. On the other hand, if it should turn up somewhere else— in somebody else's house—then it might do him plenty of good." They exchanged a thoughtful look. "You said last night that you proved he didn't do it. How come he was arrested? Didn't you let the sheriff in on this proof?"

They leaned against the cabinet (where Mrs. Henshaw might so easily have hit her head; only she hadn't) and smoked a cigarette while Rachel explained.

"I see," he said when she had finished. "He didn't push Mrs. Pierce. Ergo—" Okay; so he was a sucker for a cleft chin. His intentions, however, were strictly dishonorable. "Ergo he didn't push Mrs. Henshaw. Sounds logical to me. A little subtle for the sheriff, maybe. He's going to want something more solid. Which brings us back to the candlestick. You covered the cellar, you said?"

"Every inch. I know all the hiding places, and it's not down here. Whoever did it must have taken the candlestick away with them. No telling where it might be, by now. In the river, maybe. Or buried somewhere."

"Unless the idea was to plant the whole thing on Hartley. In which case they might tuck it away where it would do him the most harm. Let's take a look at your father's office."

It was an easy place to search. There wasn't much in it; Dr. Craig himself had bought most of the equipment when he first came to Coreyville. There was a rolltop desk, cluttered now with Hartley's paints and sketch pads. A couple of empty cabinets. No candlestick. They went back to the house and sat down at the kitchen table to have a cup of coffee and consider their next move.

"I don't suppose you've heard anything from Mrs. Pierce this morning?" said Dr. Craig.

"No, and I don't expect to. She spent the night at the hotel, and all I hope is that they still have bedbugs. I—evicted her, you know."

"I heard you." Dr. Craig grinned. Rachel had minced no words with Mrs. Pierce last night. "You'll have to go some place else," she had said. "I won't have you in the house." Mrs. Pierce snapped out that she wouldn't think of staying; she wouldn't feel safe in this nest of murderers. But the last, soul-satisfying word had been Rachel's. "You're so right," she had said as Mrs. Pierce marched upstairs. "Believe me, Mrs. Pierce, you wouldn't *be* safe."

"Petty of me," she said now. "I ought to be ashamed. But I'm not. She's Mrs. Henshaw all over again, and so I had to tell her off—" All at once she was on the verge of tears, and Dr. Craig treated himself to a split-second daydream in which she dissolved against his manly shoulder, and he patted her—in a fatherly way, of course, at least at first, and—Instead, she stood up and banged the coffee pot back on the stove. "Aren't we ever going to get rid of Mrs. Henshaw? Hasn't she done enough to Hartley and me, without this? She might at least have the decency to die a natural death. But no. She's got to get herself murdered, and she's got to have a carbon copy sister to stir everybody up—"

"Me and my choice little report," said Dr. Craig. "I wish to God I'd kept my mouth shut."

"You think that would have stopped her? Ha! Nothing can stop people like Mrs. Henshaw. I ought to know. I grew up under her thumb." She sank back into her chair. All the poise, or whatever it was that made you look twice, seemed to sift out of her, leaving a woebegone, cringing child.

Dr. Craig couldn't stand to have her look like that. The discovery shook him. Danger, signalled his twice-shy brain; Beware of Getting Involved. Proceed At Your own Risk. Remember Your Dishonorable Intentions. He got up and paced the floor. "What I can't understand—" He was surprised himself at what he said next. It was as if his mind, groping around among a lot of baffling irritations, stumbled against this and latched on to it out of sheer frustration. "What I can't understand is your father. Why the hell did he keep the woman around?"

There was a brief silence. Rachel looked down at her hands; she had straight eyelashes, like funny, tiny little brushes. Slowly, painfully, her face turned red. "He had to have somebody keep house for us," she said at last, "after my mother died. What else could he do but hire a housekeeper?"

"But it didn't have to be Mrs. Henshaw. I mean, he didn't have to keep her. He must have seen what she was doing to you and Hartley, unless he was completely blind."

"Oh no," said Rachel, "Papa wasn't blind. He knew what she was doing."

"And still he didn't fire her." It *was* odd when you thought about it—and now that Rachel had stopped cringing Dr. Craig's mind seemed to be back in reasonably good working order. "It's almost as if—well, as if she had something on him."

"You mean blackmail?" Suddenly Rachel laughed—in relief? The notion crossed his mind.

"Why not? She was certainly the type for it. Just her dish of tea."

"Yes. Of course," said Rachel. "It's funny, I never thought of that before."

"What did you think? That they were—" He paused, and the tell-tale red showed in Rachel's face again. "So that's the way you had it figured out. Papa and Mrs. Henshaw, romping in the hay."

The words appalled him, the moment they were out of his mouth. Craig the diplomat, he thought in despair. Craig, weaver of the magic phrase. The Bard of Coreyville. . . .

Rachel blinked and gave a little sigh. "Yes. Why not? It's exactly the way I had it figured out. Only I never said so. Not even to myself. Don't look so scared," she added parenthetically. "Close your mouth, it's more becoming. I'm sure Freud has an explanation for it. Maybe it's the usual thing, with girls whose fathers have housekeepers."

"Maybe," said Dr. Craig rather feebly.

"Because I don't remember anything definite that I based it on. I couldn't understand why he kept her around, either, and I'd never heard of blackmail. She did have beautiful red hair. . . ."

"It must have been either that or blackmail." (She wants it to be blackmail, Dr. Craig was thinking. It must really have eaten on her, when she was a kid.) "When it comes to that, I suppose a small town doctor would be pretty good pickings for a blackmailer."

"What do you—oh. Abor— You mean Papa might have—" She let the question dangle.

"Of course he might have," said Dr. Craig brusquely. (Any doctor with a grain of humanity might have, given the right combination of circumstances. The moral being that doctors shouldn't have humane impulses.) "So let's say she did have something on the poor guy. Where does that get us?" He answered the question himself. "It gets us nowhere. Papa might have had a motive for pushing Mrs. Henshaw downstairs. Only he wasn't here to do it. A classic example of lack of opportunity. All we've done is waste time on a dead end street. We're right back where we started."

"We could search the rest of the house for the candlestick," said Rachel. "It wouldn't have to be planted in Papa's office. Any place in the house would do. Hartley's room, or mine, or Mrs. Henshaw's. Mrs. Henshaw's room. I wonder if that's what Bix—" A peculiar expression crossed her face. She did not finish the sentence.

"What about Bix? You think she knows something?"

"Of course not. How could she? She's nothing but a kid. Come on, let's start down here."

They covered the downstairs rooms without result. It wasn't a hard job; while Mrs. Henshaw had obviously been a string-saver, she had been orderly about it. A place for everything, and everything in its place. Her bedroom upstairs, which they left till last, was fanatically tidy. Even the hairpins were sorted according to size and stowed away in little boxes.

"Depressing, isn't it? All this tidiness," said Rachel. She closed the bottom dresser drawer and sat back on her heels. "And no candlestick. Whoever did it took it away. They've had plenty of time to dispose of it."

"I don't suppose Hartley saw anybody coming or going, the day it happened?"

"Not a soul. I asked him this morning, when Hugh Bovard and I went up to the court house to see him. Of course he was over in Papa's office, and he wasn't paying any attention—as usual. You know how Hartley is. Kind of other-worldly. He didn't see anybody and what's worse, nobody saw him, so who's going to believe that he was really in Papa's office and not here in the house, polishing off Mrs. Henshaw?"

"Yeah," sighed Dr. Craig.

"Hugh says not to worry." Rachel's voice quavered. "He says the whole thing's just ridiculous. He called Mr. Whitman in Chicago this morning—he's a lawyer that Hugh's known for years. Papa knew him too, and he's coming down Tuesday. Hugh says—"

"Hey! Anybody home?" called Bix's voice from downstairs.

At the sound Rachel jumped a little, shifting on her heels. She looked down at the floor, an almost comically startled expression on her face. "It moved," she said. "It sort of tilted." She shifted again, experimentally; there was no doubt about it, the wide floor board under her heels lifted slightly at one end. Dr. Craig dropped to his knees beside her and turned back the edge of the hooked rug. He felt a prickle of excitement at the back of his neck.

"Hey!" Bix again. "Where are you?"

There was nothing else to do; she had heard them. "Upstairs!" Rachel called back. Then she whispered, "Do you think we should wait?"

"Hell no. This may be important. Bix is okay." He quoted Rachel herself. "Besides, she's nothing but a kid."

There would hardly have been time to cover up what they were doing, anyway. Bix took the stairs at a good fast clip. "Hi!"

Her eyes brightened. "What's up? What you doing? Hey, the boards are loose! Doc, what you doing?"

"Appendectomy. Emergency," said Dr. Craig. "There doesn't happen to be a chisel up there on the dresser, does there?"

"No, but there's a nail file."

It was as easy as that. They did it with the nail file and Mrs. Henshaw's hair brush. A section of two of the boards lifted out, simply and neatly, exposing a large, sturdy metal box in the cavity below. The three of them stared at it.

"Ah ha," said Dr. Craig. "Mrs. Henshaw's little secret."

"What's in it?" gasped Rachel. "Is it locked?"

Bix said nothing at all.

Dr. Craig lifted it out and tried the lid. It was securely locked. "The key ought to be somewhere in this room," he said, "unless we're all off and it isn't Mrs. Henshaw's box, but somebody else's."

"Of course it's hers. She wouldn't let anybody else in here. It has to be hers." Rachel scrambled to her feet. "Keys. I saw some keys somewhere. Was it in the desk?"

"I'll look," said Bix quickly. Already she was across the room and at the desk. "Here's some keys," she said over her shoulder. "A whole ring of them."

But none of them fit. It was obvious that none of them would, but Bix and Rachel watched, while Dr. Craig tried them all. "We could force it, I suppose," he said tentatively. "Only I'm not sure it's legal. How do you ladies feel about it?"

"It would seem more legal if we could find the key," said Rachel. "Though I don't see what difference it makes, as long as we've gone this far. . . ."

Bix was sternly disapproving. "I bet it isn't legal at all. I bet we shouldn't even be in here. We ought to put it back and—"

"And forget about it? Bix, are you serious?" Rachel's eyes

flashed with temper. "Why, there might be something in there that would clear Hartley!"

"Well—" Bix shuffled her feet and looked down at the floor.

Dr. Craig watched her thoughtfully. It occurred to him that there might also be something in Mrs. Henshaw's box that wouldn't clear Hartley.

The silence was broken by the doorbell. Whoever had turned it was impatient; it had hardly stopped wheezing before the door downstairs opened and a heavy tread sounded in the hall.

"Hullo! Hullo there!"

"It's the sheriff," whispered Bix. "Don't—"

But Rachel had already called back to him. Her eyes were still sparkling with anger. "What's the matter with you? Don't you want to get Hartley out of jail? Don't you want to know what's in that box? It'll be legal now, Dr. Craig, we'll get Charlie Jeffreys to open it and—" Her voice dwindled away, and Dr. Craig wondered if it was because of his face. Could he possibly be looking as uneasy as he felt? Probably his face had nothing to do with it; after all, Rachel was as bright as he was, the potentialities of Mrs. Henshaw's box were bound to dawn on her sooner or later. Well, it hadn't been sooner. At least things were going to be legal from here on in.

"Hullo, Doc. Afternoon, Miss Buckmaster, Bix." There was a subtle change in the sheriff's manner. The general effect he had given last night was of a man who, never having heard of a roller coaster, suddenly finds himself riding on one. Today he was still on it, but he had learned something about roller coasters since last night. He was taking it calmer.

"What's that?" His round blue eyes blinked at the metal box and at its tidy hiding place (it must be Mrs. Henshaw's handiwork, thought Dr. Craig; no one else could have managed it so neatly).

"We were just going to call you," said Dr. Craig. He was surprised and pleased at how smoothly this whopper rolled out. Here was a talent he hadn't known he possessed. "Miss Buckmaster and I happened on this while we were—er—"

The sheriff waited, plainly interested, while Dr. Craig's newfound talent evaporated.

"We were looking for the candlestick," said Rachel. Evidently she had decided that honesty was the best policy. It was certainly more comfortable, thought Dr. Craig as he listened to her explanation. And—since the candlestick hadn't turned up in any place that might embarrass Hartley—it was safe enough. Good old best-policy honesty.

"You mean you've ransacked everything?" said Sheriff Jeffreys when she had finished. "My gosh. I just talked to State Headquarters, and they said for me to seal up the whole house. They're sending a guy down, he'll be here in the morning. And here you've already—"

"We meant well," said Rachel cheerfully. "And you've got to admit we've turned up something for the State guy to work on."

The sheriff conceded the point, but there was a note of bitterness in his voice as he turned back to the box. "What's in it? Don't tell me you eager beavers haven't opened it."

"There's no key, and we didn't think it was legal to force it," explained Dr. Craig virtuously.

"Good," said the sheriff. "I'll take it along with me." They watched wistfully as he took charge of their find. "Could you make arrangements, Miss Buckmaster, to stay somewhere else? Because that's what I'm supposed to do, seal up the whole house. Keep everybody out."

"We've got plenty of room," said Bix, and Dr. Craig wished he could say the same. "You can stay at our house. Hey, that reminds me. I came over to ask you to have dinner with Daddy and me. My mother isn't feeling good, but Daddy said we could drive out to Chicken Inn for dinner."

Rachel opened her mouth, but Dr. Craig opened his faster. "It's a small world, isn't it? I've already made the same proposition to Miss Buckmaster. So she's tied up for dinner."

"I—" Rachel turned quite pink. "Why, yes. He already— Thanks anyway, Bix. We'll probably see you out there, at Chicken Inn."

"Probably." On her way to the door, Bix turned, suddenly grinning. "Bless you, my children," she said before she ran downstairs.

XI

Dr. Craig helped the sheriff lock all the doors and windows, while Rachel went to her room to repack her belongings. She also changed her dress in honor of the expedition to Chicken Inn, a circumstance which filled Dr. Craig with secret elation. The dress she changed to was brown, with a couple of intriguing gold tassels, and on her head she wore what appeared to be an omelet, done to a golden turn. On her an omelet was becoming.

"Let's not talk about Mrs. Henshaw at all. Let's ignore her," she said as they got into the coupe and waved goodbye to the sheriff. "I wonder what's in that box."

"More string, maybe. Slightly used paper bags. Apparently she never threw anything away."

Rachel sighed. "Don't try to comfort me. It may be stuffed with anti-Hartley evidence, and if it is I'll never forgive myself. Never. And neither will Bix. She had the right idea. If I'd listened to her the box would be where it belongs, with us instead of the sheriff."

"Women," said Dr. Craig. "No respect for the law. You know very well—"

"I don't care what I know. Except that Hartley didn't do it, and he's in jail."

"Who else hated her? I know nobody liked her. She probably didn't have a friend in the world. But it's got to be more than that. Somebody had to hate her so much, or be so afraid of her, that they couldn't let her go on living. There can't be many people with those qualifications."

"One is all we need," Rachel reminded him. "Wouldn't it be nice if it was Mrs. Pierce? But she wasn't even in town. Neither was I, so that lets me out."

Unwillingly, Dr. Craig remembered the snatch of conversation he had overheard in the Square Deal. And unwillingly he blurted out the question. "How bad did you and Hartley want to sell the house?"

"How bad?" Rachel's voice, as frank as ever, was tinged with surprise. "Well, of course we wanted to sell it. No point in keeping it. And of course nobody was going to buy it as long as Mrs. Henshaw was one of the fixtures. But it wasn't crucial. Papa left us a little money, enough to help Hartley through college, and I make out all right on my salary. Not that it keeps me in sables—" For a minute her face took on a faraway expression. Then, belatedly, she drew herself up. "Though I can't see what business it is of yours, Dr. Craig."

"It isn't. Except that tomorrow the State guy is going to ask you all this, and plenty more. We might as well face it."

"Oh. I—I guess you're right. You mean you're giving me sort of a workout?"

"It doesn't hurt to be prepared," said Dr. Craig. "Even when you're just going to tell the truth. One thing I don't get. You say Hartley's got a little money. Then why the hell is he sticking around here?"

"Bix." Her answer was prompt and positive. "He was all set to stay in Chicago with me, three years ago. We had it all planned, I was going to get a bigger apartment, and he was going to finish high school and—And then Bix called him up. I don't know what she said. All he told me was that he'd decided to come back to Coreyville. He clammed up, and when Hartley clams up there's no use arguing. He came back to Coreyville."

"You don't like Bix, do you?" He stole a glance at her in the mirror. That omelet was one of the most effective contraptions he had ever seen. Under it her eyes seemed shot with flecks of pure sunlight. Her nose was a little bit crooked; this pleased him. So did the sudden curve of her mouth. Then there was the vulnerable, heart-breaking cleft chin. . . .

"That's just the trouble," she burst out. "I do like Bix. I wouldn't get so exasperated with her if I didn't like her. And feel sorry for her. It's a wonder she's not a juvenile delinquent, when you consider her home life."

"It must be tough, having a mother like Mrs. Bovard." She had consulted Dr. Craig once or twice, on account of her headaches. A wan, remote, cold woman. And an incurable one. Dr. Craig had felt the dead weight of hopelessness settle on him while he listened to the familiar symptoms, while he wrote out the futile prescriptions. Pills for the headaches. Pills to make her sleep. But there weren't any pills for what was really wrong with her. "It must be even tougher, having her for a wife."

"I've always thought so," said Rachel. "If Hugh philanders now and then, it's because she drives him to it. She used to be the prettiest thing, though. I remember, when we were kids, how pretty she was. She'd bring Ronnie over once in a while. I was supposed to play with him."

"She told me a little about Ronnie." Very little actually; but enough so that Dr. Craig had known the pills weren't going to help. She had known it too; that was what haunted him. She knew she was incurable. My son, my little boy, she had said—and then stopped, as if aware that talk, which might have helped once, was now as futile as pills.

"Ronnie was pretty awful, I guess, but mostly he just bored me. He could only say a few words, and he had this little whistle that he was always blowing. Once I took it away from him, only she saw me—she never let him out of her sight for a minute—and she slapped me. After that I didn't have to 'play' with him any more, which was exactly the way I wanted it, of course. I felt as if I'd pulled off something very clever." Rachel paused. "Because he really was awful. He grunted. And his tongue was too long."

My son, my little boy. . . . Poor woman, thought Dr. Craig. But poor Hugh and Bix, too. Poor everybody, if you put your mind to it.

Only he was in no mood to put his mind to it. The car hummed along the highway, and the sun glittered on the patches of stale snow in the fields, and when his eyes met Rachel's she smiled as if she were glad to be here too. He considered putting his arm around her. Decided against it, for the present. Haste makes waste, and this one showed every sign of being too good to waste. Later, after they had dawdled away the afternoon over drinks and dinner. . . . You could dance at Chicken Inn, too. There was a juke box, and quite a decent-sized dance floor.

"What are you smirking about?" asked Rachel. She looked half inclined to smirk herself.

"It's my jovial nature. Sunny Jim, they call me."

"I see." She hesitated for half a moment. "And what do I call you? I mean—Dr. Craig sounds kind of formal, and I still associate 'Doc' with Papa—"

"Childish of you. You'll have to get over it."

"Don't you have a first name?"

"I do. But it's not fit for human consumption." (It was

Cedric. He had no intention of divulging this ridiculous fact.) "You'll have to settle for Doc."

"All right. Doc. I guess it doesn't sound so—daughterly, after all."

"Not the slightest bit," said Dr. Craig, and resumed his smirking.

XII

Chicken Inn did a brisk business on Sundays. The upper crust of half a dozen neighboring towns gathered here—the lively, cocktail-drinking young crowd to dance and get tight, in a reasonably refined way; the less rollicking oldsters to eat their way through the Sunday Special, which was hearty to the point of stupefaction. The resulting atmosphere was about equal parts sportiness and dignity. After four, when the Sunday Special went off the market, sportiness won out. It was already in the ascendancy when Rachel and Dr. Craig arrived, at three thirty. The juke box throbbed; ice clattered invitingly in the shakers at the bar; voices rose a couple of degrees above normal.

Hugh Bovard, who was having a brandy with his coffee, and Bix, who was polishing off the last crumb of the Sunday Special apple pie a la mode, saw them as soon as they came in and beckoned them over.

"Have a drink," said Hugh. "You're looking bright-eyed and bushy-tailed, the both of you. What's new? Bix tells me you struck oil, or something, in Mrs. Henshaw's room."

"Did she tell you that the sheriff's got it, on account of me not being very bright?" asked Rachel drily. "Your daughter has a low opinion of my mentality, and I can't say I blame her."

Bix, who was "dressed up" in a sheer, ruffly blouse that showed her shoulder blades in back and her pathetic little incipient bosom in front, looked embarrassed. "I don't think you're so dumb," she explained. "But you sure talk a lot sometimes."

"I'll try to reform," Rachel said. "I'd love a martini," she added to Dr. Craig, who was negotiating with the waitress, "but do you think it's safe? It may loosen my tongue even more."

"Paris the thought," said Bix. "Not that it matters any more. I guess you've already told the sheriff everything you know."

"It wouldn't matter if she hadn't, you brat." Hugh was struggling to look disapproving and parental instead of amused. "The sheriff isn't here. She's among friends. Candid friends, I might add." He sipped his brandy. "There's probably nothing crucial in Mrs. Henshaw's box, anyway."

"I like to think it's love letters," said Dr. Craig. What he was really thinking was that he would have preferred to be sitting beside Rachel in the booth, instead of beside Bix. On the other hand, this way he had a better view of her. "Love letters tied with blue."

"Love letters from Francie. Cherished for all these years." The idea obviously entertained Rachel. "How is Francie, by the way? Still in the second-hand business? Still living on peanut butter and crackers?"

Dr. Craig nodded. "The man's been starving himself for years, out of pure stinginess. At this point the shock of a good meal would probably kill him, with his heart in the shape it's in. He's apt to conk off any minute." He had been called to attend Mrs. Henshaw's estranged husband only once—and that once very much against the patient's will. Francie claimed he couldn't afford doctors. But the Smileys had insisted. The Smileys were the dirtiest people in town; Francie rented from them a room that made Dr. Craig's own quarters seem like a paradise of cleanliness and order. There the old man had lain, huddled in an unspeakably dirty bathrobe, as fiercely opposed to spending money on a doctor as though he were not at the point of death.

Which he had certainly been. With a mixture of pity and exasperation, Dr. Craig remembered the bony, ramshackle body; the two cases, one of peanut butter, one of canned beans (cheaper by the case) in the corner; the little path, worn by Francie's feet, beside the sidewalk that led from Smiley's house to the second-hand shop. (Sidewalks wore out shoe leather.)

"He's been apt to conk off any minute for years," said Hugh. "Your father used to say the same thing, Rachel. He's a tough old customer, Francie is." A defensive kind of loyalty crept into his voice. "I know everybody says he's stingy. And he is, with himself. I know everybody makes fun of him and his little path and all the rest of it. But let me tell you one thing, Francie'll give the shirt off his back to anybody he likes."

"Try and find somebody he likes," said Rachel. "You're it, Hugh. You're the only person in town he'll put up with, or that will put up with him."

"He wasn't always like that. I can remember him when I was a kid, before he got married, and believe me, nobody made fun of Francis L. Henshaw then. He was the Young Man Most Likely To Succeed. A good-looking fellow, and smart. He worked for old Mr. Kincaid in the bank, and he was all set to marry one of the Kincaid girls. Then she came along. Rose. Rose Anthony she was, in those days."

"Mrs. Henshaw, you mean?"

"That's who I mean. All at once he married her instead of the Kincaid girl, and she sure as hell ruined him." Suddenly Hugh grinned. "He'll be delighted to hear that somebody murdered her."

"Maybe he did it." Bix gave a little wriggle of excitement. "Why not? He could have. He hated her enough."

"It's an idea," said Dr. Craig. But was it such a hot one? It would get Hartley off the hook, sure enough. And Francie hated her, sure enough. He had also avoided her like the plague, for thirty years. Why would he all at once go to see her, even for the purpose of killing her? "I'm not sure he could manage it. With his heart the way it is, and nothing but crackers and peanut butter to fortify him."

"Of course he couldn't have," said Hugh curtly. "Francie's tough, but not that tough. If he was ever going to kill her, he'd have done it years ago, when it might have done him some good. He's no fool."

Much as he regretted it, Dr. Craig had to agree. Not so Bix and Rachel. Neither of them said anything, but Dr. Craig caught the look they exchanged, somehow an intensely feminine look— of secret determination and hope.

"I told Daddy you're going to stay at our house," said Bix. "Can we go now, Daddy? Because you said I could go see Hartley, if they'll let me. Gee, I wish he was here now. That's a real dreamy piece to dance to."

Dr. Craig stood up with alacrity, and he gave Bix a grateful little pat as she slid out of the booth. A sweet kid, really. "What's this lethal weapon?" he asked, as he discovered, on the hook under her coat, a bright green umbrella with a heavy, carved handle.

Bix ducked her head and blushed. "Hartley gave us that for Christmas," her father explained. "If there's a cloud the size of a dime, we carry it. . . . Okay, Biscuit, don't be mad. I'm just kidding." He stood up too, with not so much alacrity. He looked, in fact, a little wistful, and Dr. Craig thought of the wan, remote woman he was going home to, stretched out, probably, with a wet cloth pressed against the headache that was never going to go away. "Behave yourselves, you two. See you later, Rachel. You're welcome as the flowers of May. We'll be glad to have you. So long, Doc."

They were alone at last. Dr. Craig slid back into the booth, this time beside Rachel. He had a feeling that he might be smirking again.

If he was, it was wasted on Rachel. "It wouldn't surprise me if Bix snitched the key to that box," she said. "I think she knew all the time there was something in Mrs. Henshaw's room, and for some reason she didn't want us or anybody else to go into the subject—"

"Then let's not. Let's dance instead. We weren't going to talk about Mrs. Henshaw. Remember? We were going to ignore her."

It turned into one of those enchanted stretches of time, when all the martinis were just exhilarating enough, all the music was dreamy to dance to, all the things either of them said were witty or charming or profound. At seven or so they ate an ambrosial dish modestly listed on the menu as Chicken in the Pot. At eight or so they floated out into the windy, wintry night, a night of briefly glimmering stars and scudding clouds.

"Heavenly," murmured Rachel. "A heavenly evening." She lifted her face joyfully to the night and wind and the long, long kiss.

A kiss, Dr. Craig reminded himself, was a kiss, and nothing more. It had no significance, except as the opening round in that fine old indoor sport where good-looking babes belonged and must be kept. Though some kisses were better than others. This one, for instance. . . .

Better. But not more significant. Any extraordinary meaning it might seem to have was coincidental, the direct result of martinis and soft music and whatever the scent was, something spicy, that Rachel used. A simple, chemical reaction, you might say. No magic. As long as he kept that firmly in mind, he was okay, he was safe.

"We'd better go home now," said Rachel faintly.

"I wish we didn't ever have to go home. I wish—" He stopped just in time. "Come on," he said, and opened the car door.

They didn't talk during the drive home. Dr. Craig was silent because he was leary of himself, after the narrow escape of that "I wish—." Rachel was silent because she went to sleep, with her head nestled trustfully against his shoulder. (The trustfulness dashed him a little; hadn't she noticed that his intentions were dishonorable?)

But it seemed a shame to wake her. He pulled up in Bovard's driveway and just sat for a minute, looking down at the slightly crooked nose and the eyelashes that were like tiny little brushes. When he kissed her she stirred and whispered, "Greg."

It froze him in his tracks. He would die, however, die a thousand deaths before he would ask who Greg was. In the first place, she wasn't even aware she had said the name. And anyway, it was nothing to him. So all right, she was used to being kissed by some hound by the name of Greg. So what of it? Nothing. Absolutely nothing.

"What are you looking so grim about?" She had straightened up, and was adjusting the omelet hat.

"I'm not," he snapped. "Here, I'll get your bag for you." He helped her out, and she stood beside him, looking a little puzzled, while he opened the trunk.

"Who's Greg?" he croaked.

"Greg? Did you say Greg?"

"You said it first. A minute ago, when I— So who is this Greg character? What's so special about him?"

"Why, nothing. I mean, he's just a—"

"Really? I've always wanted to meet a just a."

She glared at him, and he smiled brilliantly, and the battle would no doubt have been joined except that at that moment they both heard the sound.

It seemed to come from the path that ran back of the three houses in the block—Bovards' at one end, Buckmasters' at the other, Myra Graves' in the middle. It was low, like a moan, except that it had a curious overtone of indignation. More like a bitter protest than a cry for help. It grew weaker, died away, rose again. . . .

Dr. Craig took off at a gallop. "Somebody's hurt. Wait for me here," he said.

But it didn't do any good; Rachel stayed right at his heels. "Myra's hedge," she panted. "That's where it's coming from."

She was right. They found her half under the hedge, where the frozen earth was pitted with ice. She was making feeble crawling movements, and her hat with the silver buckle was jammed down over her eyes.

"Mrs. Pierce," whispered Rachel. "Oh my. Mrs. Pierce."

XIII

Mrs. Pierce lay (though she somehow still gave the effect of sitting bolt upright) on the Bovard couch and glared at everybody out of one eye. The other eye was swollen shut, the side of her face was scraped, and there was a sizable lump above her ear. But she was very much alive. In fact, thought Bix, she glared better out of one eye than out of two. More concentrated.

"Nothing serious," said Doc cheerfully. "You're going to have a super shiner, but that's all. You'll be right as rain in a couple of days."

"Nothing serious, he says! I just beg to differ with you, young man. When somebody tries to kill me, it's something serious, to my way of thinking."

It was a laugh, thought Bix, the way they all tried to look shocked. As if it hadn't even crossed their minds for one minute that this was anything but an accident. Rachel was better at it than Daddy or Doc. "You mean you think somebody—" she began.

"I don't think. I know. Certainly somebody tried to kill me. They hit me on the head and left me there to die."

Nobody quite looked at anybody else. But Doc came through with something that took the wind out of Mrs. Pierce's sails for a minute. "What were you doing back there, anyway?"

"I can't see that that's got anything to do with it."

"No?" said Daddy. "Why not? It might have everything to do with it."

"Well, if you must know, I just thought I'd check up on that sheriff. He claimed he'd locked the Buckmaster house up so nobody could get in, but I don't trust him. Not for a minute. I don't trust anybody around here."

"Very sensible attitude," said Daddy. (Bix loved him when he got that little quirk to his mouth.)

"You were nearer Myra Graves' house than the Buckmaster's when we found you," said Doc. "How did that happen?"

"See here, young man, I don't see why I should be put through the third degree, on top of everything else! You'd think *I'd* been going around hitting people over the head, instead of the other way round!"

"But, Mrs. Pierce, you really were nearer Myra—"

"All right. I was there because I just thought I'd have a word with her as long as I was at it. Anything wrong with that?"

"Did you have your word with her?"

"I never got there. Somebody sneaked up behind me and hit me over the head, and that's the last I remember till you found me."

"You couldn't have been out very long," said Doc. "Honest to God, Mrs. Pierce, you're not seriously hurt."

"Watch your language, please. It was quarter past eight when I left the hotel. It's five minutes of nine now. I was hurt serious enough to lay out there a good fifteen minutes."

"You came in about half an hour ago, Bix," said Daddy. "Did

you hear anything? See anybody prowling around the back way?"

Bix hesitated briefly before she shook her head. "But then I didn't come the back way. Peggy took me a ways, as far as Buckmaster's, and then I cut through their front yard, and Myra's, and came on home."

"It's icy back there, and dark," Doc reminded everybody. "Be awfully easy to slip and fall. You sure that isn't what happened, Mrs. Pierce?"

Mrs. Pierce propped herself up on her elbow to give him the full benefit of her one fierce eye. "Young man, when I slip and fall, I know it. And when somebody hits me over the head, I know it. Somebody killed Rose, and somebody tried to kill me, and—"

It was time, Bix decided, to make the important point. "Well, anyway," she said, "whoever it was, it wasn't Hartley. There must be two killers. Unless you're insinuating that Hartley broke out of jail to nip back there and bop you."

They all blinked. Honestly, sometimes Bix wondered about people, the way you had to practically draw a diagram before they could see the nose on their face.

Rachel spoke first. "I love you, Bix. Of course Hartley didn't break out of jail. And of course there can't be two killers. So that proves—"

"Proves that Hartley's innocent," said Bix airily. "Natch."

Their three faces—Daddy's and Rachel's and Doc's—broke into smiles of pure joy. But not Mrs. Pierce's. She snorted. "Proves nothing of the sort. I've got my own notion about who hit me, and all it proves is that Hartley's where he ought to be, in jail. There'd ought to be somebody else up there with him, is all." She turned the withering eye on Rachel, who shrank visibly. "You heard her last night. You heard her threaten me. She came right out and said I wouldn't be safe, over there in that house—not that I had any intention whatsoever of staying. A nest of murderers if I ever saw one. The boy killed Rose, and now she's tried to—"

"That's a damn lie!" Doc looked ready to explode. "I've been with Rachel all afternoon and evening. I can vouch for her myself."

"You can vouch for her! You're a fine one to vouch for anybody. Cursing and swearing. Carrying on with her, like as not. Drinking— Oh, I smelled it on you, the both of you, like to knocked me out all over again—"

"Hugh! What's the matter? What's happened?" It was Mother's voice, sad and frail, floating down from the top of the stairs. There she stood, like a ghost, one hand at her temple, the other clutching the neck of her pale gray robe. The martyr, thought Bix. Oh sure, that's all we need, is her suffering patiently all over the place. She turned her back, so as not to watch Daddy tearing up the stairs like a dog who has been whistled home. For a terrible moment she thought she was going to cry, and she wouldn't allow it, she simply would not. . . .

"Nuts!" She gave the hassock a savage kick. Anything to hold back the tears. "Oh nuts!"

"Amen," said Doc. Then he got a grip on himself. "Look here, Mrs. Pierce, I'll call Mrs. Nelson at the hospital and tell her to come and get you. Under the circumstances, I'm sure you wouldn't trust me to drive you there. She's a good practical nurse, she doesn't drink or swear, and she'll take care of your eye. You can stay at the hospital or at the hotel, wherever you'd rather. And you can leap out bright and early tomorrow morning and tell the sheriff and his pals from the state police just exactly how to run the whole show. There. Does that make you happy?" He stamped out to the telephone, looking anything but happy himself.

"You don't need to think for one minute," Mrs. Pierce shot

after him, "that I'm going to wait till morning to tell the sheriff about this. I'll call him just as soon as I've gotten some proper medical attention."

And of course she did. Not long after Mrs. Nelson had come and bundled her energetic patient off to the hospital, Sheriff Jeffreys turned up. He didn't look happy, either.

By that time Daddy had calmed Mother down and was back downstairs. He answered the door. "Oh Lord, Charlie," he said wearily. "You know as much about it as any of us. What did she tell you?"

"What didn't she tell me! She's a terror, Mr. Bovard. That woman is a holy terror. Lit right into me, all about a nest of murderers, and she don't trust me either, and—" Charlie drew a long sigh. Then he straightened his shoulders and pulled down his coat. (Making like a sheriff, thought Bix. He forgot it there for a minute.) "Well. Seems she thinks Miss Buckmaster—"

Doc did his exploding act all over again. After that he took Charlie out to show him where they had found Mrs. Pierce, and Daddy fixed a drink for Rachel and patted her on the shoulder. She just sat and stared at the floor, and once in a while she'd take a little sip of the drink, out of politeness. Bix fidgeted. She wished she could think of something to say. She wished Rachel didn't look so much like Hartley. It was no fair for her to look like Hartley; that's what it was, no fair.

"Nobody's going to believe her," said Daddy. "Even if you didn't have Doc to vouch for you, nobody would believe it. And there's one thing sure— Mrs. Pierce may not think Doc's word is worth much, but she's going to find out that nobody else in Coreyville agrees with her. He's as well liked, and as well respected, as any man in town."

Rachel brightened up at that, Bix noticed. Old Doc must be a fast worker, all right. Personally, Bix didn't go for the animal-magnetism type; but then every woman to her own taste.

He came loping back with an all's-right-with-the-world expression on his face, and without the sheriff. "We're all straight with Charlie," he told them. "He's pretty sore at Mrs. Pierce himself. That crack she made about not trusting him hurt his feelings. Says like as not nobody hit her, she just slipped on the ice and had to blame somebody for it."

Bix sighed. In a way, it was an anti-climax. It didn't get Hartley out of jail, but on the other hand it didn't put Rachel up there with him. Which was something to be thankful for, Bix supposed. Doc seemed to think so. He was looking at Rachel like she was a princess he'd just snatched out from under the dragon's nose or something, and she was looking at him like he was a knight on a white charger. The adult infants at play, thought Bix.

"I'm going to bed," she announced. "Goodnight, all." She got halfway up the stairs before she remembered something, and paused. She knew exactly where she had left it: on one of the dining room chairs. That meant going through the living room; they would all see her marching back with it. So what? It was her property, none of their business if she happened to want it with her. And she did want it. She felt all at once as if she couldn't get through the night without it—to comfort her, to prove that she too had something, somebody of her own. . . .

Let them laugh at her. She turned around and sailed back through the living room, past their questioning eyes. "I forgot my umbrella," she said haughtily.

The silence that fell was peculiar. And another peculiar thing —they weren't laughing at her. Their eyes, all three pairs of them, were riveted on the umbrella in her hand. What did you call moments like this? Clairvoyance, that was it: she knew exactly what they were thinking, she could practically see the wheels going round. "What's this lethal weapon?" Doc had said, out at Chicken Inn, and then Daddy had teased her. . . . They were remembering that, and they were also remembering that she must have gotten home just about the time Mrs. Pierce fell, or was hit. Lethal weapon. Fell, or was hit.

"Goodnight," she gulped. It was all she could do to keep from breaking into a dead run. Up in the sanctuary of her own room, she leaned against the door, waiting for her heart to stop thumping. Anyway, she had her umbrella, her good old rod and staff they comfort me umbrella. She hugged it against her. It was going to be one of those nights when she needed it.

Some nights were okay. Some nights her room seemed cozy and familiar. The lamp beside her bed was a lamp, and that was all; there was nothing under the chintz petticoat on the dressing table except the dressing table legs; nothing at the foot of the bed except her terry cloth robe and the extra blanket; nothing outside the window except the ivy, stirring harmlessly in the wind.

Then there were other nights, like this one, when all the furniture crouched, ready to spring at some secret, pre-arranged signal. The lamp turned into a fist threatening her, the window into an eye watching her. Whatever it was, hiding under the chintz petticoat, moved now and then, ever so slightly, ever so warily. Whatever it was, huddled at the foot of her bed, crept an inch toward her, stopped, waiting for the signal. And outside the window something—what? Not the ivy. Something old and evil—tapped and tapped, trying to get in.

She pulled the covers closer around her ears, and drew her knees up tighter against her shivering body. Long ago, when she was little, she used to cry on nights like this. She hadn't known why she was crying, any more than she knew now why she was shivering. She had never learned the name of what she feared. The face is familiar, she thought—and in a way it was a laugh, only she couldn't quite manage a laugh at the moment—the face is familiar, but the name alludes me.

She was still awake when Daddy came upstairs. She heard him fumbling with the light switch and then pausing—not at Mother's door, for once, but at Bix's. Oh oh, she thought, and screwed her eyes tight shut.

"Bix," he whispered. "Bix. Are you asleep?" He came over and touched her shoulder. "I want to talk to you a minute."

She made what she hoped were sleepy noises. "What? Whatsamatter?"

"I want to talk to you. About tonight. Mrs. Pierce and— You know you can trust me, Bix. You don't need to be afraid to tell me anything."

There was one weapon, Bix had discovered at an early age, that simply made mincemeat out of Daddy. She used it in cases of extremity only, because she always felt so sorry for him. But this was an extremity, and the weapon had better be in good working order or it was going to be just too bad for Miss Beatrix Bovard.

She pulled away from him, buried her face in the pillow, and uttered a small, desolate sob.

Silence. She could feel him shifting helplessly from one foot to the other, in an attempt to steel himself. Poor Daddy. It was time for another sob, or perhaps a whimper this time. She produced a heart-rending blend of the two.

"Now Bix," he began desperately.

"I'm—I'm sorry. I'm so tired, and I haven't got anything to tell you, and—and it was so awful, going up to see H-H-Hartley—"

"Don't, please don't. I didn't mean anything. Please don't cry, Biscuit." He had given up; he was begging. Mincemeat, pure and simple. She didn't pull away from his hand this time. She let him gather her up against his shoulder and pat her hair, the way he always did. . . .

Only something was happening that she hadn't planned on

and that never had happened before. The weapon got away from her; she couldn't stop the crying. It was like some terrible machine shaking her. "Daddy! Oh Daddy!" she whispered, and she clung to him.

He picked her up and sat down on the edge of the bed with her in his lap. "There. There. I know, Biscuit. I know." His arm, rocking her, was warm and solid under the scratchy tweed; he smelled of tobacco and bourbon and, very faintly, of the printing shop. The smell—in a way—of shelter and love. Except that Bix knew from way back how, at any moment, the warm, solid arm and the shelter might be withdrawn. One word from Mother, sometimes no more than a look. That was all it took. Daddy would be long gone. There was that, always to be remembered, always, always.

"Sh, sh. It's going to be all right. You mustn't worry about Hartley. Hartley's going to be all right."

He sounded so sure. Slowly, slowly, the terrible machine loosened its grip on her. He sounded so sure. . . .

After a while he turned on the light (the lamp was just a lamp, after all) and tucked her back into bed. They smiled feebly at each other. But at the sight of his face, haggard and strained with sorrow, she felt shame rush over her. Ah, poor Daddy. Poor, poor Daddy.

She made a silent vow; never, as long as she lived, to use the mincemeat weapon again. She put her hand up to his cheek, silently promising. Cross her heart. Hope to die. Then, all at once, she went to sleep.

XIV

The detective's name turned out to be Mr. Pigeon, of all things. And he couldn't have looked less like a detective if he had actually had pink feet and a fantail. Bix had expected a hatchet face, gimlet eyes, a machine-gun voice rattling out intimidating questions. But Mr. Pigeon's voice was leisurely and rather high-pitched; he was bald, portly, and snubnosed; and his mild brown eyes looked dreamily off in two different directions, neither of them Bix.

They had their "little talk"—to quote Mr. Pigeon—in the study, a small room crowded with glass-fronted book cases, the rolltop desk where Daddy sometimes worked evenings, and the picture of Grandpa and Grandma Bovard frozen forever in their wedding finery. Mr. Pigeon sat at the desk, in the swivel chair; Bix perched on the edge of the couch, wary as a fox. She expected tricks. The preliminary chatter, for instance, about school and how old are you, Beatrix, and what do you want to study in college—all that was supposed to soften her up. Pretty corny, if you asked Bix; she could have done a better job herself. But maybe Mr. Pigeon was tired. He had already had "little talks" with all the others. Bix was the end of the line, or very near it —that was how she rated with Mr. Pigeon. Which was fine, from one angle. Not so fine, from another. It was those two angles that were tearing her apart inside.

The preliminaries were over. Let's see, now, Beatrix, you've known Hartley for—how long? All my life, Mr. Pigeon, and he didn't kill Mrs. Henshaw. . . .

He didn't like her, though, did he? Of course not. Nobody liked her. That's no reason for killing her. . . .

"Maybe he had another reason." Mr. Pigeon kept playing

a little game that involved wadding up scraps of paper and trying to balance them on the edge of the cigarette box in front of him. He didn't go at it right; he didn't wad his paper pills up tight enough. They all fell into the box, and he just kept on trying again in the same old inefficient way, following the line of least resistance. "Maybe he knew about that box of Mrs. Henshaw's, and what was in it."

Another paper pill bit the dust before Bix said anything. "What was in it?"

"Money," said Mr. Pigeon pleasantly. "A lot of money, Beatrix. Twenty-three thousand dollars."

Her heart leapt up, it soared with relief. *That's all? Just money?* She bit back the questions just in time, and gave Mr. Pigeon, instead, the big eyes and the gasp of amazement he expected. "Twenty-three thou— Jeepers! That's a nice piece of change."

"So it is, so it is. Lots of people have been murdered for less."

"Sure they have. Lots of people, for lots less." She was stuttering a little, with excitement. "That means— Why, that means anybody might have killed her for the money. Anybody at all."

"Well, not quite anybody," said Mr. Pigeon. "It would have to be somebody who knew she had the money."

"Then that lets Hartley out. Because he didn't know it. He would have told me if he'd known, he always tells me everything."

Mr. Pigeon looked amused. "You're sure about that? You don't think he might have been planning to surprise you?"

"Nope. Because—" Oh well, what was the use of trying to explain? She and Hartley simply didn't have secrets from each other. But of course Mr. Pigeon couldn't see that. All he saw was the cute, boy-meets-girl stuff.

"Something else interesting," he was saying. "Where did Mrs. Henshaw get all that money? Do you have any idea?"

"Who, me?" she said quickly. "Saved it, I suppose. Kept

squirreling it away her whole entire life. It would be just like her." She hurried back to safer ground. "If it was Hartley, then why didn't he take the money? If that's what he was after, why did he just leave it there?"

"Why not? He had plenty of time—or so he thought. All the time in the world. Remember, nobody was supposed to suspect that this was a murder. Nobody did suspect it, till Mrs. Pierce came along."

"Okay, so whoever did it thought they had plenty of time. You say it's a good reason for Hartley to leave the money there. I say it's just as good a reason for anybody to leave the money there. Why pick on Hartley?"

"Well," said Mr. Pigeon reasonably, "I'll tell you why." One of his eyes gazed off toward the window; the other seemed fixed on the fresh little wad of paper between his fingers. "Of all the people that didn't like her, it looks like Hartley had the best reason for not liking her. And of all the people that might have known about her money, Hartley had the best chance to know, because he lived in the same house with her. And of all the people that might think it was safe to leave the money where it was, he'd feel the safest, because it's his house. That's how detecting goes, Beatrix. Very little juggling, very little fancy footwork. You just take the facts and put them together in the way that makes the most sense, and—"

"But you're not!" cried Bix. "All you're doing is taking the line of least resistance!" (There. The new little paper pill fell into the cigarette box, just like all the others. She had known it would.) "Hartley's the easiest answer, so you just—" She had to stop, to get her breath. "What about what happened to Mrs. Pierce last night? Hartley sure-God didn't have the best chance to do that!"

"There now, there now." Mr. Pigeon made distressed little shifting motions in his chair. For a moment one of his eyes seemed actually to look straight at her. "We're not picking on your boy friend the way you seem to think. Don't you worry, we're following up all the other leads too. When it comes to Mrs. Pierce—well, people aren't always reliable witnesses, you know. Sometimes they get worked up and make mistakes. With a woman like Mrs. Pierce, you've got to allow for a margin of error."

"You don't think anybody hit her," said Bix wearily. She needn't have worried about what might have come out in his little talks with the others. You could count on Mr. Pigeon, every time. The line of least resistance. The easiest answer. She stood up. "Well. You got any more questions to ask me? Can I go now?"

"No more questions. You can run along to school now." Mr. Pigeon stood up too, and gave her an indulgent, good-will smile. We will now have a moment of soft-soap, thought Bix. I bet he's got a daughter at home just my age, probably just exactly like me, only she's got two heads and her boy friend isn't in jail. "No more questions, and no hard feelings either, I hope. You've been co-operative, Beatrix, and I appreciate it. Something else I appreciate too, and that's loyalty. You're a loyal little person, my dear, and—"

Loyal. Loyal. Something seemed to wrench, inside her chest. "Oh, stop it," she choked out. And fled.

She found Rachel, looking hollow-eyed and lighting one cigarette from another, in the living room. She practically fell on Bix's neck. "I've been sitting here jittering, and nobody to jitter at. Isn't he ever going to leave?" As if on cue, the study door opened and Mr. Pigeon made his leisurely way down the hall and out the door, pausing to smile goodbye at them.

"I suppose he can't help it. It's his job," said Rachel. "He was nice enough to me. Only—"

"Only he's not going to find out who really did it," Bix finished for her. "Leave us face it. Hartley's it, because he's handiest."

"You felt that way too? So did I." Her next words took Bix by surprise—for no good reason. After all, Rachel had run away to Chicago with nothing more substantial in her purse than twenty-five dollars and her high school diploma. "So I guess it's up to us. Or anyway, to me."

"Us," said Bix. She made an impulsive gesture that got them involved in a solemn, awkward half-handshake. Sort of embarrassing, really. But sort of comforting, too; for a moment the wrench inside Bix's chest was hardly there at all. "Where do we start?"

"Francie," said Rachel briskly. "Francie just loves money. If he knew about Mrs. Henshaw's box, and if he knew she hadn't made a will—which so far it looks as if she hadn't—well, it seems to me Francie's worthy of attention."

"Let's go see him. Daddy said I could skip school this afternoon. Francie's not mad for me, but I am related to Daddy, so he puts up with me. Only we've got to have some excuse. We can't just walk in and say we've come to find out if he killed Mrs. Henshaw."

"I know," said Rachel. "I thought I'd ask his advice about where to sell the silver, and the clock—it's really an antique—and my mother's jewelry. Some of the furniture ought to be worth something, and we're going to need every penny we can scrape up."

They were getting into their coats when they heard Myra Graves' "yoo-hoo" from the back door. She came trotting in, looking flustered and worried. "He's gone, isn't he, that Mr. Pigeon? Listen, Rachel, I forgot to tell him about the handkerchief, and land knows I didn't do it on purpose, I wasn't trying to keep anything from him, but he got me kind of rattled, the way he said for me to remember everything about when we found her, the minute anybody tells me *that* I forget something, sure as you're born, and—" Her breath gave out. She sank down on the sofa, unbuttoned her sweater, fumbled in her apron pocket, and drew out a crumpled blue bandana handkerchief. "There. There it is, for all it's worth. Likely doesn't amount to a row of pins. Only he said for me to remember everything, and it's going to look funny for me to bring it up now. Like I was holding it back before, or maybe making the whole thing up—"

"Making what up?" asked Rachel. "Get organized, Myra. Stop looking so guilty. What about the handkerchief?"

"Why, she had it on," said Myra impatiently. "Had her head tied up in it, you know, to keep out the dust. Looked a fright. I remember it struck me kind of pitiful, I thought to myself I wouldn't be caught dead in a rig like that—"

Bix snickered. Rachel didn't quite. And Myra's plump face got redder than ever. "So I took it off of her," she finished, with dignity. "Took it off and stuck it in my pocket and forgot all about it. Do you think I'd ought to tell that Mr. Pigeon?"

Bix could never resist teasing her. "Oh brother, are you in trouble! You're going to get arrested. That's what they do with people that conceal evidence. Sure they do. Arrest them. It's a crime."

"But I didn't mean to—" began Myra earnestly. Then she relaxed. "Fresh. If you aren't the freshest young one I ever met up with. I'd ought to smack you. Rachel. What do you think?"

"Go ahead. Smack her. Oh, you mean the handkerchief. I can't see what difference it makes, what she had on. It doesn't prove anything, except that she was cleaning house, and everybody knows that already. It was her handkerchief, wasn't it? Well, then. I wouldn't worry about it."

"He wouldn't do anything about it, anyway, that Pigeon," said Bix. "Somebody else is going to have to confess before he gets his mind off of Hartley. He's in a rut."

The three of them left together, and before she turned up the sidewalk leading to her own house Myra paused, smiling fondly at Rachel. "What's this I hear about you and Doc Craig sashaying around at Chicken Inn yesterday? You're going to have all the girls in town down on you, beating their time like this."

"Look at her blush," said Bix gleefully.

"It's like I've said all along," Myra went on. "Of course he's not married to that wife of his any more. There's some that keep on saying he is and that's why he hasn't taken up with anybody here, but I claim there just wasn't anybody caught his eye. Till now. This proves it. He wouldn't be shining around you if he was still married to her, would he?" Struck at last by the expression on Rachel's face, Myra floundered in even deeper. "He's not that kind. He's a fine young fellow, Doc is. A fine young fellow."

"Oh my, yes," Rachel said at last. Her smile was brilliant and bleak as an iceberg. "Yes indeed. Dr. Craig's a very slick operator."

XV

Anything, anything at all, was likely to turn up in the window of Francie's second-hand store, because he used it for storage space, rather than display. But there were three landmarks that had been there ever since Bix could remember—the bearskin rug, the black-boy hitching post, and the stuffed canary perched on his little swing, his bill stroking the cuttlebone stuck in the side of his cage. Bix was fond of the canary, but her real favorite was the bear, his great back flattened out in the dust, his head still unbowed, as formidable as ever. His teeth were bared in an everlasting snarl; one amber eye (the other was lost, an empty black hole) glared ferociously at the world. Yes, the bear was her favorite. She gave him a tiny, secret nod in greeting.

Francie had a bell rigged up over the door that jangled out a warning whenever anybody came in or went out. It made Rachel jump, and Bix found that her nervousness was catching. Once inside, they both stopped dead, locked in a sort of stage fright. For one thing, you couldn't see much of anything; the forty-watt bulb Francie had burning toward the back didn't exactly flood the place with light. Then there was the smell, a cold, musty, old smell mixed with the fumes from the kerosene stove. It seemed to lean on you, and so did the stacks of furniture and junk that crammed the place to the ceiling. Like a jungle, with one narrow path leading back to the forty-watt bulb and the kerosene stove. Bix had the feeling that, once she started on that path, the jungle might close in stealthily behind her, choking off any chance of escape. Which was, of course, so much malarky. Kid stuff. She braced herself and called out Mr. Henshaw's name, louder than she intended to.

A shuffling sound came from the end of the path, and a wheezing. Then Francie's voice, a veiled yet shouting sort of voice that always made Bix think of a preacher prophesying hellfire. "Well, I heard you. I heard the bell. That's what it's there for. What do you want?"

Rachel picked her way down the path first, faltering out an explanation of what they wanted as she went. Bix followed, more out of shame than courage. It was all she could do to keep from peering over her shoulder to see if the furniture jungle was really closing in.

The old man, who had apparently been crouched in a ruined velvet chair beside the stove, reading, stood up as they approached. He wore a frayed, rusty-looking sweater, over what seemed to be several layers of garments even more frayed and grimy. His hair had turned white long ago, but his eyebrows were still black and beetling, like little porches over his glittering eyes. The deep hollows in his cheeks and temples made a startling contrast with his mouth; it was as if all the rest of his face was starved for the sake of that full, flexible mouth. He was smiling. Slyly, at some pleasure known only to himself. Bix shivered.

"So you want to sell the furnishings, Miss Buckmaster. Not wasting any time, are you?"

"I need the money," said Rachel.

"Money," declaimed Francie. "Root of all evil. Who steals my purse steals trash." He chuckled. "That's what they say. That brother of yours still incarcerated?"

"That's why I need the money, Mr. Henshaw. He shouldn't be in jail, and I'm going to get him out. Because he didn't kill your wife."

"Why didn't he? He should have. The woman was an abomination upon the face of the earth. Don't refer to her as my wife." He turned suddenly on Bix. "I suppose you're interested in selling the family jewels too? Does your father know you're here?"

"N-no. I just—I just—" (Stop stammering. What are you, a woman or a worm? Look at Rachel, standing there with her chin stuck out. She's not stammering. She's not scared of a skinny, smelly old man.) "Daddy doesn't think Hartley did it, either. He says it's ridiculous."

Francie began to laugh, silently. He threw back his head, and Bix could see the knot of his Adam's apple sliding up and down. "Ridiculous. Says it's ridiculous. What does he know about it?"

"He knows Hartley," said Bix. "Better than you do, anyway."

The Adam's apple did some more sliding. Then Francie wiped his mouth with the back of one long, dirty hand. "Maybe yes, maybe no. I know Hartley well enough. They're all alike, all this younger generation. Riddled with corruption. No stamina. Undermined by soft living—"

"Oh for heaven's sake," burst out Rachel. "If you think Hartley's had a soft life you're—"

"Crazy?" Francie licked his lips. "Mr. Pigeon thinks I'm crazy. Oh, he didn't say so, mind you. But I can tell, I can tell. He had that look in his eye. They all get it. Lots of people think I'm crazy. I don't mind. It's their privilege."

And their mistake, thought Bix, staring in a kind of fascination at that strange, gaunt face. It was typical of Mr. Pigeon to check Francie off as a harmless crackpot. Typical of Mr. Pigeon; very convenient indeed for Francie.

"I may be crazy," he went on, and he was smiling again, craftily. "But I'm not incarcerated. Like our friend Hartley. Incarcerated for a crime he didn't commit."

"Then you agree with us," said Rachel quickly. "You know he's innocent, too."

"Nothing of the kind. Don't know a thing about it. Care less. I'm just taking your word for it. If he did it, I'd be the first to congratulate him. If he didn't, more's the pity."

"I suppose Mr. Pigeon told you about the money your—Mrs. Henshaw had stashed away? And I suppose you were surprised to hear about it."

"Stunned," said Francie promptly. "The only commendable thing the woman ever did. Especially if she didn't make a will. Dear, careless Rose!"

"I wonder where she got all that money. It sounds—well, it sounds like backmail to me."

There was a queer silence. Francie's eyebrows rose, as if in surprise, but the glance he darted at Rachel was one of—What? Suspicion? Anger? Fear? Anyway, not surprise.

"Now, now, Miss Buckmaster, don't let your imagination run away with you," said Francie, and Bix let her breath out again, quietly. "I don't see how even Rose could dig up anybody in Coreyville to blackmail. This isn't Chicago, you know. You've been reading too much of this modern detective trash. Why don't you try Schopenhauer instead? I recommend him highly." He tapped the worn volume on the velvet chair, and then, abruptly, smacked his bony hands together. His eyes were sparkling. "There. So much for sociable gossip. Now we can get down to the real reason for your visit. I understand you want to dispose of some furniture?"

He had them licked, and they knew it as well as he did. Bix couldn't trust herself to speak. She turned away, pretending to peer at a bow-legged table that seemed to stagger under its load of chipped china and dusty gimcracks. She could hear Rachel's unsteady voice: "Yes. The furniture. There's a clock—maybe you remember it—very old—"

Hateful, terrifying old man. *I know Hartley well enough. They're all alike, all this younger generation.* . . . And Bix had just stood there with her teeth in her mouth, too dumb, too scared to fight back. No spine whatever. No brains. Nothing but this awful wrenching feeling in her chest and the disgusting sting of tears in her eyes. She blinked at the load of gimcracks. A pink lamp shade, crusted with beads. A cracked mirror with a dented silver handle. A cut-glass bowl, final resting place of two dead flies. A lot of candlesticks. . . . Yes, there was a brass one; the mate, no doubt, of Mrs. Henshaw's. A heavy, square-cornered, brass candlestick. Her hand reached out and closed around it. She turned impulsively.

"Isn't this like the one in your house, Rachel?" She held it out. "It looks familiar, somehow."

"Why, yes. Yes, I believe it is. Just like it." Their eyes met, cautiously, and then moved to Francie's face. Bix felt prickly all over. Because there was no doubt about it, Francie's face had changed, he was no longer smiling. "We always kept ours down in the cellar. Come to think about it, I haven't seen it this time. But it's probably around somewhere."

"About this clock you mentioned—" Francie began.

"It's funny you should have a candlestick just like ours," said Rachel.

"What's funny about it? A piece of junk. I've had that one around for years. Dime a dozen."

"Really? It's quite an unusual pattern. I don't think I've ever seen one—"

"A piece of junk, I said! Do you think I've got nothing better to do than stand around all day arguing with you about candlesticks? If you want to talk business with me, talk it. If you don't, get out." The veiled, shouting voice had turned into something like a snarl. "That's what I said. If you want to talk business—"

"We heard you, Mr. Henshaw," said Rachel sweetly. "Come on, Bix. I'm afraid we've taken too much of your time. Thank you, just the same."

They sailed down the path through the jungle. But at the door, just as the bell jangled out its signal of departure, Bix looked back, and it seemed to her that Francie was smiling again. Slyly, at some pleasure known only to himself.

Mr. Pigeon (they went straight up to the courthouse to see him) was very much interested, he said soothingly. He was working on the candlestick angle; so far nothing had turned up, and, frankly, he wasn't banking too much on it. But Francie's reaction was interesting; it certainly was.

"Eccentric old codger, isn't he?" said Mr. Pigeon genially. "Every town has at least one. Very bad heart, they tell me. Apt to cork off any minute."

It was already getting dark when they walked home. One streak of cold, lemon-colored light was left in the west, but fading fast. The patches of ice that had melted a little during the day were skimming over again, sealing themselves up against another long, cold night.

"I don't care," said Bix. "Francie knows something about that candlestick. He wouldn't have acted that way if he didn't. He knows what it was used for. Maybe he even knows where it is."

Rachel didn't answer. Her feet were dragging as much as Bix's. Once she drew a sharp breath—maybe a sob, maybe just a sigh. It was better, Bix decided, not to know for sure.

Dinner didn't help the situation, either. In the first place, Mother chose tonight to start recuperating; for the first time since Rachel's arrival she showed up downstairs. Very wan in her long gray robe. Very patient and sweet. She kept making lady-like conversation at Rachel, and Rachel kept trying to keep her mind on it. Daddy was so busy fussing over darling Althea— "Are you sure you're warm enough, darling? Shall I get you the afghan?"—that he hardly knew anybody else was around. It was ghastly.

Bix cooked. Elaborately—to relieve the pressure. It didn't turn out the way the book said at all. Daddy took one bite of the Spanish rice, blinked, and said, "Jesus, honey, you sure stubbed your toe when you put in the red pepper." Mother said, "Now, Hugh. It's very tasty, Beatrix dear." Bix said viciously, "Eat it, then. I dare you to," and was rewarded with a look of saintly reproach.

The phone rang, and Rachel said, very fast, "If that's—Dr. Craig, I don't want to talk to him. Tell him I'm asleep, or in the bathtub, or dead drunk, or something." It wasn't Doc, though. It was Gloria, down at the office, calling for Daddy. Old Eager-Beaver Gloria. Daddy's Girl Friday working over-time again, loving every minute of it, and never letting Daddy forget it.

Instead, Doc simply rang the doorbell a few minutes later and waltzed in, all set for the welcoming committee. Daddy's mouth got that little quirk of amusement as he ushered Doc in. "Had your supper, Doc? Here, sit down and eat with us." And one thing about Doc, he sat up and ate the rest of the Spanish rice without a whimper. They all—even Rachel—watched him respectfully.

"Nothing like home cooking," he said when he had finished. He smiled at everybody, especially Rachel, and she gave him the full iceberg treatment. She was the one that could do it, too, thought Bix; Doc's smile froze in its tracks. After that, while they were having coffee, he kept casting worried little glances at her, and Daddy had to ask him three times to pass the cream. It was kind of a diversion but after a while it began to seem ghastly too. Bix propped her elbow on the table and stared at the sugar bowl. Why doesn't she just ask him if he's still got a wife? she thought. They think they've got troubles! Hartley—

It wasn't the same, trying to talk to him up there in that gray cement room. They had been scared before, she and Hartley, but one of them had always been able to say something. They couldn't now. They just sat, paralyzed. He must be sitting there now. Helpless; but no more helpless than she was. Hartley. He had never failed her, not once in all her life, and she was failing him. . . .

"I move we migrate to the comfortable chairs," said Daddy, getting up. "Wait a minute, Althea darling. Wait till I get the couch fixed for you." He went into the living room and turned on the light beside the couch. It flickered several times before it stayed on. "Looks like we need a new bulb. There. I guess it's all right—"

Right then was when it happened. The splintering crash; Daddy's voice, sharp with alarm: "What in the hell—"; a faint scream from Mother; the rush of all their feet.

Someone had thrown a rock through the living room window.

It lay in the middle of the rug, as incredible as a visitor from Mars.

Doc Craig moved first. "Hey, there's a note," he said, "a message—" Wrapped around the rock and held there with a rubber band was a scrap of paper on which were pasted words cut from a newspaper. It was not a long message.

> "Warning R. B. and B. B. Mind your own business.
> You know what I mean. You will be sorry if you
> do not."

Doc read it out word by word.

"What?" said Daddy crossly.

"R. B. and B.B." whispered Rachel. "Bix! That's us. R. B. and B.B." her hand, colder than the rock itself, gripped Bix's.

And Bix tore away from her. She tore away from all of them, standing there like so many wax dummies, and rushed to the broken window. A stream of winter air hit her face; it was like a drink of achingly cold water.

"Listen, you out there!" Her voice screeched into the darkness. "Listen to me! You can't scare me. I'm not going to mind my own business! You hear me? I'm going to—"

"Bix, get away from there! Bix, you crazy kid—"

She turned then, and screeched at them. It seemed to her that the sudden gust of wind which sent the curtain cracking inward struck straight through her too, straight to the wrenching place in her chest. Splinters of glass crunched under her feet; she clenched her hands against her chest, and it was rending her, splitting her, once and for all, in two. "I don't care!" she screamed at the whole world. "I don't care! I love Hartley! Do you understand? I *love* Hartley—"

XVI

And then nothing in the room moved except the curtain. Hugh stood at the bottom of the stairs, with one foot on the first step and his hand clamped on to the bannister. In her headlong flight Bix had flung away from him—even from him. He looked defenseless, thought Doc, like a man dazed by a stroke of lightning. Althea huddled in the corner of the sofa with her hands over her eyes. Not crying; simply shutting out the world, closing up like a touch-me-not against the rude hand of reality. As for Doc himself and Rachel, they seemed rooted here in the middle of the room. He stole a glance at her face. It looked the way his felt: blank. He was still holding the rock in his hand.

And only the curtain moved, twisting in the draft, making a faint whipping sound. It seemed to Doc that the air still throbbed with Bix's voice crying love and defiance, that the space in front of the shattered window still held the imprint of her figure—weedy yet staunch, absurd yet somehow majestic. Yes; majestic. . . .

Althea was the first one to speak. "Hugh. The window, Hugh. It's so cold."

"Yes, darling." He turned, like a machine jerking back into action. "I'll fix it. We'll put something up." He came over and put his arms around her for a moment. Apparently it steadied him. "First, though, I'm going to call Charlie Jeffreys and Pigeon and tell them what's been going on here. I'd like to know how they can fit this in with keeping Hartley in jail. Because it doesn't fit. That's all." He flashed a reassuring smile at Rachel. "Also, I'd like to know how they're planning to protect you and Bix. Maybe that threatening letter is somebody's idea of a joke, but I'd rather not take a chance on it."

"Lord, no." Doc looked down at the rock in his hand. He still didn't quite believe it. "R. B. and B. B. That's what I don't get, why they picked you two. What have you been up to?"

"We went to see Francie Henshaw this afternoon," said Rachel. (But she wouldn't look directly at him; she was talking as much to Hugh as to him. What *is* this? he thought, as he had thought a dozen times during dinner. She couldn't still be brooding over the Greg thing. They had both forgotten that in the excitement of finding Mrs. Pierce. What the hell was eating on her?) "And when we mentioned the other candlestick he got all upset and practically threw us out."

"The other candlestick?" Hugh stared at her. Kept on staring, while she explained it all. He hunched his shoulder nervously. "Francie? Of course he's a queer old party, but I can't believe that Francie—"

"Oh, Hugh," said Althea in that tired, sweet voice of hers. "Queer old party! Why don't you admit what everybody else knows? You're always so determined to stick up for these crackpot friends of yours."

He flushed a little, at the weary scorn in her tone. (She really is a bitch, thought Doc, in her own quaint way.) "He did act suspicious, Hugh," said Rachel. "And then, to have this happen right afterwards—it's too much of a coincidence."

"I suppose it is. But he couldn't have killed Mrs. Henshaw. He hasn't got the physical strength. Besides, I dropped in on him that afternoon, the way I do every day or so, and there he was with his nose in a book. Not one bit different from any other day. He couldn't have done it."

"He knows who did, then. Or something. He knows something he's not telling. Bix and I went right to Mr. Pigeon, and he said—Well, he said we were very co-operative. He seems to think Francie's just a harmless eccentric."

"Very convenient," said Doc. "For Francie."

Hugh sighed. Then he went out into the hall to the telephone. Doc shifted from one foot to the other, and Rachel took a tentative step away from him and then decided to stay where she was, after all. The lesser of two evils, no doubt. He was no red-hot favorite—she had made that clear enough tonight—but she would still rather be paired off with him, as it were, than with Althea. Which gave Althea a pretty low rating. The feeling, Doc decided, was mutual. Not that this set Rachel apart; Althea's cold indifference took in the whole world. She had forgotten how to love anybody—assuming that she had ever known how. "My son, my little boy. . . ." She had once known how, all right. Only all her heart had been spent on Ronnie; she had none left, thought Doc, she was bankrupt.

There she sat, pale, genteel, and bankrupt. "I must apologize," she said, "for Beatrix and the way she behaved—"

"No!" The flat, rude contradiction startled Doc, who had produced it, as much as it did Althea. He felt his face getting red. He gulped and went on. "Bix doesn't need anybody to apologize for her. The way she behaved was—was—you ought to be—"

"A fine thing," said Hugh, back from his session at the telephone. "Can't get either one of them. Charlie's wife says Pigeon called him a while back, but she's got no idea where they went. This is great. Just great." He cast a curious glance at Doc's face. But he didn't ask any questions. "Oh well. We'll get them eventually. Come on, Doc, how about we fix up this window some way?"

"Sure." As Doc turned, his eyes met Rachel's at last, in a silent, important question. *You think the way I do about Bix, don't you? She was wonderful, wasn't she?* And her whole face glowed with the fervent answer: *Yes. Of course. Wonderful.* For only a second, though. She remembered whatever it was that was eating on her, and snuffed out the glow.

All the same, Doc felt better.

XVII

Mrs. Smiley shooed the cats off the supper table and made another pass at her bleached, upswept hair, which tottered like a ruined castle on top of her head.

"That's just it," she told Mr. Pigeon and Charlie Jeffreys. "Mr. Henshaw ain't home yet. I don't hardly know what to think. Because he's always back, right on the dot of six. Like Smiley says, we set the clock by him."

They hadn't set the clock lately, apparently. It sat on the back of the stove, a drunken-looking pink alarm clock minus one foot, its hands pointing irresponsibly to half past one. Charlie Jeffreys glanced at his wrist watch. "It's after seven," he said. "And he's not down at the store. We tried there."

"Madonna honey," Mrs. Smiley addressed one of the three young Smileys who sat on the floor, all eating something red and sticky, all absorbed in comic books, "Madonna honey, run up and take another look, there's a good girl. Though I know we'd of heard him, we always do. He uses the outside stairs, you know, but he always taps on the kitchen door, looks in and says Good evening, and that's how I know it's six o'clock." Her face, caked with the remains of some other day's make-up, took on an expression of genuine concern. She fumbled worriedly at the belt of the bedraggled, flowered housecoat which seemed to be all she was wearing. Mrs. Smiley's figure, like her face, was large and amiable. "Smiley ain't back with the truck yet, or I'd of sent him out to look. We've been uneasy about him, ever since he had that bad spell with his heart, back in the fall. Madonna honey, you heard Mama. Run up and—"

"Never mind," said Mr. Pigeon. "We'll take a look ourselves, if it's all right with you."

Of course it was all right with Mrs. Smiley. "I better take you up. There's a bad place in the stairs. I keep at Smiley and at him to fix it, but you know how men are. Now I just wonder where that flashlight got to. . . ." It turned out, after some searching, to have gotten into the bread box. From under the sink Mrs. Smiley plucked a shapeless sweater and threw it around her shoulders. Then she opened the back door and led them up the rickety outside staircase to Francie's room, on the second floor.

"Mr. Henshaw!" she called before she opened the door. "Mr. Henshaw! You in there?"

Her voice trailed away forlorn and unanswered on the chilly wind. Slap-slap went her soiled lavender satin slippers; the door clicked open, and in a moment she had turned on the unshaded bulb that dangled from the center of Francie's room. For such a small room, it held a great many things, among them an unmade bed, a kerosene stove, an ancient electric plate, a dusty shelf crammed with books, and Francie's stock of canned goods—but not Francie himself. There was a strong, stale smell of peanut butter, kerosene, and unwashed wool.

"He don't like for me to make his bed for him," said Mrs. Smiley. "He'd sooner fix everything for himself. 'Just leave me alone,' he always says. 'Just leave me be, I know the way I want things.' " Suddenly her big, blurred face seemed to crumple up; her eyes moved in belated alarm from Charlie to Mr. Pigeon, back again to Charlie. "What do you want with him? What's happened? Sixteen years he's lived with us, and he's never been late before. Six o'clock on the dot. Something's wrong! Something's happened to the poor old soul!"

"Now, now," said Mr. Pigeon soothingly. "Don't worry, Mrs. Smiley. We'll find him."

Maybe so, but Charlie didn't see exactly how, at the moment. Of course the old guy couldn't just vanish. But it wasn't like looking for somebody who might have stopped in at the pool hall for a beer, or gone to the movies, or dropped in on some friends for a visit. Francie never did any of these things. If he wasn't at the store or at Smiley's, you could bet he was loping along that little path of his, on his way from one place to the other.

Only tonight you would have lost your bet. Silently Charlie followed Mr. Pigeon down the shaky staircase and out to the Chevvy. He looked back at Mrs. Smiley; she was standing in the kitchen door, wiping her eyes on her sweater sleeve. Not any too bright, thought Charlie, and pig-sty dirty; but good-hearted. You had to give her that. Or maybe all that worried her was losing out on the rent, in case something had happened to Francie. No. She'd called him Mr. Henshaw, and that clinched it, somehow, for Charlie. She thought enough of him to call him Mr. Henshaw.

"We could have looked for the candlestick while we were up there," he ventured as he started up the Chevvie.

"It'll keep," said Mr. Pigeon. "Let's look for the old man first."

"Okay. Where to?"

"Somebody must have seen him when he left the store. Unless he sneaked out the back way, for some reason. And even then—"

Down town three establishments were still open: the pool hall, the drug store, and the Square Deal Cafe. Mitch, who ran the pool hall, produced a fishy stare when Charlie asked if he had seen Francie. "Who, me? You nuts, Charlie? Francie Henshaw never drank a beer or played a game of pool in his life." No, he hadn't noticed Francie going past; and neither had any of the customers, though the kid from the filling station thought maybe he had. But he wasn't sure.

Same story at the drug store.

But Erma, the Square Deal waitress, perked right up at Charlie's question. "Sure I saw him. He came out of his store a little before six, as usual, but then he didn't go right on up the street, like he always does. That's how I happened to notice him. He stopped in front of the Tribune office, sat down on the bench where people wait for the bus, you know, and I thought don't tell me Francie's going somewhere on the bus, or waiting to meet somebody—"

"Was he?"

Erma shrugged. "The bus don't get in till 6:45, and by that time I was too busy to notice. I just saw him kind of hanging around there, is all. The Tribune office was already closed, I know that, so he wasn't stopping in to see Mr. Bovard the way he sometimes does. So that's why I thought of the bus, even though it seemed awful early for anybody to be waiting for it."

Charlie pounded back out to the Chevvie and passed this on to Mr. Pigeon. For what it was worth. The 6:45 bus went back to Westburg, among other places, and Westburg was where Mrs. Pierce lived and where she and Mrs. Henshaw had grown up. Mr. Pigeon thought it over and decided it might be worth while to follow the bus and see if Francie really had caught it.

"Okay," said Charlie. "Here we go." It was the only lead they had. And something told him it was going to be a wild goose chase.

XVIII

Out in the Bovard woodshed, Doc held the flashlight while Hugh scrabbled around among the odds and ends of lumber until he found what he wanted. "This'll do it," he said, pulling out a strip of beaverboard. "We can tack this up over the window for tonight. Let's take in an armload of wood, too. Maybe a fire in the fireplace will cheer us up." He grinned, rather wanly. "I guess we can use a little cheer."

"Amen," said Doc. "You don't happen to know what's eating

on Rachel, do you? I mean, even before all this business with the rock she didn't act—well, the way she did yesterday. Unless it's just my imagination working overtime. . . ." He paused, hopefully.

Hugh snapped off that bit of nonsense without ceremony. "It's not. She's sore at you about something, my boy. Don't ask me what. Women. I can't figure 'em out. Why don't you ask her?"

A good question. One that might have occurred to Doc himself, if he had a lick of sense, which it seemed he hadn't. "Well. All right. Well, I guess I will."

Hugh was busy with the piece of beaverboard, maneuvering it through the woodshed door. "Do my eyes deceive me, or have you gone overboard for Rachel?"

"Good Lord, no!" Doc dredged up a reasonable facsimile of a light laugh. "Thanks a lot, but no thanks. It's against my principles, that sort of thing. She's just a good-looking babe, that's all."

"That she is," said Hugh drily. Doc could see his face now—the deep lines running from nose to mouth, the quirked eyebrow that was ordinarily humorous, but that looked at this moment so mortally sad. "I wish you luck with your principles. And I wish to God I'd been bright enough to play it your way. If I had it to do over again—"

Doc waited.

"Oh hell. Let's face it. There's no reason to believe I'd be any brighter, the second time around."

A good guy, Hugh. About as good as they come, thought Doc, and definitely as unlucky. Let this be a lesson to you, just in case you show any signs of going overboard. And don't kid yourself, you've been showing them. The way you fired up about Bix, for instance. That was partly because . . . Okay, so Rachel's different, she isn't Althea. It doesn't change the principle. She's just a good-looking babe. That's all she is, and don't you forget it.

The open fire turned out to be quite a success. They sat around it—after the window was patched up—with drinks and cigarettes, and even Rachel seemed to relax in the mellow warmth. She held out her hands to it: good big hands, for all her slender wrists, and once or twice she went so far as to smile at Doc. It was almost possible to forget the rock lying there on the coffee table. Hugh made a passable joke of the extra precautions he took, locking up doors and windows, and of his trips out to the telephone in the hall. Mr. Pigeon and Charlie Jeffreys were still among those missing at eleven.

"I give up," said Hugh, yawning. "Let's go to bed, Althea. You young folks can set up as late as you want to. Just be sure you lock the door, Rachel, when Doc leaves."

"I'm sort of sleepy myself," said Rachel. But tentatively.

"You can't go to bed yet," Hugh told her. "You've got to finish your drink. Good night, kiddies."

Mr. Cupid Bovard, thought Doc. Not too subtle, maybe, but you had to give him A for Effort. One thing, the setting was made to order: cozy fire, dim lights, soft music purling out of the radio. He stretched out in his chair and stole a quick look at Rachel, stretched out in hers. The thing to do was to plan this campaign. The surprise attack? The encircling movement? Or the marking-time, it's-your-move routine, designed to wear down her resistance?

She turned her face toward him, and instantly he lost track of his cool plans. One bound, and he was out of his chair, kissing her with all the finesse of a high school kid on his maiden date. He got what he deserved—no co-operation. Not that she resisted. She just sat still, detaching herself from the whole proceedings. He balanced himself on the arm of her chair and (be nonchalant) started to light a cigarette. Which was another error, advertising as it did the unsteadiness of his hands.

"All right," he said. "Let's have it. I'm sorry I asked you who

Greg is, if that's what you're sore about. Maybe he's a ball of fire, this Greg. Maybe I ought to be flattered that you got me confused with him. I'm just not used to—"

"No. Greg's not a ball of fire. He's just—somebody I used to know." The words seemed to surprise her a little, but then she nodded, as if they were, after all, what she had meant to say. "That's all. I called Greg, late this afternoon. Because I felt so— But he didn't have time to talk. He was due at a dinner party."

So much for the Great Greg. Him and his dinner parties, Lord love him. But the fact still remained. . . .

"What is it, then? What's wrong? Yesterday things were— well, quite a bit different."

"Yesterday." She clasped her hands in her lap and regarded them thoughtfully. "Now that you mention it, I guess things were different yesterday."

"So what's happened? Why the difference? After all, I'm the same sweet kid." There. He was doing better, he was hitting his stride again.

"I'm sure you are," she said pleasantly. "Or should we say the same slick operator?"

"Look here, Rachel, let's stop playing games and—" (But that was all wrong. The point was to keep the whole thing on the game-playing level. Good clean fun, with no chance of getting involved or hurt.)

"And what? I'm just an amateur at these games of yours, you know. You're the expert." She said it bravely enough, but all at once something happened to her face. Her mouth started trembling, her eyes fluttered shut, and—well, this time it was no high school kid kiss. It was like yesterday. Too much so for safety.

"Please," she whispered. "No. Oh, please no." She pulled away from him and sat up straight.

"Don't look like that." Somehow, he discovered, he had wound up on his knees beside her chair. He was past caring. "Darling. Tell me. Tell me what's wrong."

"I'm ashamed to," she said. "Because it makes it look as if I—" She took a breath and finished, very fast. "After all, what possible difference can it make to me, whether you have a wife or not?"

A wife. The same slick operator. These games of yours. A wife.

She was waiting. "Oh," he said feebly, "that."

"Yes. That." The cleft chin tilted up, very proud, very vulnerable.

"Here's how it is. Rachel darling, I owe you an explanation—" He swallowed. Why was it that you never sounded phonier than when you were breaking your neck to tell the truth? "It's very simple, really. Believe me, I never meant to—"

He heard the noise, and stopped talking. She heard it, and stopped listening to him. A stealthy thump from the direction of the kitchen. They leaped to their feet and waited tensely. The thump came again.

"Probably nothing. A loose shutter," explained Doc. "You wait here while I take a look."

"Certainly not. Here. Here's the poker. I'll take the shovel."

They crept through the dining room (and the poker made him feel like a fool, only there was the rock, lying back there on the coffee table, the rock and the unlikely note) and noiselessly pushed open the swinging door that led to the kitchen.

XIX

Wild goose chase was right. Charlie Jeffreys shifted from one foot to the other and tried to figure out whether Mr. Pigeon was looking at him or at the bus driver, a fattish young man whose mouth, at the moment, was full of apple pie. He had had just enough start on them, had gotten all the way to the end of the line before they caught up with him. Westburg. The Westburg Eatery, Open Day & Nite. Charlie leaned against the counter and waited for the bus driver to dispose of his mouthful. He knew right now what the answer was going to be. Already the bus driver was shaking his head.

"Nope. Didn't pick up anybody at Coreyville."

"Any passengers get off there tonight?"

The bus driver swilled down some coffee and thought a minute. "Yep. Two dames with shopping bags. I picked them up in Red Rock; they'd spent the day there shopping. Yackety yackety about bargains, all the way to Coreyville."

"Anybody meet them?"

"Nope. They took off up Main Street and I got out and stretched my legs and smoked a cigarette."

"Anybody hanging around there in front of the Tribune office? Anybody sitting on the bench? An old guy, maybe, kind of a funny-looking skinny old guy?"

"Nope. Nothing doing at all. Had the bus to myself till I got to Red Rock. A bunch of high school kids got on there. No funny-looking skinny old guy." The bus driver went back to work on the apple pie, and Charlie followed Mr. Pigeon out to the car.

So back we go to Coreyville, thought Charlie. He's there some place. Got to be. And it's anybody's guess what the old devil's been up to, while we've been kiting around chasing that so-and-so bus. It'll be well after eleven before we get back. Plenty of time for plenty of things to happen.

He watched Mr. Pigeon settling down comfortably in his corner. "Now, now," said Mr. Pigeon, as he had said to Mrs. Smiley. "Don't worry, Sheriff. We'll find him."

XX

Refrigerator, stove, sink glimmered like massive ghosts in the silent kitchen. Doc took another cautious step forward and tried to decide whether or not to turn on the light. The swinging door behind him, where Rachel still paused, was half-open, letting in a finger of feeble light. It seemed to feel its way across the big kitchen to the opposite wall with its two doors, one opening into Hugh's study, the other on the back stairway that led to the second floor. Doc stopped dead in the middle of another step. That stairway door was moving inward, very, very slowly. He tightened his grip on the poker, waited while the door inched open and the shadowy figure slid through. Then he plunged across the linoleum and grabbed. At the same moment Rachel flicked on the light.

"Bix! What in the hell are you up to?"

"None of your business! Let go of me!" She stopped wriggling, and some of the scared look faded from her big eyes. She was wearing that beat-up, over-size leather jacket and a pair of slacks. "Jeepers, you don't have to twist a person's arm off."

He put down the ridiculous poker and glanced at Rachel, who had her hand over her mouth—no doubt holding back a laugh. Okay, so he was a figure of fun. After all, the poker and shovel had been her idea, not his. He glared at Bix.

"What's the big idea, prowling around like this? Naturally we took you for a burglar. Where do you think you're going?"

"Out," said Bix. She clamped her mouth shut again.

"Listen, you two," said Rachel, "stop snapping at each other, or you'll have everybody else awake, and that's not going to be any help. Or maybe—" She paused by the table, watching Bix. "Maybe that's what we ought to do. Wake up your Dad and—"

"No," whispered Bix. But she stuck her hands in her pockets and made one more stab at defiance. "I guess I've got a right to go out for a breath of fresh air if I want to."

"Oh, stop it. Breath of fresh air, my eye. We know what you're going out for."

"Do we?" inquired Doc.

Rachel paid no attention to him. "It's not safe, Bix. Stop trying to muscle in on Mr. Pigeon's territory. He may not be a thunderbolt, but he knows how to deal with this better than you do."

"Why doesn't he deal with it, then? He can't even be reached. I heard Daddy trying to get him all evening. He can't even be reached."

"For all you know, he may be down there right now. Probably he is."

"Okay, if he is, I'll help him."

"Help him do what? Down where?" put in Doc. "Will one of you dames kindly explain—"

"Down at Francie's store, you dope," Bix flashed back at him. "Hunting for the candlestick."

"For Lord's sake," said Doc. "You mean to tell me you were planning to—"

"Not was. Am." She looked him in the eye. "Try and stop me."

"But Bix, you can't go down there by yourself!"

"Oh, can't I!" She leaned toward him, and he could see the tear streaks on her thin, tragic child-face. It was like the moment when she had stood in front of the broken window with the curtains whipping out and her hands doubled up against her chest. She was whispering now, not screaming; still, it was like that moment. "You make me sick. All of you. 'Poor, poor Hartley. That poor, dear boy.' Well, why don't you do something about him instead of just standing around talking about your bleeding hearts? And now you're trying to keep me from doing anything. You're scared of a crazy old man! You're scared of a rock and a little busted glass! You make me sick!"

It didn't make any sense at all. And yet Doc felt the crawl of shame; his coward eyes shifted under Bix's gaze; he cleared his throat and ran his fingers through his hair. He couldn't think of anything to say? Nonsense, he assured himself. He could think of all kinds of arguments. He was simply taking his time choosing which to use first.

He didn't get a chance to use any of them. Rachel crossed over to Bix. She didn't touch her; she just stood beside her. "All right then, Bix. I'll go with you."

He opened his mouth to protest, but the look on Rachel's face stopped him. An intense look, aimed exclusively at him, telling him something without words. Telling him he was out-voted, for one thing. But more than that. Appealing to him to play it her way for now, to take her word for it, to trust her. It was all there, in the almost imperceptible tip of her head, the flicker of her eyelid. He looked back at her helplessly.

Women. You couldn't win. Maybe you didn't even want to.

"We'll need our coats," he said at last. "Wait here. I'll get them." While he was closing the door to the hall closet, he thought he heard a rustling from upstairs. He waited for Hugh's voice, meanwhile busily preparing his explanation. Rachel and I decided to run downtown for a cup of coffee, or a nightcap, or a bite to eat. Taking Bix with us (in case her absence had been noticed, upstairs). But Hugh didn't call down to him. He might have imagined the rustling. No, there it was again, the kind of sound a woman's robe might make. He thought of Althea and her insomnia and her long gray robe. He tried to peer up the stairway, but could see nothing. After a minute the rustling stopped too, and he went back to the kitchen.

They let themselves out the back door with hardly a sound, and set off down the alley three abreast, with Doc in the middle, firmly gripping Rachel's arm on one side, Bix's on the other. He hoped this was the accepted bodyguard procedure. Crazy, he thought; an absolutely hare-brained expedition. . . .

"The least we can do," Rachel was whispering in his ear. "Humor the poor kid. It's awfully lonesome, sometimes, being sixteen. Pigeon's probably already down there, or if he isn't we won't be able to get in—"

"What?" asked Bix suspiciously. "Why don't you talk so I can hear you?"

"We're figuring how to get in the place. You got any ideas?"

"We'll find some way." Bix gave a confident little skip. There was something contagious about her faith, something satisfactory—Doc admitted it to himself—about the whole project. It beat sitting at home, waiting for somebody to throw another rock.

He still couldn't quite believe the rock, anyway. Just as he couldn't really believe that this alley—dark as it was, dark as a pocket—was bristling with weird and wonderful dangers. Sure it was dark; this was familiar, pokey old Coreyville on a winter night. Quiet; except for the wind which made a faint, sad rattling in Myra Graves' lilac hedge, the sound of a car starting up a couple of blocks away on Main Street, and the ring of their own footsteps on the frozen ground. Ordinary, Coreyville noises. For the life of him Doc couldn't get alarmed about them.

They cut across the vacant lot opposite the Buckmaster house and turned down the back street which brought them, by way of another alley, to the rear entrance of Francie's store. Nobody met them or jumped out at them. A dim night-light burned in the grocery store next door; Francie's place was wedged in between it and the barber shop. Bix took out her flashlight and turned it on the weather-beaten door.

"I don't see any signs of your friend Mr. Pigeon," she was saying smugly. "No doubt he's already been here— Hey! Maybe he has! Because somebody has. The lock's busted." The flashlight beam gave a jump of excitement, then settled again on the padlock, which—no doubt about it—had been forced. They needn't have worried about how they were going to get in.

"Solves problem number one. All we have to do is walk in," said Bix, and prepared to suit the action to the word.

"Now wait a minute." Doc pulled her back, none too gently. "This is funny. What if they're still in there? Whoever broke the lock, I mean. Francie wouldn't bust into his own place. It's got to be somebody else."

"There's only one way to find out," said Bix. "Go in and see. You're scared to, I suppose. Well, it was nice seeing you. . . . Hey! What's that? Down past the barber shop?"

The world's oldest gag, and Doc fell for it. The flashlight beam swerved for a split second down the alley, he turned wildly and stared—at nothing, of course—and by the time he had a brain cell working, she was through the door. The witch. The damn, obstinate, slippery little eel of a witch. He forgot about Rachel (until she gasped) and said several things out loud. Then he followed Bix through the door. Rachel grabbed at his sleeve. "Wait for me. I'm coming too. Here. I've got a lighter." In the flicker of the little flame her eyes looked enormous. "I'm sorry," she whispered. "I didn't think it would be like this."

"Who's blaming you?" he said. "Come on."

There was a cold, stale, kerosene stink. The lighter didn't really help much. They kept bumping into things—sharp-cornered things, things with knobs and splinters, things that jangled or teetered or clattered. Once or twice there was a scurrying sound up ahead that could have been mice or Bix, take your choice. Wherever she was, she was lying low. Clutching her flashlight and biding her time. Unless somebody had been waiting for her. . . . His insides gave a lurch. Did he dare call out her name? Supposing whoever it was (if there was anyone) hadn't got to her yet, was just waiting for a sign? He played the lighter over another few feet of clutter and moved forward.

"Like a jungle," whispered Rachel. "Isn't it?"

It was. Hide-and-seek in the jungle. Come out, come out, wherever you are. One thing was for sure: he was It. Whatever happened to Bix or Rachel, he was to blame. They weren't responsible—Bix because she was sixteen and in love, Rachel because she was Hartley's sister—but he had no excuse. A real, aged-in-the-wood, bona fide meathead.

They had groped their way into what seemed to be a comparative clearing. Doc blundered against Francie's chair, just missing the kerosene stove. Up ahead lay more jungle, even vaster than the one they had covered. It was no good; they could stumble around in here all night and get no place. "I've got my bearings now," said Rachel in a low voice. She had stopped too; her hand was pressed tight in his. "There's a light, right about here. I remember. Let's—Let's turn it on and get it over with. If there is anybody in here they've already got us spotted, so—"

"Okay," he said after a minute. "Where is it? Turn it on."

"Oh nuts." It was Bix's voice, close at hand, and sagging with disgust. "I give up. Only will you please kindly not bitch everything up by turning on the light?"

"Bix! Where are you? Are you all right?"

"Why wouldn't I be?" She turned the flashlight on her own face briefly; it loomed up disembodied, dust-streaked, but undamaged. "I'm right here. Where else? If you turn on that light somebody's going to notice it from the street and come busting in and spoil everything. So will you please kindly—"

"Will you please kindly excuse me while I wring your neck?" burst out Doc. "You and your low tricks! Sneaking in here behind our backs, and then playing possum. Why the hell didn't you—"

"Temper, temper," reproved Bix. "I just figured I'd save time and avoid an argument."

"Sure. And maybe get yourself exterminated. God knows who's been prowling around in here. May still be here, for all you know."

"Nobody's showed up yet," said Bix airily. "And they've had plenty of time. Here. This is what we're looking for. Another one like this." The flashlight shone on a heavy brass candlestick. "Come on. Let's get busy."

"Busy nothing. We're getting out of here. I mean it, Bix."

"You promised—" she began, and he could see what was coming up. The routine that had trapped him before: the you-make-me-sick, scared-of-a-crazy-old-man business.

He wasn't having any more. "That was before I knew somebody else was going to have the same idea." He reached up and floundered in a wide circle above his and Rachel's heads, searching for the light. Found it. Francie's forty-watt bulb gave out with a foggy yellow glow; as it swung back and forth the shadows seemed to leap and flee every which way in terror. Doc stopped the swinging. Dusty velvet chair; cheerless stove; bow-legged table loaded with junk; a nightmare clutter of furniture, almost ceiling-high, stretching into the gloom ahead. Was someone lurking there, watching and waiting? There was no sound.

He braced himself and met Bix's eyes. She was standing beside the table, grasping the candlestick in one hand and the flashlight in the other. Her face was white with the fury of one betrayed; oh Lord, he thought, she'll never forgive me, poor kid. That was the trouble with being sixteen—everybody was against you. Lonesome, Rachel had said. Awfully lonesome.

"Okay," she said stonily. "So we advertise. I'm still going to look, till somebody stops me."

And Doc, she left no doubt, wasn't the man who could stop her. She turned and set off up the path toward the front of the store, an absurd, exasperating, indomitable figure. He glanced at Rachel. She looked as if she didn't know whether to laugh or cry.

"Look then, damn it," he said, and he took off after her, herding Rachel along with him. "But we stick together. I still insist on that."

(Long Lars, the night watchman, was sure to notice the light in the course of his rounds and investigate. Besides, by this time Doc himself was finding it hard to believe that their friend the lock-breaker was still around. Surely he wouldn't have passed up all these golden opportunities to dispose of Bix, or all three of them, and nip out the back door. What had he been after, anyway? The candlestick? But that didn't make sense. If it was Francie, why would he break his own lock? And if it wasn't Francie, what was wrong with leaving the candlestick here, where it would implicate Francie and no one else?)

"Here," said Bix. "Make yourself useful. Hold the flashlight, will you?"

Doc obeyed meekly enough, while Bix began her search. Rachel helped. They opened drawers, they clambered up on tables and chairs and peered in corners. All they found was plenty of dust. (Ten minutes, and still nobody from the street had spotted them. Where was Long Lars? Drinking coffee, probably; chinning, in his monosyllabic way, with Erma over in the Square Deal, instead of tending to his duties.)

"How about the window?" asked Doc. "Plenty of junk there." He swept the flashlight beam over the incredible array: hitching post, chafing dishes, a child's rocking chair, a moth-eaten bearskin and a stuffed canary in a cage, urns half as tall as Dr. Craig and a set of teacups no bigger than thimbles.

"Why not?" said Rachel. "It might be Francie's idea of a joke, to hide it in the window. Providing he's the one that hid it, of course. Those vases are plenty big enough—"

"Wait a minute!" said Bix. Her voice was hushed, shaky with excitement; her eyes, as far as Doc could make out, were riveted on the head of the bearskin. A mean-looking customer, all right, with its yellow jags of teeth and its two fiercely gleaming little eyes. Still, it was nothing to go into a trance about. He swiped the light once more across the window, and Bix let out another muted yelp.

"His eyes. He's only supposed to have one eye. . . ." She darted past Rachel and Doc, and leaped up into the window, knocking over a chafing dish and throwing the stuffed canary into a fit of delirious swinging. The teacups expired in a series of dainty crashes while she scrabbled under the bearskin.

The candlestick was there, tucked up under the bear's head, where the flashlight had caught its brassy glint through the one empty eye socket. Bix rubbed it against her leather jacket. Then she held it aloft triumphantly, like a warrior displaying a battle trophy. All she could do was squeak. "Oh, boy! Oh, boy! Oh—"

"That's it," Rachel was babbling. "Bix honey. That's it. . . ."

Doc thrust the flashlight into her hands and lifted Bix out of the window bodily. She felt light and brittle as a bird, and inside the leather jacket she was shivering violently. He didn't feel any too steady himself.

"You found it." He forgot that she was never going to forgive him and hugged her, and he forgot that Rachel was mad at him and hugged her too. Everybody forgot and hugged everybody. "You did it, kid."

Their little love fest didn't last long. They were jarred out of it by noises from the back of the store. The tread of feet, cautious but resolute-sounding; voices demanding, "Francie? Hey there, Henshaw!" The figures of Charlie Jeffreys and Mr. Pigeon emerged in the foggy yellow light back there in the clearing. They raced back with their find, all yammering at once.

"Where the hell were you all night? Somebody threw a rock through Bovard's window, and we've been trying to get you. . . ."

"Look! The candlestick! We found the other candlestick!"

"And somebody else has been prowling around down here, because the lock's busted. . . ."

"Sure," put in Charley. "That was us. Trying to find Francie. We figured maybe he'd had a heart attack and was still in here. That was after we got back from Westburg. We been all over looking for him."

"Francie? You've been looking for Francie? Where is he?"

Charley opened his mouth and then shut it again, more in sorrow than in anger.

Even Mr. Pigeon sounded less tranquil than usual. "We haven't found him yet. He's disappeared. Hasn't been seen since before six. Now let's get this straight about the rock and the candlestick and the rest of it."

Bix thrust her trophy at him. "I guess this proves it wasn't Hartley. He couldn't have hidden it here because he never came in here. I guess now you'll have to let him out of jail. He couldn't have thrown the rock, either. It has to be Francie."

"We'll see," said Mr. Pigeon cautiously. "We'll see. Maybe there'll be some fingerprints to help us, unless you've smeared them all up."

Bix's eyes got big. "I didn't think. All I did was pull it out from under the bear, and—" (But Doc had a vivid little picture in his mind of her standing in the window, rubbing the candlestick on her jacket before she held it up in triumph. Had that really been a thoughtless gesture? Of course. It must have been.) "Can we go now?" She was practically jumping up and down with excitement. "I want to go home and tell Daddy. And Hartley. I want to tell Hartley—"

"In a minute." Mr. Pigeon took out his handkerchief and wrapped it around the top of the candlestick before he picked it up gingerly. "Let's have the other candlestick, the one that's always been here. And let's see just where this one was found." They moved in a little procession toward the front window. Questions. Answers. Doc listened, with a kind of objective interest, to his own voice explaining. The rock thrown through the window. The three of them setting out on their expedition. The search. He was making it all sound quite likely, he was convincing himself that it had actually happened. Rachel explained, too, and she left her hand where it belonged, pressed tight in his. All in all, things were looking up; life in general seemed a pretty good deal.

And then he noticed that Bix was gone.

"The kid?" said Charley, looking startled. "Why, she was here just a minute ago."

"She's probably raced off home," said Rachel. Very calm and sensible. Except that Doc felt her hand go suddenly tense. "That's what she wanted to do, and you know how she is when she makes up her mind."

He knew, all right. And he was turning into a hysterical old maid, because nothing could have happened to Bix in these few minutes, there was absolutely no cause for alarm. . . .

"Bix!" they called. Their voices sounded curiously muffled in this crowded place. As if they were all being slowly strangled, thought Doc. "Bix! Where are you?"

There was no answer at first. They were halfway to the door when they heard the muffled cry: "Let go! Let me go!" and running footsteps. Doc got out into the alley first. So he saw her first —the pitifully slight figure, like a bundle of old clothes, huddled against the back wall of the grocery store. His hands flashed into action, apparently of their own accord, searching for the pulse (and finding it, oh thank God, finding it), groping gently over the cropped head, afraid of what they might find. They paused at Bix's neck, and the others were here by now, with flashlights, so he could see that childish neck, smaller at the base, like a jointed doll's. No marks there. Nothing but a graze across her mouth, where she had scraped against the wall.

"Which way? Which way did they go?" Charlie Jeffreys was stammering with the strain of getting set to run both directions at once.

Bix's eyelids quivered and opened. Her beautiful gray eyes looked straight up into Doc's, trying to tell him something, and her swollen lips moved stiffly. It was hardly words that came out. Though it might have been, at that. It might have been, "I— fell—"

"We heard you yell. Whoever it was got scared and ran."

"Which *way?*" pleaded Charley, and when Bix pointed, not very positively, toward the barber shop he shot off.

"Who was it, Bix? Who grabbed you? Can you tell us? Did you see them?"

She closed her eyes, and her dirty face twisted grotesquely, trying to hold back the tears. She could not do it. They squeezed out—the terrible, difficult tears—and as she turned her head, once, from side to side, they trickled back across her temples.

Doc gathered her up in his arms. "Never mind. Don't try to talk any more. You're going to be all right, Baby—"

From down the alley came a hoarse yell, a thudding of foot-steps. They turned to see the lanky figure of Long Lars the night watchman bearing down on them at full tilt, his fantastically long shadow flying along beside him. Long Lars was by nature a man of few words; these had now deserted him. His scraggly reddish moustache worked up and down; one arm flailed out, gesturing urgently.

At last a scattering of broken words struggled out past the

moustache. "Back yonder. The old man. Old Francie. Sheriff found him. Looks dead to me."

Next, thought Doc. The line forms to the right, and no jostling, please. Just another quiet winter night in familiar, pokey old Coreyville.

Still carrying Bix in his arms, he headed down the alley toward his next customer.

XXI

Once in a while they came snooping around, poking at him, and it was an indignity, in a minute he was going to open his eyes and tell them so, he didn't have to put up with it, and he wasn't going to. In a minute. In just a minute.

The skimming was beginning again, though; better wait till it let up. Faster and faster. Higher and higher, with nothing to hold him down. Like the first time he ever rode on a Ferris wheel. And when was that, in the snarl of yesterday and today and tomorrow? Never mind, it had been some time, because the skimming was like it. The same delicious qualms, the perilous rush of wind, the world tilting crazily. . . .

"Go easy on him, will you?" somebody said. (Now? Or some other time? Close at hand? Or way off somewhere?) "He's not up to much. Whatever he was doing last night, it nearly finished that heart of his. It's a miracle he's pulled out of it at all."

"He seems to be resting comfortably now," said another voice. A ridiculous, know-it-all kind of voice. And there was a murmur about all right, then, no hurry. . . .

Resting comfortably. The fool woman. I am dying, thought Francie with a certain relish; that's what the skimming is, I am dying, and the fool woman says resting comfortably.

Why don't you go ahead and die, then? Francie knew who that was, all right: his old acquaintance the commentator (audible only to Francie) had been asking just such impolite questions for years. A crusty old party, the commentator; Francie had a sneaking fondness for him. *Why don't you go ahead and die, then? What's keeping you?*

Something remained to be done. That was what was keeping him. Something important that he had to do first.

You already did it. Don't you remember? Brain like a sieve. You already did it, and you hid the candlestick—that was pretty smart of you, hiding the candlestick the way you did.

Pretty smart? It had been a masterly touch. Of course he remembered. But that wasn't what he meant. Something else—an important, final something that he had to do. It would come to him, as soon as the skimming sensation let up. He couldn't be expected to remember everything while he was sailing through the air at this dizzy pace.

"How are you, Francie?" said someone. This time Francie knew it was now and close at hand. His eyes jerked open, and for an appalling moment everything was clear—one of the faces bending over him belonged to that new-fangled young doctor (he'd charge you for breathing if you didn't keep your eye on him) and the other face was Mr. Pigeon's, and the third belonged to Mrs. Know-it-all Nelson, who ran the hospital. . . . The hospital! So that was what they had done with him behind his back! Horror-struck, he took in the clean, bare room, the antiseptic smell, the smooth sheet over him. They had stuck him in the hospital at God knows how many dollars a minute, just as they had threatened to do last fall. The Smileys—those mental incompetents, those base and treacherous Smileys—were responsible for this, and they would answer for it. But later. All in good time. Just now, it was more than he could bear. He closed his eyes, and off he skimmed.

"How are you, Francie?"

How do you do, Mr. Henshaw. I'm pleased to make your acquaintance. . . .

The hospital, Dr. Craig, the Smileys—already they were out of sight, left far behind; and Francie, pleasantly conscious of his height, the elegance of his recently acquired moustache, and his new straw hat, was standing in the vestry (Wednesday evening choir practice) being introduced to the new choir member. Miss Rose Anthony, formerly of Westburg, who had very kindly consented to lend her voice to the soprano section. I'm pleased to make your acquaintance. She said it with a kind of demure slyness, as if already he and she had some sweet, terrible secret, and in the churchly dimness her face seemed to bloom like an unearthly flower. What was bewitching about that face with its waxy pallor, its sharp features and down-curving mouth? She was not a pretty girl, Miss Rose Anthony; not even if you considered her hair, which was hidden, when he first saw her, under a large, ornate hat. And yet, all during choir practice, he was acutely aware of her and of his own uncontrollable impulse to watch her. Time after time he succumbed and let his eyes slide toward the soprano section, and each time Rose caught him at it. No matter how hastily he looked away, he could not escape her subtle, knowing smile, hardly more than a twitch of her mouth. I know, she seemed to be saying, I know, and you will know, before very long. Something shameless about her, from the beginning; shameless and tainted with evil. So that their little game in the choir loft—the guilty, split-second trysts between his eyes and hers—became a travesty of other, wholesome flirtations. The whole thing was like that, and it was played out against a background of sunshiny innocence that made the taint all the more evil. And all the more irresistible. It was as if Rose Anthony awoke in him a perverse taste, unsuspected until now, that spoiled all other pleasures for him forever.

The world that she poisoned was not so much his as Etta Kincaid's. It was Etta's native land—a happy little world of lawn parties and dances and ice cream socials—into which she had drawn him with all the strength of her warm, merry heart. To him it was all new (he had grown up in an orphanage) ; a miracle of apple-blossom freshness, like Etta herself. "So you're engaged to Etta Kincaid," Rose Anthony said to him. "How nice. And you work down at the bank, for her father. How nice." Thus, with a flick of Rose's tongue, was love reduced to expediency.

The monstrous part of it was that no one else saw Rose as he did—the serpent in this miniature Eden. "She does have a sharp tongue," Etta admitted. "But then she doesn't really mean it. Poor thing, she's getting over an unhappy love affair. That's why she came here and took the job in the millinery store, you know, to get over it." To the pure all things are pure. Etta and the rest of the crowd rallied around, cheerily bent on helping Rose forget her unhappy love affair. He alone knew that it was a myth: Rose had never heard of love. He alone was singled out for those sly, demure glances of hers, the half-derisive, half-inviting little smiles. Could it be because Rose and he were somehow akin? The same breed of cats? The idea revolted him. And yet. . . . And yet. . . .

"Can you tell us what happened last night?" asked Mr. Pigeon. "What were you doing in the alley?"

"Summerhouse," Francie corrected him. What were you doing in the Kincaid summerhouse? What were you doing there with Rose Anthony, while Etta and the other innocents drank lemonade on the veranda?

She pulled off her hat, and the moonlight spilled down on her breath-taking hair, on the ghostly whiteness of her arms, on her heartless, haunting face. It was like a collision, that first kiss. Violent, and without tenderness. Then he was engulfed: Rose's body seemed to go boneless and plaster itself against him, her arms twined around him mercilessly, her tongue plunged against his, avid as a snake. And he was lost. He was lost.

He did not know this immediately. He believed that he could find his way back to Etta's fresh little paradise and live happily forever after. The long feverish summer was over before he knew that he could not.

"How did you feel about your wife, Francie?" Mr. Pigeon was saying sociably. "You didn't like her much, did you?"

"Despised her," Francie whispered. "An abomination."

Etta had asked him too, on one of those tense, painful evenings spent away from the crowd. Just the two of them, as Etta wistfully put it. She didn't understand, she faltered in a voice so strained that it no longer sounded like hers, and he got a glimpse—dimly, through the haze of his own misery—of what it was costing her in pride and courage to ask. "But you always said you didn't like Rose, Francis. Why, if you don't like her—"

Why, why? How was it possible to be captivated by what he most despised? Rose's conversation, petty and drenched in spite; her laugh, invariably malicious; her sharp fox-face; her too-white hands that knew so well what they could do to him—everything about her was exquisitely odious. "I don't know why," he told Etta. Looking into her clear, dark-blue eyes, he felt again a surge of hope. Etta was here, she was real, loving him and beloved; Rose was a bad dream, a delirium, a disease—but not an incurable one. Of course not incurable.

"I'm through with her," he said to the face above him, which seemed half the time to be Mr. Pigeon's and half the time Etta's. "I'm through with her for good and all."

"Of course you are," said Mr. Pigeon. Or it may have been Etta. Because she believed him, each time he said it to her. So did he. Neither of them could believe that he was lying, any more than they could believe that he was really lost.

He made one last effort to save himself. For a whole week he managed to stay away from Rose. Then—choir practice evening again—she waylaid him, outside the church. A mournful fall twilight: smoke in the air, and the dead leaves drifting down. "I'm in the family way," said Rose in a hard, triumphant voice. "What are you going to do about it?" She waited a moment, her face lifted in insolent challenge. "Well? Do you want me to tell your darling Etta and her dear old daddy? What a surprise it's going to be to them. Oh mercy me, yes." His hand reached out and closed over her wrist, and she shrank back as if he had struck her. "You do and I'll kill you," he whispered.

"Of course you're through with her," repeated Mr. Pigeon gently. "Whoever killed her saw to that."

He should have killed her, there on the church steps. He wished to God he had. Because of course she was lying. By the time he found it out (or had he known it all the time, in that dark, shameful part of him that was akin to Rose?) the pattern of his life was set forever in ruin and hate. He and Rose were already absorbed in the vicious wrangling of their marriage. Etta's father and mother had whisked her away to Chicago; she wrote him one desolate little letter, and he never answered it because there was nothing to say, he could not even bear to think of her name or go past the Kincaid house where the grass was withered now and the veranda sunless and empty. He knew what people were saying about him: that he was no good, living off Rose the way he did (he had not even tried to get another job after he resigned at the bank); that—they declared!—you wouldn't know he was the same person, they sometimes wondered if he was all there, he acted so queer, not even speaking to you on the street if he could help it. . . . Let them say it. Let them think he was crazy.

"You think I'm crazy, don't you?" he said to Mr. Pigeon.

"Why no, Francie, not at all," said Mr. Pigeon, ever so heartily. "You gave us quite a time last night, but of course nobody thinks you're crazy. I expect you had a very good reason for throwing that rock through Bovard's window. Didn't you?"

Now he figures he's tricking me into something, thought Francie indulgently. As a matter of fact, he had forgotten about the rock and the note. He remembered now, though. Doc Buckmaster's girl (wanted to dispose of her furniture! Ha!) and the other one, the skinny little one.

"None of their business," he told Mr. Pigeon. "Time somebody taught them a lesson. Snooping around. Asking questions."

Mr. Pigeon nodded. "After you threw the rock, what did you do? Where did you go? Back to the store?"

Francie paused, trying to unsnarl it in his mind, trying to feel his way back through what seemed to be a long, dark, blank stretch. The rock in his hand, and then the crash, and then somebody screaming. "She hollered out the window," he said cautiously. "Hollered that she wasn't scared, she wasn't going to mind her own business—"

"And so you went back to the store, or hung around in the alley, waiting for her. Is that what you did, Francie?"

He had the wit to snap his eyes shut. He needed a minute to get his bearings. A false move, a step missed in the dark. . . . "Snooping around," he murmured. (That had been safe, before.) "Asking questions."

Apparently it was working again. "They asked about your wife, I suppose," said Mr. Pigeon. "And the candlestick. And the money your wife had, hidden away. Where did she get that money, Francie? Did you ever give her any, after you separated?"

But Francie was skimming again, he had lost the thread. Only the last word rang in his ears. Separated. Separated. "Get out, then," Rose used to shrill at him. "Go ahead and leave me. Who's going to keep you if I don't? Who'd give a crackpot like you a job? You can't leave me! You'll never leave me, unless I kick you out!" He must really have been crazy in those days, because he believed her. For three whole years he believed her. (The happiest years of Rose's life, no doubt. What bliss it must have been to her, to know that he was so completely, so abjectly, dependent on her.) As for Francie himself, he lived in a trance of inertia, bound to her body and soul, hugging his hateful chains. People began calling him Francie, instead of Francis or Mr. Henshaw. The few people, that is, that got near enough to him to call him anything. He avoided everybody he could. He took long, frenzied, nocturnal walks—but always, always, he went back to her. . . .

It was Hugh Bovard who first jolted him out of his inertia. Unknowingly; to this day Hugh didn't know that the afternoon he fell off his bicycle was a milestone in Francie's life. Hugh and the bicycle came bucketing down the sidewalk, swerved to avoid a kid on roller skates, and shot across the yard where Francie was raking leaves, to wind up in a jumble of spinning wheels and scattered school books at Francie's feet. "Why don't you look where you're going?" snapped Francie. "Fool kid!" But Hugh was too busy picking himself up and trying out his gangly arms and legs to notice. "Gosh, Mr. Henshaw," he said cheerily, "just missed you, didn't I?" He grinned, and Francie became aware of a strange tugging sensation around his own mouth. It was some time since he had smiled at anybody, and the reason he was doing it now was—well, for one thing, it was some time since anybody had called him Mr. Henshaw or treated him in this offhand, uncurious way.

To cover his confusion, he bent down and started collecting some of the papers and books. Caesar's Gallic Wars. A red, ink-stained volume that took him back to his own school days. He flipped the pages; they were battle-scarred, the margins crowded with laboriously pencilled translations, hardly any of them correct. "This isn't right," said Francie—and that was how it began. Hugh stared at him, as at a gold mine. "You mean you can read that stuff right off, just like that? Holy smoke, Mr. Henshaw!"

It was an odd sort of project to get involved in—translating Caesar for a rattle-brained high school kid—but for some reason it was gratifying to Francie. He liked Latin, he kept telling himself; he didn't give a damn about the kid, he just liked Latin. Or maybe it was the flattery. Hugh was as open-hearted as a puppy: He thought Francie was swell, and said so, frequently. Anybody would have felt flattered by that, of course. But for Francie there was a more subtle flattery in Hugh's casual acceptance of him as a fellow human being, extraordinary only because he could read Caesar just like that. It was unselfconscious on Hugh's part, as natural to him as breathing, and it was balm to Francie's blighted soul. Months passed, though, before he admitted, even to himself, that the two of them were fast friends. Occasionally Hugh brought him little offerings—tickets to the basketball games (he never used them, of course), a bird-book (he still had it), memo pads filched from Bovard Senior's printing shop. Then one day he thrust a wad of money into Francie's hand. "Because I owe it to you," he said sternly. "I've been saving, out of my allowance." There were seven one-dollar bills, a fifty-cent piece, a dime, and a nickel. "You don't owe me anything," whispered Francie. "I don't want your money." But Hugh was already half-way down the steps. "Why not?" he said. "You've earned it."

He had earned it. Fascinated, he looked down at the money in his hand. It was his, his very own, and the sight of it seemed to kindle in him a tiny, wavering spark. The spark never went out. Through the rest of Francie's life it grew into a steady, devouring blaze, and as it grew its whole nature was changed. Because they could say what they liked (and he knew, all right: skinflint, stingiest man in town) but that first spark wasn't avarice at all. It was a glimmer of pure hope, such as a prisoner might feel, coming upon a rusty tablespoon in his cell and seeing in it the promise of freedom. So Francie, staring at the first money he had earned in three years, saw not money but a tool, a means of escape. He had earned this; therefore he could earn more, and with money he could buy freedom. Or at least a piece of freedom.

He could, and he did. ("It's about time," Rose said, when he got the job down at old man Frederick's second-hand store. But he caught the flash of alarm and secret fury in her eyes. She saw as well as he did, she knew what was coming.) Was it any wonder that he became obsessed with money, that he grew in time to regard this precious tool as the goal itself? He had nothing else. . . .

"Where did your wife get that money, Francie?" repeated Mr. Pigeon. "Have you any idea?"

He kept his eyes closed, though his mind once more set up a weary bustle. This again was shaky ground: he must move cautiously, if he was to accomplish whatever it was that remained to be done. What was it? What was it? He almost had it, only it slipped away, and he was so mortally tired.

"Hey there, old-timer," said a different voice, and it was the one he had been waiting for, the only one that gave any meaning to the whole snarl. His eyes flew open, and there was the face of his boy—not really a boy any more: a man, as luckless in his way as Francie himself—but his, his friend.

He tried to say, "Hey there, Hugh, my boy," the way he always did, but his voice went back on him. A great wave rose inside him and broke in a triumph of recognition and affirmation. He knew what the important thing was now; in one exultant flash he seemed to see the pattern of his own life, cross-grained yet somehow meaningful. A sob burst out of him, and his old acquaintance the commentator had his usual unflattering say: *Making an exhibition of yourself. At your age. Bawling like a baby.* He didn't care.

"What have you been doing to him?" said Hugh roughly. "For God's sake, can't you see he's worn out? You don't need to worry, he's not going to get away from you."

He started to say "Wait," but they were already too far away to hear. Never mind; they would be back, and next time it wouldn't slip away from him. He had it all clear now; it was just a matter of hanging on till he got it done, and after that there would be nothing to keep him at all.

"Don't try to talk any more. Go to sleep now," Hugh told him. "They've tired you out."

Yes. He was tired. He would like to have told Hugh a lot of things, but right now he was too tired. "Don't worry about me," he said before he let his eyelids close. "Don't worry, my boy."

XXII

Doc and Mr. Pigeon paused when they got outside Francie's room and looked thoughtfully at each other. "Funny," said Doc, "his reaction to Hugh. Seemed to break him all up."

"Oh, I don't know. After all, the old guy's human. As far as I can make out, Hugh Bovard's the only person in the world he cares anything about. Wouldn't it break you up, to think you'd tried to choke your only friend's daughter?"

"It wasn't much of a try. Not a mark on her throat, though Bix insists it hurts. I know—" He held up his hand, anticipating Mr. Pigeon's answer to that one. "Francie's old and not very strong, and she yelled before he could get a good grip on her. He didn't really commit himself on the point, just now."

"No, but he was fuzzy about other things too," said Mr. Pigeon comfortably. "Like when he came out with 'Summer-house.' Did you hear him? It's anybody's guess, what he meant by that. His mind's still wandering a bit, that's all."

"Could be. Could also be he's fuzzy like a fox. Because he was clear enough about the rock. When you come right down to it, that's all you really got out of him—he threw the rock, and he hated his wife."

"Now, now. No use making things hard for ourselves. Not at this stage, anyway. Another session or two with him will probably clear everything—"

"Well." Hugh shut the door to Francie's room behind him and turned a cold, hard eye on Mr. Pigeon. "Proud of yourself? It must be great sport, badgering an old man when he's about to die anyway. It must take real guts."

Mr. Pigeon blinked mildly. "Believe me, Mr. Bovard, I don't do these things for the sport of it. I'm trying to solve a murder. I'm trying to find out who attacked your daughter last night."

"I realize that," snapped Hugh. He flushed slightly.

"Not everybody would be as quick to forgive as you, Mr. Bovard. Or maybe you don't think Francie did it." He waited courteously, while Hugh swallowed a couple of times and hunched his shoulder.

"I suppose—I suppose he did," he said at last miserably.

"It looks like it," agreed Mr. Pigeon. "It looks like, after he threw the rock through your window, he went back to his shop, maybe just to warm up before he went on home. He may have been there when Jeffreys and I came looking for him. He could have hidden easily enough, we didn't really search the place. We didn't know about the rock, but he undoubtedly thought we did know and were after him. He may even have still been hiding there when Bix and the others came along, or he may have just started home, seen them, and hung around in the alley till he got a chance at Bix. Luckily, it wasn't enough of a chance. He heard us coming and beat it, and that's when his heart gave out —naturally enough—and he collapsed."

Hugh was silent a moment. "Did he tell you all this? Did he admit it?"

"It all fits in," said Mr. Pigeon. "Tell me, Dr. Craig, what are Francie's chances? Is he going to pull out of this?"

"Ordinarily, I'd say no. Last night I would certainly have said no." He glanced back, mentally, over the long, precarious night; half a dozen times he had thought to himself this is it, it's all over. "But— Well, he made it. I don't see how he could have, but he did. Plain will power, maybe. Or maybe he's just too mean to die. I'll be honest with you, after last night I don't trust my own judgment."

"I've never seen him as bad as this. He didn't even make a fuss about being in the hospital." Hugh ran his hand over his forehead wearily. "I know you have to do your job, Mr. Pigeon, the same as anybody else. But hell, I've known the old boy most of my life, and I just can't believe he's a—a murderer. He couldn't have done it. He was right there in his shop that afternoon. I dropped in and spent an hour or so with him."

"Nobody knows just when Mrs. Henshaw was killed," Mr. Pigeon reminded him. "Some time before four thirty, but that's all we're sure of. Then there's the candlestick. It's too much of a coincidence, finding that in Francie's shop. Plus the fact that he's admitted the business with the rock last night. Oh, he's in it, all right. He's in it up to his neck. As for motive—well, you never can tell about these eccentric old birds. They get notions. They brood over some little thing, magnify it till it turns into what is, to them, perfectly good grounds for murder. It happens all the time—people that get killed for picking their teeth, or wearing the wrong color necktie. You can pick a motive practically at random, with a character like Francie."

Plausible enough, thought Doc. A very plausible guy, Mr. Pigeon. Look at the tidy little case he had cooked up against Hartley. "Anyway," he said, "it's got Hartley off the hook."

Hugh brightened. "That's right. At least Hartley's cleared. I understand he's already been up here to see Bix. She must be walking on air."

"Just about," said Doc. He was too bone-tired to pursue the vague uneasiness, or doubt, or whatever it was, that flicked its tail across his mind. With an effort he straightened up (if he kept on leaning against the wall here he was going to be asleep on his feet) and started down the hall. "Come on, let's take a look at Our Heroine. You haven't seen her yet, have you, Hugh? That's right, she was asleep when you were here earlier this morning."

"Is she really doing all right?" asked Hugh.

"Bouncing back in fine shape. Youth, you know, youth. Actually, it was more a matter of shock than anything else. Though I don't like to think of what might have happened if we hadn't got there when we did."

"Don't," said Hugh. Suddenly he put his hand on Doc's arm. "You know, Doc, you want to forget all that stuff you were saying last night, about how it was your fault for letting Bix and Rachel go down there. All that stuff. I know Bix, when she sets her mind on something. I don't blame you, and you mustn't blame yourself, either."

"I still think I acted like a meathead," said Doc. "But I haven't got the strength to argue with you." He opened the door to Bix's room and looked inside. She was perched on the window sill, hugging her knees and staring out at the wan winter morning. "Hey, you. Get back in bed and make like a patient. There's a guy out here wants to see you. Claims he's a relative."

"Daddy?" She scrambled to her feet; her robe, which seemed too big in some spots and too little in others, gave her the scrawny, pathetic look of a half-grown bird. Her eyes flew from Doc's face to a point behind him, where Hugh must be, and she spread her arms in a wide, theatrical gesture. "Daddy, darling! You're here at last!"

This is what comes of seeing too many movies, thought Doc. Even Hugh looked a little startled. Then he hurried into her waiting arms. Over his shoulder Doc could see Bix's face, eyes closed apparently in rapture. Aside from the scraped mouth, she looked quite blooming—the result, no doubt, of Hartley's visit.

"How are you, Biscuit? Doc tells me you're doing fine. . . ." His hands touched her neck tenderly, and she drew back, shuddering. "Poor baby."

Bix mustered a brave smile. "It's not so bad, really."

"She'll be back to normal in no time," Doc assured them both. "The same fresh brat. I just hope you'll always be as lucky as you were last night."

"Who was it?" asked Hugh. "Have you any idea, Bix? Try to think. Was there anything you saw or heard or felt that would identify him?"

Doc had noticed it before: Bix could look blanker than anybody on earth when she wanted to. Her face at this moment was about as expressive as a door knob. "I didn't see anything. They came up behind me, whoever it was, and grabbed me. They threw something over my head so I couldn't see or yell, and then they grabbed me by the neck and—and that's all I know."

"Was it somebody tall?"

"I guess so. I don't know."

"What about what they threw over your head? Was it a coat or a scarf or what?"

"Something dark and heavy. I don't *know*, Daddy." Her eyes suddenly got dark and distressed-looking. "It all happened so quick. I've told you everything I know."

"I'm sorry, honey. I just wanted to check with you. Pigeon's convinced it was Francie, of course."

Her face had gone blank again. "Aren't you? Who else could it have been?"

"Nobody, I guess. I just don't see—" He broke off and gave her a cheerful pat behind. "Let's skip it. Whoever it was, it wasn't Hartley. The well-known silver lining. It clears Hartley, once and for all. Let's forget the rest and be thankful for that. How is the lad, anyway?"

"He's—wonderful," breathed Bix, and Hugh and Doc grinned at each other.

"Utterly, utterly," said Doc. "I just hope he appreciates the chances you took for him, young lady. I just hope he's properly grateful."

"Why should he be grateful?" Bix's eyes flashed. "He'd do the same for me."

"Okay, okay. Watch your temperature."

Hugh picked her up and started tucking her back in bed. "Your mother sent you her love." He was trying, rather clumsily, to make this sound off-hand and natural. "She said she hopes to get over and see you this afternoon."

"I bet," said Bix. Then she bit her lip, and both she and Hugh flushed.

The situation called for something deft in the way of a subject-change, but nothing suitable occurred to Doc. He kept shifting from one foot to the other and clearing his throat. It was Mrs. Nelson, bringing in Bix's lunch tray, who finally came to the rescue. All three of them greeted her with open relief. "Here we are," said Doc. "I've got to make some calls, but you can stay a while longer, Hugh. Eat hearty, Bix. If you behave yourself there's no reason why you can't be out of here tomorrow."

"Tomorrow?" There was an odd note in Bix's voice, and again Doc was aware of that uneasy impression flicking across his mind, just out of reach. In a moment, though, she was gushing away in her best cinema style. "Oh Daddy, did you hear that? I can maybe go home tomorrow!"

He plodded down the stairs, collected his coat and bag, and was just about to go out the door when Hugh came tearing after him. "Doc, Doc! Come back! There's something wrong—she can't swallow!"

He hurried upstairs again, to find Bix sitting bolt upright in bed, rigid with alarm. "I can't," she whimpered. "I just can't swallow."

"It came on all at once," Mrs. Nelson reported. "She'd eaten half her soup, and all at once her throat just seemed to close up. . . . " She let her voice trail away. Behind her rimless glasses her shrewd eyes looked frankly puzzled.

And that was the way Doc felt after he had examined Bix. He could find nothing wrong with her, aside from the superficial scratches on her face, which couldn't possibly account for this dramatic new development. Besides, she had had no trouble whatever in swallowing a hearty breakfast earlier in the day. Was it hysteria, then? A sort of delayed shock reaction?

Mrs. Nelson put it in a slightly different way. "I think she's putting it on," she told Doc matter-of-factly, after he had given Bix a sedative and done his best to reassure Hugh.

"But for Lord's sake, why?"

Mrs. Nelson shrugged. "Maybe she just wants attention."

"She's already got it," said Doc. "And will have, for some time to come. And don't think she doesn't know it. She's no fool."

"No, she isn't. She's a sensible kid. Plenty of backbone. Not like that mother of hers. That's why I don't think she's hysterical."

"One thing's sure, she'll have to stay here till she snaps out of this. I told her so." He paused, recalling Bix's pitiful little sob when he had warned her about having to stay in the hospital. But there hadn't been any tears in her eyes. "You'd think she'd be sitting on top of the world, with Hartley cleared and all."

"Oh, she was," Mrs. Nelson assured him. "Lively as a cricket. Chattering away to Mr. Bovard and me about going home tomorrow, and then all at once she stiffened up and said she couldn't swallow. Scared Mr. Bovard out of his wits. I don't know, I had a feeling right from the start she was putting it on."

Doc sighed. "Well, keep an eye on her. She'll probably sleep most of the afternoon, and she's better off not having any company till this evening."

"Nobody at all?"

"Nobody at all. Hartley can wait till after dinner, and her mother—"

"Ha," said Mrs. Nelson. "That's one visitor we don't have to worry about. She wouldn't cross the street to see Bix if her life depended on it."

XXIII

It was a rugged day for Doc. He had a long list of calls, and when at last he got back it was to find an office full of coughs and sniffles and aching joints—all the afflictions of February—waiting for him. Fortified by a container of coffee from the Square Deal, he worked his way patiently through the lot of them. Back to the hospital for another quick look at Francie and his other patients there. He gulped down something or other at the Square Deal and called it dinner, but for all his haste it was quarter to nine before he rang the Buckmaster doorbell. Rachel had moved back home in the afternoon.

"You poor creature," she greeted him—and the words were

music to his ears; they made him feel deliciously sorry for him-self—"you must be exhausted."

"Oh well. I'll live." He achieved a martyr's smile. It was all he could do to keep from purring. The red glass chandelier cast a tender glow on Rachel's face; it caught the sheen of her smooth hair and lit up her eyes. He forgot that he was a poor ex-hausted creature and took her in his arms.

Queenie looked out from the library door, and, when she considered that things had gone far enough, uttered a short bark of disapproval.

"Our chaperon." Rachel gave a little laugh. "Come on in by the fire. We'll have a drink and catch up on everything. Oh Doc, I'm so—"

Happy. That was the word she didn't need to say. It oc-curred to Doc that happiness was very becoming to Rachel. She had lost all her worries—including, for the moment, the one about whether he was married or not—and the effect was pretty dazzling.

Hartley, who was standing in front of the fireplace, looked different too. Still shy and awkward (he apparently couldn't decide whether to treat his stretch in jail as a joke or to ignore it) but it seemed to Doc that his voice had lost some of its old quality of uncertain, apologetic mumbling. It was going to take time, but who knew, Hartley might even get so he'd hold his head up. (It had always annoyed Doc, the way the kid ducked his head, as if he half-expected somebody to swat him.)

"How's Bix? The Nelson dame wouldn't let me see her this afternoon, and Hugh said—"

"I can't find anything wrong with her physically," said Doc, "and I'm not a psychiatrist, so your guess is as good as mine. Better, in fact, because you know her better. What is your guess, Hartley? Could she be scared of something?"

"Scared?" Hartley paused in the act of poking the fire; his

face was turned away. "What's she got to be scared of? The whole thing's settled. Francie's It, poor, ornery old boy, and they've got him. He's thrown his last rock and killed his last wife and choked his last Bix."

"And damn near drawn his last breath. He'll never live to be brought to trial."

"I'm glad of it," said Rachel firmly. "Have they found out yet about the money? She must have been blackmailing Francie too."

"What do you mean 'too'?" asked Hartley sharply.

"Just an inkle of mine. About why Papa kept her around all those years. Think nothing of it."

"Think nothing of it! Rachel, have you lost your mind? You're suggesting that she blackmailed Papa? Doc, let's draw the poor woman a diagram, she doesn't know what blackmail is. Look, it's like this. A can't blackmail B unless A's got something *on* B, and—"

"All right, smarty. You're not telling me anything I don't know. It's not so fantastic."

"It is. Completely fantastic. Papa's life was an open book. The reason he kept her around was because he was too busy to find somebody better for the job. It wouldn't have been any cinch, you know. He probably tried, and when he didn't have any luck he just gave up and kept her."

Rachel stuck out her chin. "I don't believe it."

"All right, kids, try to get along," said Doc. "Pigeon spent the afternoon snooping around in Francie's finances. He's got money, all right. No necessity for him to live the way he's been doing all these years. He's just stingy. Oh, he's not rich, but it seems he ran onto a real antique now and then, and cleaned up. All strictly cash, according to a couple of Chicago dealers that Pigeon talked to. They say the cash thing was a peculiarity of Francie's. And he kept hardly any records, so there's no telling how much he's made in the last thirty-odd years. Or how much of it he may have turned over to Mrs. Henshaw."

"I wonder what she had on him," said Rachel. "Because, according to the authorities, A can't blackmail B unless A's got something *on* B—"

Hartley gave her a friendly half-poke. "He was probably paying her to stay away from him. Look, Doc, can I go see Bix now? Don't you think this No Visitors business has gone far enough?"

"Run along. I've already told Mrs. Nelson to throw you out if you stay too late. And if you can figure out what's eating on her, let me know. It beats me."

"He's changed, isn't he?" Rachel asked eagerly, the moment the door shut after Hartley. "Did you notice how he talked back to me? He never used to do that, not even with me. He'd just get stubborn and clam up. It was the only defense he had against Mrs. Henshaw." She sat down on the hassock beside Doc's chair with her hands clasped in her lap; her face was alive with happiness. "We're going to sell the house as soon as we can, and Hartley can use the money for art school. We're free. Free. Both of us. We're rid of her at last."

"I suppose you'll be going back to Chicago," said Doc. He said it against his better judgment. All the danger signals were flashing their little hearts out, and it made no difference, he could not stop. "No reason for you to stick around here, I suppose."

"I haven't decided what to do about my job yet," Rachel chattered on. "I talked to my boss today, he's been awfully decent about it all, and he'll hold the job for me for another week or so if I want him to."

"It'll take a while to get rid of the house, won't it?" asked Doc. "It's big and old-fashioned, and of course Coreyville's an out-of-the-way place."

That was what Joan used to say. Joan. His wife's name could

still produce in Doc the familiar pang—the old reflex, remnant of the grief that had once torn him to pieces. This out-of-the-way dump, Joan used to say. This God-forsaken little hole. He should have known better than to bring her here, of course. He should have faced the truth. In Chicago it had been possible to gloss it over. But in Coreyville there were no diversions for Joan, no excitement, no shelter from the merciless glare of truth: Joan did not love him. It had been perhaps more of a shock to her than to him. Not that that made it any easier for him to bear. She had cried when she left. Quite a little storm of tears. He still didn't know how he had summoned the strength to let her go. It hadn't been pride; that was one of the things love did to you—it stripped you of pride. So it must have been the extremity of despair, the knowledge that to follow her would be merely to postpone the final, inevitable parting. Sooner or later; and he had chosen sooner. A form of emotional mercy-killing.

And now here was Rachel. . . . "Stop making it sound like a white elephant," she was saying. "So all right, it hasn't got picture windows. It's a good comfortable house, and somebody's going to want to buy it. Mr. What's-his-name, the butcher, wanted it before, only of course he changed his mind when he found out Mrs. Henshaw went with it. As far as that goes, Hartley can tend to selling it. I don't have to stay here for that, if I decide I want to keep my job."

Doc nodded bleakly. No reason why she should stay here at all. He felt left out and forlorn, and it didn't help a bit to remind himself that it was, in a way, his own fault. What had he offered her that she couldn't get in Chicago? Fun and games. The bargain offer, available everywhere. Everywhere was right. Especially Chicago.

Still, he had thought that she'd—Well, didn't she even *care* any more whether he had a wife or not? Here he was, all primed to tell her the God's truth (yes he was; he might as well admit it) and she didn't even pay any attention.

"I'm not a slick operator," he said in a loud, contradictory voice. "You said last night. I'm not a slick operator."

"No?" She tilted her head, smiling a little, waiting.

"No," he said weakly. His mouth felt dry. "And I want it to make a difference to you whether I have a wife or not, because I—"

She was still waiting. This was going to be tough. To begin with, he was breaking a three-year-old habit of silence. "I've never talked about Joan to anybody," he said. "That's her name. Joan. I've never told anybody about her. I don't know why, exactly."

Maybe it had been hope, at first: for most of the first year he had kept himself going with the standard wishful thinking (the letter, special delivery, or the telegram that might come at any moment: "Darling, I can't live without you," the telephone that might ring in the middle of any night, the train or the bus or the car that might bring her back). It would have been bad luck, of course, to talk at that stage; wishes that were not kept secret never came true. And afterwards it was shame, in a way; an unwillingness to confess to his own failure.

He took the plunge. He wanted to. He couldn't bear not to talk about Joan any more. "I was in love," he said, "and she— well, she wasn't. Maybe, if we'd stayed in Chicago, we could have made out. For a while longer, anyway. She liked excitement and parties, and as long as she had them it kind of made up for the other."

(Had it been that way, he wondered, with Rachel and the Greg character? He reached out and took her hands.)

"We didn't get a divorce right away, when she went back to Chicago. No particular point to it. Then, a year or so ago, she decided she wanted to marry somebody else. So she got a divorce. I didn't mean to make a mystery out of it. I just never felt like talking about it to anybody till now, because I—"

"Never mind," whispered Rachel. "The important thing is. . . ."

Yes. The important thing was the way her eyes were lit up. For him. She was not Joan. She was Rachel; that was the important thing. He drew a sigh of relief, and in that moment his canny, safe-and-sane resolutions crumbled away to dust. So all right, if he got hurt he got hurt. He was like Bix, he didn't care if it was dangerous. It was still worth it.

She's got you, he told himself. Brother, are you sunk.

He hadn't felt so good in years.

XXIV

It was quite a while before they changed the subject. Then Rachel asked about Bix, and he told her the whole puzzling business. He even tried, not very successfully, to pin down the vague impression that had flicked across his mind occasionally throughout the day. "Somehow I feel as if she's scared. Not of what happened to her last night. Something else. She seemed all set up at the idea of going home tomorrow, and yet—"

"She's a funny kid. Cagey. Like Hartley. You can't get much out of either one of them. Mrs. Henshaw's box, for instance. I've got a feeling Bix knew there was something in Mrs. Henshaw's room. She didn't want us to open the box, remember? I suppose she was scared there was something in it that would make things even worse for Hartley."

"One thing about her, she's a woman of action," said Doc. "I'm willing to bet that if anybody socked Mrs. Pierce it was Bix and her umbrella. That was to clear Hartley too, of course.

But what I don't understand is last night. Maybe she just wasn't thinking when she rubbed the fingerprints off the candlestick, and then again—She couldn't have thought Hartley's prints were on it. And anybody else's would have been good for our side."

"She wasn't thinking, then. She just did it automatically."

There was one other thing. "She said something funny when I first got to her, there in the alley. At least I think she did. It sounded to me like she said 'I fell', as if she had some notion of making out that nobody grabbed her, she just fell. Only why in the hell would she?"

"She wouldn't. You must be mistaken," Rachel said at last. "You heard her yourself, afterwards. She made quite a story about being choked."

They studied each other a moment in silence. All right, then, Doc was thinking, Bix isn't scared of anything because she's got nothing to be scared of. This can't swallow business is just delayed shock.

He wished he was surer of it. He had a special feeling of responsibility for the kid; they had a good deal in common, he and Bix. Tonight had taught him that.

Suddenly Rachel jumped up. "Let's go see her. It's not too late. Come on. Let's just go see how she is."

"Hartley's still here," Mrs. Nelson told them when they got to the hospital. "I told him he could stay till ten. Mr. Bovard's been and gone. She didn't eat her supper, but I did get a little milk down her. You can't tell me. That child's putting it on, and when she gets hungry enough she's going to decide she can swallow as well as ever."

She was so right. Doc and Rachel walked in on an interesting little scene: patient and visitor were polishing off a spread of hamburgers and candy bars. Bix had her mouth full; at sight of them in the doorway she swallowed, guiltily but efficiently. She had the grace to blush.

"Congratulations," said Doc. "You seem to have made a re-markable recovery." He brushed aside Hartley's bumbling, half-hearted explanation and ushered him out before either he or Bix could protest. "Sure, sure. Your visiting time's up, Hartley. You've done your duty. I want to examine my patient."

His patient watched, wary-eyed but silent, while he gathered up crumbs and wrappers and stuffed them in the wastebasket.

"Now." He sat down beside her, mechanically felt her pulse. It was jumping a bit. And why not? "Why did you try to fool us, honey? Don't look at me like that. I'm not going to bully you. I'm just curious."

"I didn't—" began Bix. She trembled her lip piteously and buried her face in the pillow. Almost a flawless performance. Only she couldn't resist peeking at him, out of the corner of her eye, to observe the effect. Rachel, standing at the other side of the bed, made soothing noises. But she raised her eyebrows at Doc and gave a helpless little shrug that expressed his own feel-ings pretty accurately.

"We want to help you," said Rachel. "But we can't, if you won't tell us what you're scared of."

A muffled gulp from Bix. No other answer.

"You are scared, aren't you?" said Doc. "Why, Bix? Why are you scared to go home?" It was one of the wildest shots in the dark he had ever made, but it hit the mark. He felt the sharp-boned little wrist between his fingers stiffen and jerk away. Bix sat up straight, her telltale eyes hurrying from Doc's face to Rachel's, her fists pressed defensively against her chest. Before she could decide what tack to take, Rachel collected herself (she had looked as startled as Bix for a minute) and pressed the ad-vantage.

"You can't be scared of your Dad, Bix. Is it something about your mother? Is it on account of your mother that you don't want to go home?"

Woman's intuition, thought Doc. Never underestimate it.

"She hates me," whispered Bix. "She's always hated me. She said so."

"But you've never been afraid of her before." Rachel paused. "Or have you? Bix, you've dodged this one long enough. I want you to tell me the truth. Why did you call Hartley when he came to Chicago three years ago? Why did you get him to come back here? Were you afraid of your mother then?"

Bix drew a long, shuddering breath and closed her eyes. "My mother. Yes. Mrs. Henshaw came to see her—"

"Mrs. Henshaw!" Doc gasped it out. "You don't think your mother had anything to do with this Henshaw business!"

"Yes. No. I don't know." Bix wadded up a corner of the sheet, smoothed it out, wadded it up again. Her eyes were fixed —but unseeingly—on her busy hands. She was staring at something quite different, a three-year-old memory that could still daze her with terror. "She came to see my mother, and I saw her, and she looked—terrible. . . ."

"What did she come to see your mother for? They weren't friends, were they?"

"No. Oh, no. She said to me, 'Is your mother home, dearie?' and her eyes kind of slid around all over, like a—like a ferret. And then my mother came, and there was this awful scene—"

"But what about, Bix? What was it all about?"

"I don't know. I keep telling you. They told me to get out. 'Get out of here.' Said to me, 'What are *you* hanging around for? Get out of here and stay out.' So I went and hid, but I could still hear. Only not what they said. Just sort of screeching and so finally it stopped and I couldn't stand it, I called Hartley." She wasn't faking this performance. She was shaking all over, uncontrollably; her teeth clicked against each other.

"There, there." Rachel put her arms around the thin shoulders; her own face was pale and big-eyed.

"But that was Mrs. Henshaw, Baby," said Doc. "No reason to be so frightened of your mother." Though it might not be so far-fetched, at that. Terror could put some pretty fancy twists into a kid's mind.

"It was—both of them. The way she looked at me. Shoved me out. Said to me, 'Get out of here and stay out.' " Again the shuddering gasp. "I felt like I couldn't stand it without Hartley. She hates me. She looked at me that same way last night, after the rock came through the window. I saw her hating me. She's sorry he didn't kill me. . . ."

Oh Lord, thought Doc, like as not it's the truth. "Now look," he said, "you can depend on me. I won't send you home as long as you feel like this. I think you're probably off the track about your mother, but it's still a deal. I promise. You don't need to pull any more phony symptoms on me."

"You can come stay with me," said Rachel. "Or something. We'll figure out something."

If they had to, they could just tell Hugh the truth. It wouldn't be exactly news to him, poor guy. It might even be the best thing for all the Bovards, to get this mother-daughter antagonism out in the open at last. Just as it seemed to have done Bix good to unload. She was still crying a little, but in a relaxed, relieved way.

"Can't Hartley come back just to say goodnight to me?" she quavered.

"Spare us the schmaltz," Doc told her. "Okay. If he's still around—and I suppose he's waiting outside to challenge me at dawn or something—he can come in for five minutes. No more. I'll have Mrs. Nelson time him."

He paused at the door, looking back at her, propped up on her pillows, waiting to say goodnight to Hartley. Something in her expression struck him. It wasn't exactly like the moment when he had caught her peeking at him to see if he was melting.

But there was no doubt about it: she was looking damn pleased with herself.

XXV

Myra Graves had the nicest kitchen in the world, Rachel thought contentedly as she slipped out of her coat and settled down in the old splint-backed chair. Nothing was changed since Rachel's childhood; that was what made it so satisfactory. Myra had even kept her old wood range—for company, as she said—and it seemed to purr in unison with the tortoise-shell cat curled up on her little oval rug in front of it. The hand pump for rain water still stood beside the sink; the red geraniums sunned themselves on the window sill; the familiar blue and white dishes looked out like old friends through the glass doors of the cupboard. And Myra herself, in her rick-rack trimmed apron, was bustling around baking a batch of molasses cookies that smelled just the way Rachel remembered. Heavenly.

"I'll sit down and have a cup of coffee with you soon as I get this last pan in," Myra said. "Seems like old times, having you run over of a morning. Doesn't it?"

"Except I always used to have troubles. You must have gotten fed to the teeth, listening to all my woes." Rachel stretched her arms and smiled. "I got no more troubles no more."

Myra's eyes brightened. "You mean he hasn't got a wife, after all?"

"Not at the moment. But he's going to have one, if I have anything to say about it. And I think I have."

Myra tried to look shocked. "Why, Rachel Buckmaster! That's not a very ladylike way to talk."

"I don't feel ladylike. I feel—"

"What about him?" said Myra hastily.

"I don't think he feels ladylike either."

She laughed, and Myra gave up and laughed with her. "Tell you the truth, Rachel, I don't blame you a bit. Doc's a fine young man, and it's high time somebody made up his mind for him. Go to it. That's what I say. Go to it." She thumped her rolling pin enthusiastically. "Not that he's been resisting any to speak of, anyway."

"That's right. He started it. I think." Rachel gazed off into space and let herself wallow. "It doesn't seem possible, Myra. This time last week I'd never even heard of Dr. C. W. Craig. We've only known each other four days. Just think of it! It doesn't seem possible."

"Well," said Myra briskly, "looks like it's happened, possible or not. My land, Rachel, stop looking so moony-eyed. I don't know but you're easier to put up with when you've got troubles. After all, there's been other things going on too. What about Francie? Do they arrest a man when he's about to die anyway?"

"That's what Mr. Pigeon's trying to decide. He keeps talking about loose ends that have to be tied up."

"Loose ends!" echoed Myra. She drew up a chair, planted the coffee pot on the table between them, and settled down for a good gossip. "Where's any loose ends? Francie did it, didn't he? I thought he as good as admitted it."

"He admitted throwing the rock through Bovard's window. He admitted that he hated Mrs. Henshaw. Doc was there when Mr. Pigeon questioned Francie, and he says that's really all it amounted to."

"Seems to me like that's plenty," said Myra. "He threw the rock to scare you and Bix out of looking for the candlestick. So he must have known that's what she was hit with. How would he know that if he hadn't done it himself? Why else would he hide it? And the reason he did it was because he hated her. . . ." Her voice trailed off into uncertainty.

Rachel sighed. "It really is a loose end. He'd hated her for years. What happened to make him kill her right then, after all this time? Even peculiar people don't commit murder without a special reason. It would be different if they ever saw each other, but as far as anybody knows they hadn't exchanged a word for years."

"Maybe they did see each other," said Myra tentatively.

"In Coreyville? Without anybody knowing about it?"

"Not very likely, I guess. Still, secrets have been kept here. Look at Mrs. Henshaw. Hiding all that money away, and nobody knows where she got it."

"Myra." Rachel cleared her throat and tried again. "Myra, you knew Papa as well as anybody in town. Do you think she could have gotten it from him?"

She wasn't sure what she had expected Myra's reaction to be. Indignant protests, probably, like those Hartley had thrown at her. Reproachful reprimands for a daughter who could ask such a question. She got something quite different. Myra didn't say a word. She just blushed. A rich, guilty red.

"You've thought of it too, then?" said Rachel in a low voice.

Myra gave an odd little shake to her head, as if something hurt her. "Of course I thought of it. A long time ago. She— Rachel, she must have had some hold on him. It doesn't make sense otherwise. He loved you and Hartley."

"I know." Conscientiously Rachel trotted out Hartley's arguments. Give them another chance. See how they sounded to Myra. "But he was busy and overworked. Housekeepers don't grow on trees. He probably couldn't find anybody else for the job."

Again Myra's head jerked in that little gesture of pain and something like pride. "After Mr. Graves passed on—" Myra always referred, thus formally, to her husband; it called forth in Rachel's mind an unapproachable figure, not at all like the easy-going Mr. Graves she remembered. "After Mr. Graves passed on, he could have had me for a housekeeper any time he wanted. I thought the world and all of your Papa, Rachel."

The mournful, quiet words seemed to tremble in Myra's cozy kitchen, mingling incongruously with the kettle singing on the stove and the spicy smell of cookies. Even Myra, thought Rachel. Even jolly, warm-hearted, forthright Myra had not escaped the Henshaw blight. There she sat across from Rachel, staring into her coffee cup like a child about to cry, her worn hands idle, for once, in her lap. "She must have had some hold on him," she repeated.

"Maybe he—had an affair with her," ventured Rachel.

And once more Myra surprised her. "No. I thought of that too. So I asked him."

"You asked him?"

"Yes." Myra gave a rueful little smile. "I guess I haven't always been so ladylike, myself. I asked him, and it wasn't that. I could have told. Your Papa was one of the poorest hands at lying I ever ran across. It was something else."

"But what, Myra? What? Have you any idea at all? It's important to me, somehow. . . ." She didn't know exactly why. If Papa's money, not Francie's, had filled Mrs. Henshaw's box, of course, it meant that Francie had some other motive. But how could she go to Mr. Pigeon with anything as flimsy as this? I just have a hunch she was blackmailing my father. . . . Preposterous.

Myra was shaking her head in resignation. "It beats me. Always has. Always will. Whatever it was, it's buried with her. And good riddance. Mrs. Pierce took the body back to Westburg for the funeral, so Mr. Manning was telling me. Buried her yesterday."

"Poor Mr. Manning. He had such a nice service all planned for her here."

They tried out rather weak smiles on each other; close as they were, they had never had a conversation quite like this before. It seemed so odd to think of Myra with sorrows of her own, as confused and uncertain beneath her brisk cheeriness as Rachel herself. It seemed so odd to feel as old as Myra.

"There," cried Myra, jumping up and whipping the tin of cookies out of the oven. "All but burned them, sitting here gabbing. I thought I'd take some up to the hospital to Bix. Or is she well enough to go home yet?"

"No, she's not home yet." Rachel paused. "Myra, do you believe everything Bix says?"

"More or less. As much as I do any kid that age. Why?"

"Well, when Doc and I went to see her last night she went on about how she doesn't want to go home, she's scared of her mother, and then she told this tale about Mrs. Henshaw coming to see her mother three years ago. . . ."

Myra listened, open-mouthed. "I never heard of such a thing," she said when Rachel had finished. "What in the world's got into the child?"

"You don't believe it, then?"

"Why, I don't know what to think! Of course she and Althea never have hit it off, but—Scared of her! Scared to go home!"

"She isn't a normal woman, you know," said Rachel. "I never thought much about it when I lived here, but it's different when you come back and see her. It just isn't normal for a woman to waste her whole life grieving over a son like Ronnie. That's what she's done. She's ruined her own life, and Hugh's, and it looks as if she's done plenty of damage to Bix, too."

"Of course she has. She never loved her. Never paid any attention to her, if she could help it. I know for a fact Hugh used to take Bix down to the Tribune office with him, if they didn't have a hired girl at home, just to make sure the poor child would get fed. With Ronnie Althea'd been just the opposite.

Wouldn't let him out of her sight. I declare, I used to wonder how she stood it—lugging that great hulking lump of a kid around, and coaxing him to eat, and trying to teach him to walk and talk. She practically watched over him while he slept. It made you sick to see her—"

"I know," said Rachel. "I remember Ronnie."

"What they should have done, of course, was put him in an institution. But she wouldn't hear of it. Your Papa suggested it once, and she flew at him with the butcher knife. Yes she did. Threatened to kill him."

"Maybe Bix knows what she's talking about, after all. Maybe she's got a right to be scared of her mother."

"Oh, now, Rachel—" But it was an automatic protest. Violence, after all, had been done. All over again, Rachel felt the impact of it: somebody had murdered Mrs. Henshaw; somebody had tried to murder Bix. (Somebody? Francie, of course. Francie.)

"I never knew Althea and Mrs. Henshaw to have anything to do with each other," said Myra. "Friendly or otherwise. What could Mrs. Henshaw have gone over there for? Unless it's all just one of Bix's made-up stories. She does play-act sometimes."

"Something scared her," Rachel pointed out. "She was scared enough to call up Hartley and get him to come back. She might lie to the rest of us, but I don't think she'd lie to Hartley."

"No, she wouldn't," said Myra decisively. "She'd never lie to Hartley. What does he say about it?"

"Backs her up, of course. Claims it was all just the way she says, and he came back to 'protect' her. Though I don't know just how. Moral support, I suppose. He just keeps saying he couldn't leave her alone, with nobody to depend on. You know how those two are. They've stuck together like fly paper, all their lives."

"How about Hugh? Was he supposed to be in on this business three years ago?"

"Bix didn't mention him," said Rachel. "Just Mrs. Henshaw and her mother. . . ."

XXVI

"Three years ago?" Hugh was saying in a puzzled voice. "Mrs. Henshaw went to see Althea and made a scene three years ago?" He leaned back in his swivel chair and frowned at the ceiling.

Portrait of a man wracking his brains, thought Doc. He felt suddenly irritated with everything—the racket of the linotype back there beyond the front office; the creaking of Hugh's chair; his own foolish, hesitant voice saying, "That's what Bix told us. Hell, Hugh, I don't want to meddle in your business. But she is my patient, and she's got this notion about not wanting to go home on account of her mother. I know Althea isn't very well, so I thought rather than go to her—"

"Good Lord, yes!" Hugh thumped himself upright and stared at Doc in a kind of anguish. "I'd break your neck if you'd bothered Althea with all this nonsense."

"It isn't nonsense," said Doc unhappily. "Not all of it, anyway. You know as well as I do that Bix and her mother—well—"

The door to the back room opened and Gloria Johnson, jiggling and switching in one place and another, came in with a handful of proofs.

"Oh, good morning, Dr. Craig. Excuse me, Mr. Bovard, but I just wanted to ask you—"

"Later," snapped Hugh. "Don't bother me with it now. Do us a favor, will you, Gloria? Go back and discuss Life and Literature with Fritz for half an hour or so. I'll let you know if I need you."

The end of Gloria's nose quivered; her perfect-secretary smile was replaced by an expression at once wounded and forbearing. "I'm terribly sorry, Mr. Bovard. I didn't realize. I'm terribly sorry." She switched out again, and for a moment the air throbbed with tender, womanly understanding.

Hugh cleared his throat. "To get back to Bix—" He stopped, helplessly. "What in the hell do you do, Doc, when the two people you love hate each other?"

"Well—"

"I'll tell you what you do. You do all the wrong things. You keep pretending it isn't so. Hiding your head in the sand. You ignore so many danger signals and smooth out so many crises that you lose track of what's real and what isn't. You keep trying to make up for it yourself somehow—which is quite a trick, considering how busy you are pretending it isn't so. And you keep hoping. That's the biggest mistake of all. You keep hoping."

Doc kept his eyes carefully fixed on his own feet. He needed a shoeshine. "No use blaming yourself. It's natural enough to try to make the best of an unfortunate situation."

"Natural maybe. But it's all wrong. I should have faced the fact years ago. I should have given up and sent Bix away to school or wherever it is you send kids when their mothers don't want them."

"It's not too late now," said Doc. "For Bix."

Hugh's face twisted. "But for Althea—"

"I don't know. I'm no psychiatrist."

"It wouldn't help if you were. I've tried that, too. She didn't—co-operate. What was the use, she said, it wasn't going to bring Ronnie back."

In his mind's eye Doc saw Althea's remote face and heard her voice: My son, my little boy. Beyond help, and aware of it; perhaps willing it, choosing to be lost.

Hugh's eyes—gray, like Bix's—were fixed on him imploringly.

"It might work for Althea, too. Even now. Maybe, if Bix were gone—She'll be going away to college next year anyway. If it was just Althea and me, maybe I could—"

Doc sighed. The biggest mistake of all. To keep hoping. "Maybe. Meantime, something's got to be worked out for Bix. I promised her I wouldn't send her home as long as she feels this way, and I won't. She's afraid of her mother, whether there's any real reason for it or not."

"There can't be any real reason," said Hugh. "It's ridiculous. Althea wouldn't hurt a fly. She has a horror of any kind of violence. Bix is simply imagining things."

"I was hoping you'd know something about this Mrs. Henshaw business. Lord knows what Pigeon's going to make of it—"

"Pigeon!" Hugh's voice rang out in genuine surprise. "Why would he make anything of it?"

"He's a great little guy for loose ends. Keeps worrying away at what he calls the loose ends in the case against Francie. There are some, you know. Such as motive. Immediate motive, that is. You said yourself, yesterday, that you couldn't believe it. Pigeon does believe it, but at the same time he's got those loose ends on his mind. He's not overlooking any bets. He wants to know about all the quarrels Mrs. Henshaw ever had in her life—and believe me there were plenty of them. The butcher, the baker, and all the rest. Pigeon's been after all of them."

"I don't blame him. I'll be glad to tell him anything I can remember—" Suddenly Hugh's face darkened. "But I won't have him going to Althea. I won't have it!" He brought his hand down flat on his desk, and the photographs of Althea and Bix jumped nervously.

Doc continued to stare at his feet. He certainly did need a shoeshine. After a moment Hugh went on more quietly, "Tell me again what Bix said. When was this? Three years ago?"

"Shortly after Dr. Buckmaster died. Hartley was in Chicago, because that's when Bix called him, at Rachel's, and got him to come back."

"So that's why he came back," said Hugh. "I always wondered."

"So did Rachel. That's how she pried all this out of Bix."

"And it was just between Althea and Mrs. Henshaw? I wasn't there?" Something began to dawn in Hugh's face. "Hey, wait a minute. I *was* there. That must have been the time I came home and found her—Of course I was there." He leaned forward and gave a short laugh. Embarrassment and relief, equal parts. "Poor Bix. She's got it all mixed up."

"I don't doubt it," said Doc. "She's a prize mixer-upper when she puts her mind to it." An inherited trait? The notion just brushed through his head. Apparently all three Bovards had done a passable job of bollixing themselves up. "So you were there? You know what she was talking about?"

"Sure I know what she was talking about. Though how she hooked it all on to Althea—Well." Again Hugh gave the short, embarrassed laugh. "You understand I'm not exactly proud of this little episode. It's not something I'd care to see published, if you know what I mean. It was me that made the scene."

"Yes?" said Doc. He waited.

"Okay. Here goes. I came home one night and found we had company. The late lamented Rose. She hadn't come to see me. In fact, she was quite put out when I showed up earlier than usual. I spoiled all the fun, because I knew what she'd come for. Althea didn't, thank God. She still doesn't. Any more than Bix does."

"What had she come for?"

"Gossip," said Hugh promptly. "She'd got hold of a piece of gossip that would have—upset Althea, so there she was, all set to spread the glad tidings. She did things like that, you know. Automatically. She didn't have anything against Althea—or me either, as far as that goes. She was just spiteful in general. Trouble-making was as natural to her as breathing. So when she got hold of this silly piece of gossip—"

"Silly? You mean it wasn't true?"

"No." Hugh swallowed. "Unfortunately, I don't mean that. It was silly, but it was also true. Everybody does silly things, now and then. There was a girl in town that winter, a school teacher. A nice little thing. Very pretty. And—Well, I told you I wasn't proud of this."

And Rachel had told Doc something, too. *If Hugh philanders now and then, it's because she drives him to it.* He remembered it now; it clicked neatly into its place.

"I don't suppose we were very bright about it," Hugh was going on doggedly. "Coreyville isn't the ideal locale. Anyway, here was Mrs. Henshaw with this tasty morsel."

"It's a wonder she didn't blackmail you," said Doc. "It was right up her alley."

"Probably figured it was too small potatoes. Which it was, sure enough—much as I would have hated for Althea to hear about it. She wasn't in good shape at the time, anyway, and I wasn't going to have her bothered with anything extra." He half-smiled, bitterly. "Hell, maybe I'm kidding myself. She might not have turned a hair."

That would be Doc's guess, but he refrained from saying so. "So what did you do?"

"I blew my top. I walked in and she gave me this sly stuff about how sorry she was Althea was feeling so poorly, she'd just dropped in for a little visit—God, the woman was a bitch! —and I don't know, I just blew up. I told her what she could do with her neighborly impulses. Told her to get out and stay out."

The phrase struck a chord in Doc's memory. "Did Bix hear all this?"

"Bix? I don't think—No, of course she didn't. I bundled Althea upstairs first, and then I had sense enough to get Bix out of there too. It was nothing for a kid to hear."

"What did you say to her? Bix, I mean."

"Why, I don't know. Told her to get out, I guess. I don't suppose I minced any words with her. I was too sore for that."

Hugh might not remember exactly what he had said to Bix, but Doc was willing to bet that he himself could quote it, word for word. *Get out of here and stay out. What are you hanging around for?* Bix had simply transferred those cruelly cutting words from the father she loved to the mother she hated. You didn't have to be a psychiatrist to figure that out. She might have done it consciously, with some idea of protecting Hugh; or unconsciously, because it was too painful to remember the other way.

"You mean," said Hugh, "she's been brooding over this for three years? Mixing it all up in her mind, somehow twisting it around so it would be Althea's fault?"

"Looks like it. I suppose you've always meant security to her, and so when you blew up and snapped at her it was too much for her. Like the Rock of Gibraltar turning into cardboard. Nothing left to hang on to."

"Except Hartley," said Hugh. "Hartley's never let her down." His face looked empty and defenseless; for a moment it merged, in Doc's mind, with Althea's. Both haunted. Both lost. He couldn't tell which face was which. Then, with a little shake of the head, a straightening of the shoulders, Hugh got his identity back. His reassuring, familiar identity —a guy with maybe more than his share of troubles, but definitely not defeated by them.

"I figure it this way," said Doc in a burst of relief. "She got over the first scare—on the surface at least—because Hartley came back and you got back to normal. But Mrs. Henshaw getting herself killed kicked it all up again. It's been a real rugged week for Bix, you know. Anything that happens to Hartley happens to her too, in a way. On top of that, it's not exactly restful to have somebody grab you and choke you. So she gets scared all over again, and by this time, as you say, she's twisted everything around so as to blame her mother. God knows, she may even suspect her mother of choking her."

Hugh's jaw dropped. "You're not serious!"

"Not really. I just mean she's overwrought and confused and very much aware of the fact that her mother doesn't love her. With that combination, you can't expect logic, in the ordinary sense of the word. Though I suppose to Bix it seems perfectly logical."

"I suppose it does." Hugh hunched his shoulder. "To me it's fantastic. Fantastic. I guess I've been hiding my head in the sand too long to grasp it. The mentality of an ostrich. That's just the way I feel. You got any ideas, Doc? What would you do if Bix was your daughter?"

"Well—" The flush of Doc's little triumph (for it had, he felt, been a pretty shrewd analysis for an amateur) faded abruptly. Here it was, what he had always said about psychiatry: So you find out you're the way you are because you hate your mother. So what do you do about it? He was suddenly aware of the strain in Hugh's waiting face, the deep lines that weren't going to be eased by spouting theories. "Is there any place Bix could go for a visit? Grandparents? Aunts? Uncles? It might help if she got clear away from her mother for a while."

"There's my sister in St. Louis," said Hugh. "Bix likes her, and she's got a couple of kids about the same age. Do you think Bix would leave Hartley? I mean, I can't see myself making her do something she doesn't want to. . . ."

"You nor anybody else," Doc told him. "Believe me, your daughter has a whim of iron. There's nothing to do but sound her out. If she won't go away, then we think of something else. Rachel suggested that she come and stay with her a few days. How would you feel about that?"

He looked away from Hugh's face quickly. Okay, Bright Boy, he said to himself, how would you feel about it? How would you like it if your only child would rather go to the neighbors'—would rather stay in a hospital—than come home?

"Whatever she wants," Hugh said after a minute. "Just so Althea's kept out of it. . . ."

Those two phrases, it occurred to Doc, summed up most of Hugh's life. He must have been saying them, thinking them, feeling them, for years. What other course had been open to him? To give Bix whatever she wanted (only he couldn't give her the important thing) and to shield Althea (only it was too late; the mortal blow had been struck long ago).

Perhaps Hugh was thinking the same thing. He did not get up when Doc rose; slumped at his desk, he raised his hand rather absently in a gesture of goodbye. And when Doc looked back from the street, he was still just sitting there, staring at nothing.

XXVII

It was one of the more peculiar half hours of her life, thought Rachel. For one thing, she was all out of practice on The Social Call. And this was a Call, all right; the atmosphere of gentility —engraved cards, lace-edged handkerchiefs, ladies sipping afternoon tea—spread through the library like a delicate fragrance.

Except that the Caller was Althea Bovard, of all unlikely people. There she sat (she who seldom made a social gesture of any kind) complete with hat and gloves and correctly pleasant expression.

"It was so nice of you to come," said Rachel, and realized that she had already said it at least twice before. Her own costume bothered her; she had been ready to step into the shower when Althea rang the bell, and her good old fuzzy bathrobe and mules struck her as not the accepted attire. The hour bothered her too. Too late for lunch. Too early by a couple of hours for afternoon tea or cocktails.

She was visited by inspiration. "Would you like a glass of sherry?"

"That would be very nice," said Althea politely. Apparently she meant it, too. Drank hers right down without ceremony, and didn't demur when Rachel gave her a refill. It set Rachel to wondering whether a bottle might not figure in Althea's withdrawn way of life.

"I must tell you, Rachel, how much I appreciate your asking Beatrix here for a while." Althea removed one glove and patted her lips daintily with her handkerchief. "I realize, of course, how anxious she is to get out of the hospital, but it's just more than I can undertake to have her at home until she's fully recovered."

Rachel blinked. This wasn't exactly the way she heard it, but let it go. "I'm looking forward to having her. I'm sure she'll be no trouble at all."

"I'm afraid I've had to neglect Beatrix a little this winter," the faint, sweet voice went on. "I haven't been at all well myself, you know. These really splitting headaches."

"I'm so sorry," said Rachel. What she was actually feeling was exasperation. How the woman could sit there and talk about her headaches when her own daughter had narrowly escaped being choked. . . . "Bix seemed to be getting along fine when I saw her last night. It was lucky for her somebody turned up in time."

"Yes, wasn't it? That is, if—Oh, I probably shouldn't even be mentioning it. But Beatrix is inclined to dramatize herself, you know. Such a difficult age, isn't it?"

"You mean you think she just made it up? Nobody really grabbed her?"

"I've never been able to understand people who do such things. But of course you know much more about what happened the other night than I do. After all, you were there, weren't you? I didn't even hear about it till in the morning. I was so upset— you know, when the window got broken—that I took a sleeping tablet and slept right through all the excitement. I really don't think I could manage without Dr. Craig and his sleeping tablets."

"I'm sure Bix didn't make it up," said Rachel. Of course she was sure; she had heard the running footsteps in the alley, after Bix cried out. And yet hadn't she herself suspected Bix of embroidering a few other facts, now and then?

"Hugh hasn't told me many of the details. He's so anxious for me not to be upset. But I gather it was Francie Henshaw. Did Beatrix—or the rest of you—see him?" Althea took another drink of sherry and ran through the handkerchief-patting routine again. Her cold, pale eyes, however, remained fixed on Rachel.

"Nobody saw him," Rachel told her. "Bix says he threw something over her head so she couldn't see, and by the time we got there he was gone. We just heard him running away."

"He's always been—queer. But then aren't we all?" A genuine, engaging smile crossed Althea's face; Rachel remembered how pretty she had been, years ago. "As I said, I probably shouldn't even have mentioned Bix's habit of romancing. Hugh says she'll outgrow it, and I expect she will. . . . Thank you, just a drop. Mrs. Henshaw's—death has affected us all. Even me, and I hardly knew the woman."

She paused, with an air of significance that puzzled Rachel. After all, why make such a point of hardly knowing Mrs. Henshaw? Nobody had said otherwise. There was, of course, Bix (who was probably going to outgrow her romancing) and the story of Mrs. Henshaw's visit to her mother. . . .

"I didn't even know her to quarrel with," said Althea, and smiled again. "It's been years since I've been inside this house. Not since I used to bring Ronnie over—"

Oh my, thought Rachel, here we go. I knew she'd get around to Ronnie eventually.

The doorbell saved her. "Excuse me," she said, and hurried out to answer it.

There stood Mrs. Pierce, looking somehow armed to the teeth, primed to fight for her rights, no matter what the odds. She wasted no breath on pleasantries.

"We're here for Rose's belongings," she announced. The car in which she had arrived was parked out in front; the challenging gesture of Mrs. Pierce's head indicated that it was loaded with auxiliary troops and heavy artillery. "My son-in-law drove me up from Westburg, and we're here to get Rose's clothes and whatever else belonged to her. No reason in the world why you should keep—"

"No reason whatever," agreed Rachel. "I've already packed everything up. You're welcome to it. Won't you come in?"

Suspiciously, Mrs. Pierce entered. She followed (alert for possible treachery) as Rachel, intending to make her excuses to Althea, opened the library door.

What happened next was a kind of stifled explosion from Althea. The sherry glass slipped from her fingers and shattered on the floor as her eyes fastened on Mrs. Pierce; her whole face seemed to shudder and go slack.

"No, no," she gasped. "It can't be. You're dead, you're dead. It can't be—"

"Dead, am I!" Mrs. Pierce drew herself up. "Well, we'll just—"

"It's all right," put in Rachel, who by this time had a grip on things. "I'm sorry, Althea. I forgot you've never met Mrs. Pierce.

It's Mrs. Henshaw's sister. Mrs. Pierce. I took her for Mrs. Henshaw, too, the first time I saw her."

Althea put her hands up to her eyes and gave a little moan. Hugh ought to be here, thought Rachel uneasily. He knew what to do with Althea when she got into a state; Rachel didn't. She tried a timid pat on Althea's shoulder and launched into an explanation of Mrs. Pierce's presence. It was punctuated by snorts from Mrs. Pierce herself.

"What if I do look a good deal like Rose? I don't see that that's any reason for anybody to take such a fit. Just tell me where Rose's things are, Miss, and I'll leave you and your friend to yourselves."

"They're upstairs in the hall," said Rachel with relief. "Why don't you go on up? I'll be with you in a minute."

Althea waited for the door to close behind Mrs. Pierce before she took her hands away from her eyes. It was awful when she tried to smile. The atmosphere of gentility had been shattered with her sherry glass; her hands shook visibly as she fumbled into her coat. And her murmurs of apology and assurance (she was all right now, just her nerves, so silly of her, Rachel mustn't worry) did not hide the fact that this was flight.

Rachel stood at the door and watched her go down the walk. She looked very fragile in her gray caracul coat and little feather hat, and she swayed slightly—whether from the shock or the sherry or a combination of the two was anybody's guess. Just as it was anybody's guess why she had come in the first place. It was odd, the remnants of The Social Call that stuck in Rachel's mind. Althea's sleeping tablets, that made her sleep right through all the excitement. Bix and her dramatic tendencies. And that neat little phrase, "I didn't even know her to quarrel with."

Had Althea planned those remnants to stick in Rachel's mind? She hadn't planned on Mrs. Pierce. That was one thing sure.

Mrs. Pierce had walked in, like a ghost from the grave, and exploded The Social Call and Althea along with it.

There was an indignant-sounding thump from overhead.

"I'm coming, Mrs. Pierce," called Rachel, and started up the stairs.

XXVIII

It was the same routine, Rachel found, all the way down Main Street. At the post office, where she stopped to pick up the mail; at the butcher shop, where Mr. Havelka cut a steak for her with loving artistry and told her exactly how to cook it; at the grocery and Elaine's Beauty Shoppe and the Square Deal Cafe, where she stopped for a coke and a chat. The same routine. Why, hello, there, Rachel! How are you? You're looking fine (or wonderful, or pretty as a speckled pup, depending on the sex and disposition of the exclaimer). How's it seem to be back? How's the old home town look to you?

It looked pretty good, at the moment. Better than it ever had before. The change was not so much in Coreyville (except for the sign above the drug store: Dr. C. W. Craig) as in Rachel herself. She felt free of Mrs. Henshaw, really free at last. Mrs. Pierce's departure, with her sister's belongings, had cut the last tangible bonds. And the afternoon's tour of Main Street had given her a healthier perspective on Althea's visit. It seemed not so much peculiar now as pathetic—the fumbling attempt of a neurotic woman to behave, for once, in a normally friendly way.

She paused a moment, outside the cafe. Where to now? Home? She had pretty well made the rounds; but she still felt mildly sociable, and like as not Hartley was up at the hospital with Bix. Her eye fell on the Tribune office with its big front window where

three giant ears of squaw corn—largest grown in the county—
were on dusty display. She could stop in and bandy a few words
with Hugh. If he wasn't too busy he might even like to come
home with her for a drink.

She went in, and was effusively greeted by Gloria Johnson—
Eager-Beaver Gloria, as Hartley and Bix called her. Rachel could
see their point, all right. Gloria positively oscillated with help-
fulness, with admiration, with earnest explanations.

"Oh, Miss Buckmaster, Mr. Bovard's going to be terribly
sorry he missed you." Gloria quivered all over at the tragedy of
this circumstance. "He's gone to the hospital to see poor old Mr.
Henshaw. I understand he's very low, and Mr. Bovard's so faithful about visiting him. He's wonderful that way, you know. Such
a fine character. Won't you sit down? He may be back any minute, and it would be such a shame if he missed you. Maybe you'd
like me to call him? I'll be only too glad—"

Rachel rallied enough strength to put the brake on at this
point, but further resistance was beyond her. She said feebly all
right, she might sit down for a minute or two—

"Oh, not that chair, Miss Buckmaster!" cried Gloria. "This
one's much more comfortable! Here, let me pull it a little closer
to the radiator, so you'll be sure to be warm enough. Can't I hang
your coat up for you? It's so smart-looking, I've admired it every
time I've seen you. Do let me hang it up for you."

Rachel clutched her coat, obscurely determined not to let it
out of her hands, and perched on the edge of the chair. "Don't let
me keep you from your work," she said, more curtly than she intended. (Sure enough, the end of Gloria's nose twitched in a
wounded way, and Rachel felt ashamed. But irritated too: somehow Gloria asked for it.) "You're probably up to your ears in
something," she added with a conciliatory smile, "and I don't
want to interrupt you."

She was immediately, thoroughly, forgiven. "I'm way behind

on my filing," Gloria confided, with a rueful glance at the pile of papers on her desk. "Sometimes it just gets away from me. I feel there's so many other things to do that are more worthwhile. You know what I mean? Naturally I try to take as much of the burden off Mr. Bovard's shoulders as I can, and if I can be useful to him in other ways, why, I just feel that's more important than the filing."

"I'm sure you're right," murmured Rachel, because some comment seemed indicated.

"I just love my job." Gloria's face—spotty, almost painfully sincere—took on a dedicated expression. "Mr. Bovard's the most wonderful man to work for in the world. Oh, I know he's supposed to be quick-tempered. He does get mad sometimes, but when he does it's for a good reason. You know what I mean? It's justified."

Again some comment seemed indicated, and Rachel groped mentally. I'm glad to hear you testify? Amen, Sister Gloria? All the possibilities that occurred to her had a distinct religious flavor.

Her gropings turned out to be unnecessary, anyway. Gloria carried on without encouragement. "Besides, I feel that a person with so much on their mind, it's no wonder he loses his temper once in a while." She let a delicately significant pause fall, while she turned to her desk and began pawing away at the papers. "Poor Mrs. Bovard, I mean. It's a terrible worry to him. Not that he ever says much, of course. But I can tell. I'm funny that way. I can tell."

I bet you can, thought Rachel. She took a speculative look at Gloria's figure—the trim little waist, the lush tempting swell above and below. God had done all right by Gloria in some departments, and it was unlikely that those departments were wasted on Hugh. Gloria asked for it, in more ways than one.

"Like all this past week, he's been so edgy, and Fritz says it's just pure orneriness. But I know better." Gloria nodded wisely. "It's poor Mrs. Bovard. Not feeling well again. I can just sense it. She's been doing so well all winter, too. Up till now."

Rachel felt a flicker of genuine curiosity. All this past week. That would be, roughly, since Mrs. Henshaw was killed. Last night's session with Bix rose again to haunt her, and the puzzling visit from Althea this afternoon. "What got Mrs. Bovard upset this time, I wonder?" she asked.

But Gloria's psychic powers apparently didn't extend beyond Hugh. "You never know. A delicate person like that, it could be anything. Sometimes if somebody just mentions Ronnie, it sets her off all over again. And then, right away, it shows on Mr. Bovard, and everything gets on his nerves."

"Maybe he's just worried about Francie. And Bix. He certainly got all upset about what happened to her."

"I know." Gloria's eyes brightened. "Isn't it awful, to think of that old man doing a thing like that? Killing his wife, and then trying to choke Bix, when Mr. Bovard's been such a wonderful friend to him, all these years—Oh, Miss Buckmaster, here's your brother! Hello, Hartley! How are you?"

"Hi, Gloria." Hartley came in, the collar of his windbreaker turned up against the cold, Queenie at his heels. "What's up, Rachel?"

"Nothing. I just stopped in to say hello to Hugh, only he's up at the hospital. Any chance of your giving me a ride home?"

"I might, if you play your cards right." He lounged against the corner of Gloria's desk, watching her busy hands as they sorted and stacked. He ran the tip of his tongue along his upper lip; Rachel recognized his teasing expression. "Some secretary you are! Really, Miss Johnson, just look at that desk! An eyesore. A blot on the Tribune escutcheon."

Gloria bridled happily. "Isn't it a sight? I was just telling Miss Buckmaster, I'm way behind on my fil—" She gave such a sudden gasp that Rachel, who was putting on her coat, turned to see what was wrong. Gloria's face (except for the spots) had turned as white as the envelope she was holding in her hand. It was a long envelope, still sealed, with Hugh's name printed on it in neat letters. "Oh, my! How could I have forgotten? Oh, Mr. Bovard'll never forgive me!"

"What's the matter? What's wrong?" Even Hartley looked concerned.

"I forgot to give it to him." Gloria's voice was hushed and bleak. "It came way last week. It came the day Mrs. Henshaw was killed, I remember because we were all excited and mixed up, and that's how I forgot to give it to him. It must have gotten stuck in with the stuff to be filed and—Oh, my!"

"Oh now, look," said Rachel. "He's not going to blame you for a little thing like that. Maybe it's nothing important, anyway. Why don't you open it and see what it is before you end it all?"

She reached for the envelope, and Gloria gave another gasp of alarm. "Oh, you mustn't *open* it! I never open those letters when they come. Mr. Bovard always wants all the personal ones turned over to him."

"What do you mean 'those letters'?" Hartley asked. "How do you know who they're from if you never open them?"

"I don't know who they're from. I just recognize the printing. And the envelope. They always come in a long envelope like this. There was one a few days before this one. He'll be mad at me," wailed Gloria. "He'll be furious."

"I doubt it," said Rachel. But she felt a little click somewhere in her interior, as if something there were being alerted. "After all, anybody can overlook a little thing like a letter."

Hartley was staring at the envelope, too. He even picked it up, and then flicked it back on the desk with what was meant to be a casual gesture. A long white envelope, neatly printed, fatter than an ordinary letter. As if it might contain another envelope.

What was so extraordinary about it? Why should she feel again the little click—of curiosity, or recognition, or whatever it was? Anybody might get such a letter; anybody might write it. Lots of men were fussy about having their personal mail turned over to them, unopened. And poor little Eager-Beaver Gloria was just the type to magnify a trivial oversight into the blunder of the century.

"Don't worry about it, Gloria," she said. "It's probably nothing important, anyway."

"I know, but—" At that moment the phone on Hugh's desk rang, and Gloria leaped like a rabbit. Then she got a grip on herself, switched across to the other side of the office, and intoned, in her best girl-Friday manner, "Tribune office. . . . I'm sorry, Mr. Bovard isn't in just now. May I take a message?"

Her back was turned to Rachel. Hartley's too; or at least partly. He was at the door, ready to leave. And something peculiar happened to Rachel's hand: it shot out, of its own accord, snatched the long white envelope, thrust it into her purse.

"Okay, Hartley," she said breathlessly. "I'm ready. Let's go." (Had he seen her? His face was suspiciously blank.)

They pantomimed goodbye to Gloria, still busy at the phone. Once in the car and on the way home, Rachel relaxed. She even began to wonder if it had really happened, her hand behaving in that peculiar way. Yes, it had. She could feel the bulge of the envelope through her soft broadcloth purse.

"Doc says it's all right for her to leave the hospital," Hartley was saying, and she realized that she had asked him about Bix and he was telling her. "He says you told Bix last night she could stay at our house for a while, and so I thought—"

"Of course. Why don't you bring her over for dinner tonight? I got a fine big steak, and Doc's coming, and we'll have a party." Their eyes met, startled and pleased at the idea. It would be the first time she and Hartley had ever had a party, company of their own in their own home.

"All right. If you want to," said Hartley, as if it happened every day. But his eyes kept their shine. "All right. Swell."

What a nice, shy creature he was! She felt suddenly giddy with happiness, and close to him, closer than at any moment since her return.

"Remember how we used to pray that Mrs. Henshaw would go away?" she asked. "That she just wouldn't be there in the morning? Now that it's come true I can hardly believe it. But it is, she's gone forever. Somebody killed her, and I don't really care who."

"What do you mean you don't care who? We know who. Francie."

"I know." She hurried on, absorbed in her own feelings, bent on opening her heart. She could do it with no one else, not even Doc. Hartley alone would understand what she meant. She could even tell him about the letter. "It has to be Francie. I know it in a way, and yet in another way I don't know it at all, I don't believe it. Do you, Hartley? Do you believe that Francie—"

"What are you talking about?" Hartley's voice cracked at her; when she turned and saw his face alarm sprang up in her, without warning. "What's the matter with you, anyway? 'You don't know it at all, you don't believe it.' For God's sake, Francie's practically confessed. What more do you want?"

"Hartley—" she whispered, but his face did not change. It remained the face of a stranger, furious and alarming.

"You better cut it out, that's all. I'm telling you. You're going to be damn sorry if you don't. You better keep your mouth shut and stop trying to make trouble. Can't you let well enough alone?"

They were home. He turned sharply into the driveway and

jolted to a stop. Neither of them spoke while Rachel collected her packages and purse and got out of the car. How bleak the yard looked—dark already falling, and the trees stiff and naked in the biting wind. Behind her she heard the car door slam and Hartley's feet following her, gaining on her. She became aware of an unreasonable impulse to run. To run some place very fast. Only there was no place to run but the house.

And when Hartley caught up with her it was, after all, only to help her with the packages and to say, in a low, shame-faced voice, that he was sorry.

"It doesn't matter," she said. She kept her eyes on the ground, as if she too were ashamed. She hurried into the kitchen, turned on the lights, went on into the front hall to put her coat away.

When she came back and looked in her purse, which she had left on the kitchen table, the long white envelope was gone.

XXIX

It was Bix who salvaged the party. She was in high spirits when she arrived, and she stayed that way, blissfully oblivious of everybody else's mood. Which was far from festive, though they all tried. Hartley, never very dependable socially, was by spells over-talkative, over-silent. Poor Doc, in fine enough fettle when he arrived, caught the jitters from Rachel. So much so that very soon all he was capable of was long, anxious looks at her and jumpy little smiles when she caught him at it. She couldn't help it, she simply could not focus her mind on anything but Hartley and the letter. What had he done with it? Burnt it? Torn it up? Returned it? Hidden it? Plenty of opportunity, she supposed, for him to have done any of these things. When he built the fire in the library, for instance. Or when he went upstairs to clean up and change his clothes. Or when he went back to the hospital to get Bix. . . .

Hugh, who stopped by with an overnight bag for Bix, was least festive of all. He acted so befuddled, so unlike himself, that for a moment Rachel wondered if he could be drunk. Then it came to her: he was too miserable to make sense. Losing Bix—for that must be the way it seemed to him, as if he had lost her forever—had taken the heart out of everything for him. He still had Althea, though. Poor Hugh, thought Rachel. He still had Althea. As much of her as he had ever had.

Still preoccupied with her own problem, she brought him a drink and sat down beside him. "I suppose Gloria told you I paid you a call this afternoon? See what you miss when you don't tend to business?" (And has she broken down and told you about the letter yet? She must be out of her mind, poor kid. Now that it's disappeared, she won't know what to do.)

"What?" said Hugh. "Who? Oh. Gloria." He seemed to make an effort at concentration. "I haven't seen Gloria. I didn't go back to the office."

(So she hasn't told him yet. She's probably still there, tearing the place apart looking for it. Unless Hartley returned it to her. Only wouldn't he have told me, wouldn't he have asked me what the big idea was, stealing other people's mail? Wouldn't that be the natural thing for him to do?)

"I'm sorry I missed you," said Hugh heavily.

Halfway through his drink, he rose abruptly and said he must be getting home. Bix flew to give him one of her Hollywood-type kisses, and he produced a haggard smile. "So long, Biscuit. See you tomorrow. Good night, all."

Rachel saw him to the door and paused under the red glass chandelier, watching him plod down the steps and across the yard. Like an old man, she thought; and shivered. What a long time it seemed since those mellow, convivial evenings of Papa's and Hugh's, when the sound of their voices had seemed to filter all through her, steeping her in security. They had been, to her child eyes, so solid and unchanging, and now—

The phone rang, and when she answered Gloria's voice broke over her in a distraught flood. "Oh, Miss Buckmaster, I hate to bother you, but I just don't know what to do. You remember the letter that got me so upset, when you were in this afternoon? It's disappeared, simply vanished, I've turned the whole office inside out and it's simply not here, and I wondered if by any chance you or Hartley might have picked it up, by mistake, you know, and—"

She ran out of breath. It was time Rachel said something, anyway. But what? Never mind, Gloria, I stole it, a slight case of kleptomania, think nothing of it. A family trait. Because guess what, Hartley turned right around and stole it from me. . . .

"Hold on a minute, will you, Gloria? I'll ask Hartley." She had been afraid to ask him before. She was still afraid, she discovered; she was going to have to do it quickly or her courage would fail again.

"Hartley!" she called, and when he came out into the hall she blurted it out. "Gloria's in a sweat about that letter again. Says it's disappeared, and wonders if we picked it up by mistake. Have you got it, Hartley?"

"Who, me?" He was giving her the exasperating blank stare he used to reserve for Mrs. Henshaw, the I-don't-know-anything-about-anything expression. She forgot about being afraid.

"Hartley, I could shake your teeth out—" she began, but he gave a little hiss of warning: Bix had stuck her head out the library door and was saying hurry up, she wanted to dance.

"Tell her you don't know anything about it," he said, very quick and low. "And for God's sake tell her not to tell Hugh about it."

She searched his face; it told her nothing. She felt the obscure alarm creeping back over her. And the helplessness. After all, what else was there to do? "I'm awfully sorry, Gloria," she said into the telephone. "We don't seem to find it anywhere. . . ."

Back in the library, Hartley and Bix were engaged in what they called dancing. It looked more like a do-or-die athletic contest to Rachel. Their faces set in the grim expression of football players hitting the line, they flung each other at arms-length, banged back against each other, whirled and twisted at violent angles. Queenie had retreated under the couch for shelter; Doc was on it, with his feet drawn up and a strained expression on his face. It seemed like the safest place. Rachel joined him.

"Who's ahead?" she asked, and he grinned feebly.

"You got me. All I know is they're in there pitching. Ever see so many elbows in your life?"

Rachel never had. Something else caught her eye, as Hartley crouched for another assault, his jacket flying out like a sail taking the wind. The envelope was there, in his inside pocket. Not burned or torn up or even hidden. Right there in his pocket. Her breath caught in excitement.

"Let's play the other side," said Bix as soon as the record ended. "It's better, anyway. More zing."

"Look at them," said Doc in wonder. "Not even winded. Let's get out of here, Rachel. I feel like I'm aging rapidly."

"Wait a minute," said Rachel. Because while it was true that they weren't winded, they were warm. Bless their energetic little hearts, they had worked up a sweat, and if there was a God, Hartley was going to take off his jacket and. . . .

Yes. She could hardly believe her luck. Just as the music blared out afresh (more zing, sure enough) Hartley shrugged out of his jacket and flung it across the foot of the couch. His eyes were half-closed, his face rapt. He had forgotten the letter and everything else except the call of the wild.

A moment's fumbling, and Rachel was at the door. "Come on, Doc. Let's make a run for it. You can help me with the steak."

Hartley had opened the letter. She leaned against the kitchen table, the envelope jumping in her hands. She had been right: there was another slightly smaller envelope inside. It was addressed to Mrs. Althea Bovard, and as Rachel stared at the familiar, prudish-looking handwriting, it seemed to her that the solid floor under her feet shifted and shook in a kind of slow-motion disintegration. Hartley had opened the inside envelope too. It took less than a minute to read the short message inside. It took less than a minute for the world to fall apart.

"What's up? What's the matter?" Doc was standing right beside her, but his voice seemed to come from a long way off. Her ears rang with tears; she could feel them streaming down her face while she stuffed message into envelope, envelope into envelope.

"Put it back," she sobbed. "Put it back. I never read it, I never saw it. Oh, please. Put it back. . . ."

XXX

She wouldn't tell him what it was all about. That was what threw him. It wasn't enough for her to dissolve like this—and dissolve was the word, all right: she just leaned against the kitchen table with that letter in her hand, her face ugly with tears, and went to pieces. But that wasn't enough. She had to go secretive on him, too. And how could he help her, how could he fix things for her, if he didn't even know what was wrong? What did she mean, treating him like a kid, not old enough yet to be told the facts of life?

"Tell me what's the matter. What's happened?" he kept asking, and all she did was shake her head and stuff the envelope into her pocket (she had on kind of a swishy skirt and a black sweater; and that he approved of, that sweater was definitely for Rachel).

He had seen her snake the envelope out of Hartley's jacket, and he had caught sight of the name Bovard, and that was apparently all the information she considered him capable of coping with.

"Well, then, stop emoting," he said crossly. "If it's none of my business, spare me the tears."

That jolted her out of it a little. "Oh Doc, I'm so sorry," she said, and she might have gone on from there, except that at that moment the two acrobats came romping out from the library, yammering for food. They would.

Rachel turned around, quick, and began rummaging in the refrigerator, and he covered up for her as well as he could. Not that it took much doing, with Bix. She was so full of girlish glee that she wouldn't have noticed if Doc himself had been crying his heart out. (As a matter of fact, Bix was looking downright pretty tonight. Hadn't had a chance to hack at her hair for some time, apparently; and those great luminous eyes of hers made up for everything else.) He wasn't so sure about Hartley. He never was exactly sure about Hartley. The kid had spent so much of his life in mental hiding from Mrs. Henshaw that he was apt to keep his face closed up for everybody else, from force of habit. A real master of the deadpan. And of course he must be mixed up in this letter business; it had been in his pocket.

He had to hand it to Rachel, the way she got a grip on herself and went through with the party. All during dinner he kept thinking: Later, they would shake the juvenile element later, and he would get the whole story out of her or know the reason why. All he had to do was bide a little time.

But, like they say, the best laid plans. They were having coffee in the library, and he was just getting set to remember an errand he had to do ("Come along, Rachel, keep me company. Let the kids do the dishes.") when who should turn up again but Hugh

Bovard. He couldn't remember whether he had put bedroom slippers in Bix's overnight bag or not; so here he was, with a sadlooking pair of scuffs. Bix turned up her nose at them.

"Those old things! Why, Daddy, of course I have my others! I had them with me at the hospital."

"Well, I couldn't remember," said Hugh forlornly. He looked so grateful when Rachel offered him a cup of coffee that Doc decided it wouldn't actually hurt him to bide a little more time.

A queer kind of absent-mindedness seemed to clamp down on everybody except Bix, who chattered away about the pros and cons of visiting her aunt in St. Louis. Luckily, few comments were necessary; Doc had a feeling nobody could manage much beyond an occasional nod or shake of the head. He certainly couldn't. At that, the others were better off than he was: they knew what they were thinking about. All he could do was flounder.

At last Bix ran down. "Oh, I meant to ask you," said Hugh, lighting another cigarette, "what's all this fuss about Gloria and some letter that she found, or didn't find, or whatever? I gathered from what she said to me that she'd called you about it. That's all I did gather, I must say. A hysterical type female, if I ever saw one."

Hartley's face stayed blank. But Rachel's was a dead giveaway; her spoon jittered against her saucer. "She called you?" she stammered. "I told her not to—I mean, why should she bother you when like as not it'll turn up tomorrow and probably isn't important, anyway. . . ." She started to lift her cup for a casual sip. Decided against it.

"She claimed she couldn't sleep with it on her conscience." Hugh's eyebrow quirked in amusement. "That conscience of Gloria's. Definitely over-active. I expect you're right, it's probably nothing important, anyway. Did you see the letter?"

Rachel gulped, and before she could do any more damage

Hartley spoke up. "Sure we saw it. Down at the office. It turned up in a bunch of other stuff, and you'd have thought it was a million dollar check, the way she went on about it. Said she should have given it to you way last week, that you'll undoubtedly have her shot at dawn—"

"Oh now, look," said Hugh. "I'm not such a terror as all that. I guess I do raise a little hell with her now and then, but I don't know, she kind of asks for it."

"I know what you mean." Rachel was over-eager, too quick to snatch at a diversion. "She affects me the same way. Brings out the bully in me. Isn't it funny how some people can do that to you?"

Hugh nodded, but he didn't pursue the side trail. "I still don't get it, though. So she mislaid a letter and then found it. Why call you up about it? Or me either, when it comes to that? What's all the shouting about?" He looked half-puzzled, half-exasperated.

"It disappeared again," said Rachel desperately. "That is—"

The telephone rang. Saved by the bell, thought Doc, as she hurried out to the hall to answer it. Hartley escaped by the simple method of starting the record-player again; Bix brightened right up, all set for another scrimmage; and Hugh settled back in his chair with a fatherly smile. Maybe he was really worried about the letter, maybe not. If he was, he wasn't telling Doc. God forbid that anybody should tell Doc anything.

"It's for you, Doc," said Rachel from the doorway. "Mrs. Nelson at the hospital."

Francie, of course. It was a miracle he had held on this long. The shots had kept him comfortable, in a half-coma; nothing could mend the broken-down machine that was Francie's heart.

It was still sputtering, though. "He insists on seeing you," said Mrs. Nelson's forthright voice. "Says you've got no business going away and leaving him when he's dying. And he wants Mr. Bovard, too. I haven't called him yet, thought I'd let you decide.

He doesn't look a bit good to me, and I can't get him quieted down."

"I'll be right over," said Doc. "Bovard's here, so I'll bring him along. Tell him we'll be right over. Did you give him another shot of—"

"I did not," snapped Mrs. Nelson. "He won't have it. Says he's got a right to die in his right mind if he wants to, and I don't know but I agree with him."

"Okay. Hold everything. We'll be there."

Back in the library he explained briefly. Hugh was already on his feet, prepared for the message. He had forgotten about the letter, but Doc caught a flicker of relief in Rachel's eyes when she heard that Hugh was leaving too.

"You'll call me when you get a chance, won't you?" she asked wistfully. "Please call me, Doc."

"Of course. Don't worry."

A futile bit of advice: she was obviously going to sit here and stew—and somehow it wouldn't seem quite so much as if he were abandoning her, if only he knew what she was going to stew about. He couldn't explain the reluctance he felt at leaving her. After all, she wasn't alone, Hartley and Bix were there too. Hartley. . . .

Halfway down the porch steps he turned; she was standing in the doorway, her hands clenched in the pockets of her skirt. The letter must still be there. He took a step back toward her. "Why don't you call Myra, ask her to come over and keep you company?" He said it fast and low. "The kids will probably want to go out somewhere."

"Yes, I will. I'll call Myra. That's a good idea." She latched onto it so eagerly that he felt more uneasy than ever. (Did Hartley know yet that the letter was in Rachel's pocket now, instead of his own? What would he do when he found out?)

"I wish I didn't have to go," he said.

But there was nothing else to do.

XXXI

"Hey there," exclaimed Hugh when they walked into Francie's room. "This is more like it! You're looking like yourself again!"

It was true that at first glance the old man seemed to have rallied. Propped up against the pillows, glittering-eyed, gaunt and unshaven, he had recaptured some of his old air. That arresting, even rather majestic air of a legendary character, like one of the early prophets, or the Ancient Mariner. But his pulse—flickering, now rapid, now almost gone—told a different story. And his voice was hardly more than a husky whisper. Hanging on from sheer stubbornness, by the skin of his teeth; and just as well aware of it as Doc was. His eyes softened when he looked at Hugh, but he didn't waste any strength on pleasantries.

He asked right away for the sheriff and Mr. Pigeon. He'd been asking for them as well as for Doc and Hugh, it seemed, but Mrs. Nelson had put it down to the vagaries of a wandering mind. Francie treated himself to a brief snort.

"Get them," he whispered. "Make it official."

So that was why he was hanging on. A full-dress confession. Hugh wheeled abruptly, crossed to the window, and stood there with his back to the others. He might have been looking out at the view, except that the blinds were drawn, there was nothing to see. No help from him. Doc hesitated by the bedside, held by the fierce urgency in Francie's eyes. He remembered what Mrs. Nelson had said over the phone. Says he's got a right to die in his right mind if he wants to. Why not with a clear conscience, too, if that was what he wanted?

"Go ahead," he said to Mrs. Nelson finally. "Call them."

They waited in silence—Francie with his eyes closed, hoarding his meager store of energy; Hugh at the window, staring at the view that wasn't there; Doc with his fingers on the bony wrist, as if by holding the pulse like this he could keep it from flickering out.

It took Mr. Pigeon and Charlie Jeffreys ten minutes to get there. Mr. Pigeon ambled in; Charlie tiptoed, his face as solemn as a funeral. He jumped slightly when Francie (obviously already a corpse in Charlie's mind) opened his eyes and spoke.

"Write this down." Francie's voice, reduced as it was to a whisper, still had a ghostly ring of authority. They did what he said, all of them. Hugh joined the circle at the bedside because Francie wanted him there. His skinny fingers clamped on to Hugh's hand, holding him, and often as he talked his eyes would turn to Hugh's strained, sorrowful face. Something between them, thought Doc, a powerful current of sympathy or loyalty or whatever it was that had sparked their incongruous friendship in the first place.

Charlie did the writing. His ball-point pen traveled soberly over the paper, tracing a path that from time to time (much to Charlie's chagrin) faded out almost entirely. An appropriate instrument, it seemed to Doc, to record Francie's wavering, husky story.

"I killed Rose Anthony Henshaw," he began with ceremonious relish, "because I hated her. I'm glad I did it." He watched to make sure Charlie got that down.

"No other reason? Such as money?" One of Mr. Pigeon's mild brown eyes was trained on the foot of the bed, the other on the head. This lent a note of polite detachment to his part in the proceedings.

"Money too." Francie's full lips twisted craftily. "She hid it. Didn't believe in banks. Didn't believe in wills, either. Didn't figure on dying, I guess. But she did."

Nobody was going to argue with him on that score.

"So you went to the Buckmaster house that afternoon," prompted Mr. Pigeon. "Thursday afternoon. And—"

"She wouldn't tell me where it was. So I killed her. Pushed her down the cellar steps. 'Go, lovely Rose'. She went, all right. Let out a squawk on the way down." He smiled, as at a rich, mellow memory.

"Then what did you do?"

"Went down and looked at her. I wasn't sure she was dead. So I hit her with the candlestick. . . . It was there. By the window."

There was quite a long pause. Charlie's ball-point pen waited, conscientiously poised. Francie closed his eyes. His face grew more mottled, his breath more labored, as if he were once more in actuality making the trip down the steps, reaching for the candlestick, crashing it down in that needless, blundering blow.

"What did you do after that? Look for the money?"

Francie's eyes stayed shut. "Didn't need to. No will. I'd get it anyway." Suddenly he shook all over, swept by a gust of soundless laughter. When it subsided he went on. "I went back to the shop. Candlestick under my coat. I hid it in the shop window, under the bearskin. . . ."

"How did you know about Mrs. Henshaw's money, Francie?" asked Mr. Pigeon gently. "How did you know, if you hadn't talked to her in thirty-five years?"

Francie's eyes flew open at that, glittering and scornful. " 'If.' Big word. 'If.' "

"You mean you did see her? You did talk to her? How often?"

"As often as I had to." (It was plain that Charlie didn't know what to make of that. But he wrote it down.)

"Let's get this straight, Francie. Let's go back to the beginning. You say you hated your wife. Why?"

For the first time, Francie's voice rose above a whisper, rose to a whirring echo of its old thunder. Hate seized him and rattled his rickety frame like an engine taking hold in a worn-out machine. "The woman was an abomination. Evil clear through. Serpent in the Garden of Eden. . . ." There was a certain grandeur, thought Doc, in the Biblical phrases; nothing half-hearted about Francie's hymn of hate. "Tricked me into marrying her. Ruined me. . . ." The grandeur drained away; something sick and sly took its place. "Only she had me. She knew it. So did I. Same breed of cats. How did I know about her money? How do you think I knew? It was mine. I paid it to her."

"You paid it to her? What for?" The moment the question was out, Mr. Pigeon looked as if he wished he hadn't asked it. Which was precisely Doc's reaction. Because what happened to Francie's face wasn't nice to watch. It seemed to crawl with slyness. Where was the Ancient Mariner now, the early prophet? He had changed before their eyes into a small boy, gloating over obscenities scrawled on a back fence.

"What for?" Francie licked his lips. Something like a snigger escaped him; his elbow jerked, and for an appalling moment Doc thought he was going to dig Mr. Pigeon in the ribs. "Three guesses what for."

Mr. Pigeon cleared his throat. As for Charlie, he bent his head so far over his pen and paper that only his ears could be seen. They were bright red.

Francie clucked his tongue at them in malicious mock-reproval. "I paid her to keep quiet about it. Naturally. Think I wanted the whole town to know I couldn't leave her alone?"

It was fantastic. But no more fantastic than the rest of

Francie's life, the part that the whole town had known about for years. Doc thought of the little path worn along the sidewalk between Francie's shop and his room at Smiley's; of the cases of peanut butter and beans; of the sizable bank account Mr. Pigeon had uncovered, and the profitable transactions with Chicago antique dealers. If you wanted to get technical, it was fantastic that Francie was alive at all. Any reasonable man would have given up and died two nights ago.

"So you'd been paying her all these years," Mr. Pigeon had rallied and was going on, "without anybody knowing you ever saw her. And you killed her to get the money back. Nobody saw you, coming or going?"

Francie shook his head. "Years of practice," he whispered, "sneaking to the Buckmaster's and back."

"What time was it? On Thursday, when this happened?"

"Two, two thirty. Didn't find her till four thirty."

"What did you do, the rest of the afternoon?"

Francie looked slightly bored. "Puttered around the shop. Read. Talked to Hugh."

"That right, Mr. Bovard? You went to see Francie?"

"Yes." Hugh's voice sounded strangled. "He seemed—the same as always."

"Did he tell you any of this? Mention Mrs. Henshaw?"

Both of them shook their heads, and Mr. Pigeon turned back to Francie. "Didn't it bother you when Hartley Buckmaster was arrested?"

Francie made a gesture like a shrug. "His tough luck." So much for Hartley. So much for all of it, in fact. Doc became aware of a slackening in Francie, a kind of mortal indifference. The strength that he had stored up so fiercely was spent, where he had meant to spend it; his mission had been accomplished; he wasn't interested any more.

But Mr. Pigeon still had questions. "You didn't care about

Hartley. But then, when Miss Buckmaster and Mr. Bovard's daughter began asking about the candlestick, you got worried. Didn't you?"

"Snooping around," murmured Francie. But perfunctorily, without rancor. "Scared them off. . . ." He hardly bothered to nod assent to the other questions. Yes, he had thrown the rock through Bovard's window. Yes, after that he had gone back to the shop. He didn't seem to hear when Mr. Pigeon asked about the attack on Bix. His eyes stayed half-open and dull; his head sagged a little to one side.

Silence. Doc could hear the tiny, busy tick of Charlie's wrist watch, a sobbing of wind under the eaves. Nothing else. It was as if they were all holding their breaths.

The knobby wrist between his fingers jerked suddenly in one more spurt of energy. Mission not quite accomplished, after all; there was one last chore.

"Sign," said Francie. "Let me sign." He sounded in a hurry and irritable, like a business man at the end of a trying day. And the spurt of energy still held, incredibly, driving the pen across the paper (which Charlie held for him) in the impatient, proud-looking strokes of Francie's signature. Francis L. Henshaw. It trailed off at the end, and the pen fell from Francie's fingers and wept blue-black tears onto the sheet.

So they had their signed confession. Charlie picked it up and held it uneasily, by one corner.

With a sigh, Francie turned to Hugh. For a moment his face lit up with gaiety and affection; it occurred to Doc that he might once have been quite a handsome man. "Give me a good write-up," he said. "In the paper. See that I get the credit, boy. . . ."

Another sigh. The spark winked out. That was all.

XXXII

The minute he could manage it, he called Rachel and told her about Francie. "So everything's all right now," he finished anxiously. "The whole thing's settled."

She made a small sound, as if she were catching her breath. But she didn't say any of the relieved things he had hoped for. She didn't say anything at all, and her silence made Doc feel irritated and helpless. What was the matter with her, anyway? Everybody else was satisfied: no loose ends left to bother Mr. Pigeon; poor old Francie granted the kind of death he wanted—in his right mind, and with a clear conscience. So why couldn't she forget about that damn letter, which couldn't possibly have any significance any more. . . .

"Rachel. Rachel, are you all right?"

"Yes. I'm all right." Her voice still sounded strained and faraway, the way it had when she first answered the phone, and he had another lurid, split-second vision of someone standing over her, threatening her.

"You're not alone, are you? Myra came, didn't she?"

"Yes, she's here." (Not that Myra could do anything, really. But it was a comfort to Doc to think of her sitting there with her crocheting or whatever, and her stock of mild gossip that ran on, whether anybody listened or not.)

"Is Hartley—Did the kids go out?"

"No. They're here too." Did her voice tremble, ever so slightly, on that?

"Listen, Rachel—"

"Doc," she broke in breathlessly. "Are you coming back? Please come back."

She wanted him. He would cling to that. Never mind the

ramifications. She wanted him to come back, period. "Of course," he said. "I'll be right there."

Hugh was waiting for him in the hall. Just sitting there on one of the straight-backed chairs, staring at the picture on the opposite wall. Hope, done up in her blindfold and blue dress. The poor guy looked dazed, done in. "Come on, Hugh," said Doc. "Nothing more to be done tonight. We might as well get out of here. I'll give you a lift home."

Neither of them spoke until they had almost reached the Buckmaster house. Then Hugh said, "I'd like to say goodnight to Bix. Okay if I come in with you for a minute?"

"Sure, come in and have a drink. I know I can use one, and you look like you could too."

He did, indeed. The street light played shadowy tricks with Hugh's face as they went up the walk, accenting the jut of cheekbone and brow, making of the eye socket an empty cavern. It gave Doc the feeling of looking at a desolate landscape. The craters of the moon, something like that.

"I know how you feel about Francie," he said awkwardly. "But maybe it was the best way, after all. I mean, he died happier than most people—"

"Yes." Hugh stopped with his hand on the doorknob. "Two good friends I've had in my life, Doc. Nobody ever had better. Doc Buckmaster, and Francis Henshaw."

Francis, not Francie. It gave Hugh's words a formal ring, like an epitaph. And a fitting one, thought Doc; an epitaph that would have suited the old boy right down to the ground.

Rachel was in the hall, talking on the phone, when they walked in. "Oh, Althea," she was saying, "I meant to call you earlier. . . ."

Something queer happened. Hugh—who had seemed in a kind of slow-motion trance for the past hour—was suddenly swift and purposeful as a cat. He whipped down the hall; Doc caught a glimpse of Rachel's startled face as Hugh bent over her, his hand closing on her wrist.

"What are you doing, calling Althea? What are you telling her?"

All at once Doc was there, too, with no recollection of having moved. "What's the idea? Let go of her. Let go." He shoved, and Hugh half-turned, eyes glaring, face dark and hostile. His right hand stayed clamped on Rachel's wrist. With his left he covered the mouthpiece of the telephone. The old game: keeping Althea out of it.

The incredible little tableau held for a minute more. Then Rachel stuck out her chin. "I'm not telling her anything. She called me, asking for you. Here, talk to her yourself."

Hugh's hand fell away from her wrist as she stood up; he put it up to his face, as if to wipe away the unfamiliar, angry mask that had been there. It was gone now. He was himself again, blinking down at Rachel in a bewilderment that matched hers and Doc's.

"Good Lord, Rachel, I'm sorry. I don't know what in the hell's the matter with me." He sat down heavily, staring at the telephone in his hand, and Doc saw Rachel's eyes soften with compassion.

"You're tired, Hugh," she said. "That's all it is. You're tired and upset about Francie. Doc, why don't you fix us all a drink?"

As he headed for the kitchen, Doc heard Hugh's voice, husky but otherwise the same as always speaking into the phone. "Althea, darling, I didn't mean to worry you, I'm terribly sorry I didn't call you. . . ."

They were all gathered in the library by the time Doc showed up with the tray of drinks. (He had dawdled, hoping that Rachel would join him in the kitchen. After all, she had asked him to come back; you'd think she could spare him a minute or two alone. But it seemed not.)

"Well, anyway, this settles it," Myra was saying. "I don't suppose it'll suit Mrs. Pierce—and if it hadn't been for her snooping around getting Hartley arrested, there'd have been nothing to settle—but I for one consider it a God's mercy Francie's out of reach of the law, where he won't have to pay any penalties. There's been enough justice done, that's what I say, murderer or not." She smoothed out her crocheting and looked around a little defiantly, as if she expected somebody to give her an argument. Nobody did.

"You mean I get a drink too?" asked Bix, bouncing a little on the edge of the couch. "Gee, Hartley, lookit. I've been promoted."

"Just one," Doc told her. "For medicinal purposes. Then off to bed with you. I don't allow my patients to sit up till all hours, carousing."

"All hours! Only eleven thirty."

Hugh gave a start of surprise. "Is that all it is? Really? I had a feeling it was something ungodly, like two thirty or three. Lost track of time, I guess, there at the hospital." He had gulped down his first drink; now he watched thirstily as Doc poured him another.

"My," said Myra, sipping hers genteelly, "it's strong, isn't it?"

"Made according to prescription," said Doc. "Recommended for its powerful relaxing properties." He leaned back in his chair, the picture (he hoped) of repose. Maybe if he set an example, the others would unwind too. God knows they needed to.

But the nervous stiffness in his own back refused to melt, and when he looked around he got a curious feeling of tension slowly, relentlessly rising. In spite of the cozy little fire. In spite of the sociable drinks in their hands, and the leisurely cigarettes. Myra had stowed away her crocheting and sat bolt upright, acutely conscious of the fact that she, a member in good standing of the

Ladies Aid and a number of other straitlaced organizations, was drinking a highball. (Acutely conscious of something else, too? Yes, Doc was almost sure that just that daring drink couldn't account, all by itself, for Myra's rigid little smile.) The kids sat on the couch, Bix with one foot tucked under her in what should have been a casual attitude, Hartley lounging beside her, his face blank yet watchful. Hugh was hunched in his chair, clutching his glass as if it was all he could do to keep from gulping this drink down like the first. And Rachel—poor desperate Rachel with the color all drained from her face, so that the lipstick on her mouth jolted you like a wrong note, and one hand clenched up tight in the pocket of her skirt. . . . Still hanging on to that damn letter, thought Doc. If she was trying to hide the fact that she had it, he had never seen a lousier job of hiding. You'd have to be blind to miss it.

What was wrong? What were they all waiting for? Because they were waiting—innocent bystander Doc along with the rest of them. Something was going to happen, that was all he knew: a crisis ahead that kept Rachel's hand frozen onto the letter, that had sent Hugh plunging down the hall in terror of what Rachel might be saying to Althea.

A flock of wild surmises scudded across Doc's mind. He had caught sight of the name Bovard on the letter, and there were three Bovards to choose from. Hugh, Althea, Bix. Supposing Bix had been telling the truth—for once in her tricky young life— about that interview between her mother and Mrs. Henshaw. Supposing she had some real grounds for fearing her mother, and supposing not she, but Hugh, had been the liar, skillfully switching the spotlight to himself. He would do that, wouldn't he, if he thought Althea needed shielding? Doc didn't doubt it for a minute. Hugh would shield Althea no matter what she had done, and no matter who got thrown to the wolves in the process. Bix, along with the rest of the world. He was an indulgent father—

possibly even an understanding one—but there was not the slightest question as to who came first with him. All Althea had to do was lift her eyebrow. Again, in his mind's eye, Doc saw that remote, ravaged face of Althea's. A violent woman, he thought suddenly; it takes violence to suffer like that. Supposing, supposing. . . .

But that left Rachel and Hartley, and—no use dodging it—you couldn't leave them out. They were in it, both of them, swiping the letter from each other. Rachel scared. Hartley wary.

It also left Francie and his confession and his clear-conscience, right-mind death.

The silence was getting pretty nerve-wracking. Even Myra, with her plump face set in a parody of a Ladies-Aid smile, couldn't seem to dredge up any conversation. There was only one thing to talk about, and nobody dared. Well, damn it, thought Doc, I dare. This had gone on long enough.

"You know," he said, "Francie did just one thing wrong. He made just one little mistake."

"Yeah," said Hartley. "All he did was murder her. Naughty, naughty."

"I don't mean that. I mean from his point of view. It was a perfect crime, almost. If he'd let well enough alone, nobody would ever have known it was a crime at all. But that's where he made his mistake. He had to go down and hit her over the head with the candlestick to make sure, and that did it. That spoiled his perfect crime."

The silence showed signs of setting in again, but Myra headed it off. "They say there's plenty of people do get away with murder. More perfect crimes than you can shake a stick at, they say. Deaths that look natural, and nobody's ever the wiser."

"Who says?" asked Hugh irritably. "If nobody's ever the wiser, how do they know—"

"I read it somewhere," Myra persisted. "According to the authorities."

"I don't believe it," said Hugh.

"I do." Bix spoke up smartly. "Why not? Say somebody's sick anyway, not expected to live. Like—" She warmed up to her subject. "Like Francie. Say somebody'd slipped Francie a shot of arsenic tonight, Doc wouldn't know the difference, he'd call it a natural death. Wouldn't he? Wouldn't you, Doc?"

Doc found it necessary to swallow hard. "I'd know arsenic," he said.

"Well, something else then. Some drug that would just make it look like Francie's heart gave out, the way everybody's been expecting it to. It could happen. I bet it does happen, lots of times. I bet—"

" 'You bet, you bet,' " Hugh mimicked, in a surprising flare of anger. "Why don't you pipe down? You don't know what you're talking about. Drugs, perfect crimes, natural deaths. It's time you learned to act like a human being instead of a spoiled brat." He paused, as if suddenly aware of the ring of startled faces, all turned his way. He made a visible effort to get a grip on himself. "What I mean is, it's irresponsible, this kind of busybody talk. Irresponsible and dangerous. You all know it as well as I do. Do you realize, Bix, what harm you could do Doc if somebody like Mrs. Pierce latched on to what you've just been saying?"

Bix's big eyes flew to Doc's face in consternation. "I didn't—" she began.

"Of course you didn't," said Doc. "Don't be so touchy, Hugh. You've got yourself all worked up about nothing. Nobody slipped Francie anything. And there aren't any Mrs. Pierces present, thank God. I started this little discussion myself, with my crack about Francie's one mistake."

"I wish he hadn't made it," Myra blurted out. She took a sizable sip and blinked.

"You're inebriated," said Doc. "Obviously headed for the gutter. And you, Bix, you should have been in bed long ago. Beat it. Scram."

She surprised him by getting up obediently. "Okay. It's not so skintillating down here, anyway. Night, Daddy. Night, all."

"Don't be mad, Biscuit." Hugh went over and stood beside her, humbly. "I'm sorry I snapped at you. Don't know what's the matter with me tonight. Please don't be mad."

"I'm not," said Bix coolly.

"Give us a kiss, then."

She lifted her face politely enough, but her eyes reflected none of Hugh's tenderness. Kids could be harder-hearted than anybody, thought Doc; they didn't seem to have heard about the quality of mercy, strained or otherwise.

XXXIII

With Bix out of the way, it seemed reasonable to suppose that Hugh would take himself off for home and Althea. Instead, he mixed himself another drink. Not that he relaxed with it. He didn't even sit down; in an uneasy attempt at casualness he propped one elbow on the mantel and stood there, his face set in a strange, tense expression that perhaps felt to him like a sociable smile. Doc began to wonder if he was afraid of Althea, too. Or maybe she was sore at him for not having called her and had told him over the telephone not to come home at all. She was capable of it. Then he noticed how often Hugh's eyes kept straying to Rachel, who still sat with her hand clutched in her pocket. She might as well be waving the letter under everybody's nose.

"Heaven's sakes, Hugh, sit down," said Myra at last. "Enough to make a person climb the walls, the way you're jittering."

"Jittering? Am I? Sorry." But he remained standing, one

hand jingling the coins in his pocket, the other fiddling with his glass. "Thinking about Francie, I guess. Francie and his one mistake."

"What I can't get over," said Myra, "is to think they'd been seeing each other all these years, and not a soul in Coreyville knew it. I wouldn't have thought it was possible. Here I was, living right next door, and I never once suspicioned. Never once."

There, thought Doc in relief, we're getting back to normal, mulling it over the way the whole town will be doing tomorrow. Perfectly natural. He added his bit. "When it comes to that, look at Hartley." (The trouble was that everybody did, literally; Hartley's eyes shifted in alarm.) "What I mean is, there he sat, right there in his father's old office, not noticing a thing, while Francie was busy pushing her down the stairs and beating in her head and sneaking away again."

Hugh gave a sudden, excited laugh. "That's the astonishing thing. The really amazing stroke of luck—that nobody saw him. Broad daylight, and yet nobody saw him come or go." He began to pace back and forth between the mantel and the little marble-topped table against the wall. As if he were on a stage, thought Doc; and indeed Hugh seemed to him a little larger than life, like an actor playing his big scene. His eyes took on a glitter, his gestures grew slower, more controlled.

"Imagine, just imagine," he said, and his audience, willing or not, was with him, seeing what he told them to, carried away—as Hugh seemed to be himself—by the power of his words. "Two o'clock in the afternoon. February. Cold and dismal. Lunchtime over. The housewives through with the dishes, the kids back at school, the business men all back down town at their stores or offices. Only *he's* not where he's supposed to be. He's hurrying along, down the back way, ducking behind the hedge. Maybe he knocks at the back door, maybe he doesn't. Anyway, there she is. Can you see her? Can you see that malicious face of hers, with the mean, turned-down mouth and the sharp nose and those red-dish eyes? Francie was right, you know. 'Evil clear through. An abomination on the face of the earth.' She was cleaning house. A mop in her hand, and that ugly dust-colored apron and her hair done up in the blue kerchief, skinned back and tied in rabbit ears in front, and the smell of furniture polish and scrub-water—"

Somebody—Rachel? Myra?—drew a sharp breath. Then si-lence while Hugh paced to the mantel, back again to the table. Absent-mindedly he slid the little table drawer open and shut, open and shut, before he went on. "Who knows what they said to each other? Who knows what set him off? Maybe it was just one of those oily smiles of hers, or the way her eyes slid around, all over him—She wasn't a big woman, just a little push would do it. A little, quick push. And then down the stairs, and the candle-stick, because by that time he couldn't stop himself, and then up again with it under his coat, and out onto the street—" Hugh's voice had sunk almost to a whisper; a rapt, triumphant smile spread over his face. "And nobody saw him. The sheer, fantastic luck of it. Nobody saw him."

Doc waited. Now, surely, would come the sigh from the audience, the slackening of tension as the curtain falls. Instead, he felt a queer ripple along his nerves. No one sighed. No one sank back in relief. No one moved at all.

It was Myra who broke the silence at last, but what she said made no sense to Doc. "How did you know?" She leaned for-ward a little, her round face dazed. "Her hair tied up in a kerchief, you said. How did you know?"

Out of the corner of his eye Doc caught the violent, quickly-suppressed jerk of Rachel's shoulders. He could not see Hugh's face; he was still fiddling absent-mindedly with the drawer of the little table. Open, shut. Open, shut. Open. . . .

"Ah." Hugh's voice had an aimless sound. "So you've still got your father's revolver, I see. I'd forgotten about it. Old Man

Schwartz made it for him, you know. His masterpiece, and old Schwartz was no slouch as a gunsmith. A beauty. Your father's pride and joy." He took it out of the drawer, stroked it lovingly.

"Don't," whispered Rachel. "Hugh, don't. It's loaded."

"How did you know?" repeated Myra. Again she was leaning forward; Doc had an impression that the question was being drawn out of her against her will. "About the kerchief. Because I'm the only one that saw it. I found her first, and I took it off of her, slipped it in my pocket even before Hartley got there. So how could you know?"

There was a sharpening in Hugh's eyes as they met Myra's, a kind of intense focusing. But he spoke to Rachel, not to Myra. "Loaded? Nonsense. Nobody's fool enough to leave a loaded gun lying around in a drawer like this."

"Papa did. You know he did," chattered Rachel. "You've heard him say it time and again. The only safe gun's a loaded gun, he always said. It's the 'unloaded' ones that do the damage."

"You couldn't know," Myra explained to Hugh, or perhaps to herself. "Unless you ——"

"I'm sure you're mistaken, Rachel," Hugh slipped the revolver back into the drawer, without, however, closing it. His voice was still pleasant and soft. "And now suppose you give me the letter you stole from my desk."

Hugh's movements were quick—the swoop of his hand into the drawer, the three or four strides across the room to Rachel—but Doc's were even quicker. He was aware of an impact, like running into a door, but of nothing more. It was startling to find, seconds later, everything changed around: himself waving the gun at Hugh with one hand, while with the other he clutched the letter that had been in Rachel's pocket. Startling and rather embarrassing: what did he do next? He couldn't think of a thing to say.

"Doc, it *is* loaded," Rachel warned him earnestly. She was

standing up now, rubbing her wrist, where a red welt showed. "Really and truly it is. Be careful, Doc, because it really and truly—"

"Shut up," said Hartley. "Stop saying the same thing over and over. The point is, the important point is—" But his eyes swung back to Hugh, and his voice trailed away.

Hugh stood still, in the middle of the room. He was breathing heavily, and his face and neck were flushed a dusky red. "I don't care about anything else," he said. "Only the letter. Althea mustn't see it."

"Oh, Hugh, why?" Rachel burst out imploringly. "Why—"

"You read it, didn't you?" A joyless smile flitted across Hugh's face. "Okay. That's why."

"What's why?" Doc had found something to say at last. "What the hell is this letter?"

"Read it," said Hugh wearily. "Give Hartley the gun. He can keep me covered. Read it, and you'll know too." He stumbled backward a few steps, found the easy chair and sank into it, with his hands dangling lifelessly down over the chair arms. Anything but a dangerous looking character, thought Doc as he handed the revolver to Hartley.

The outside envelope, the one with the cancelled stamp, was addressed to Mr. Hugh Bovard, c/o The Coreyville Tribune. The inside envelope read Mrs. Althea Bovard, and the message itself, written in a remarkably tidy, prim-looking hand, was brief but annihilating. "Ask your husband what he knows about how Ronnie died. Dr. Buckmaster knew it too, and why not? It was their doing. Very truly yours, Rose Anthony Henshaw." Doc stared at it for a long, long time. A kaleidoscope pattern of faces and voices skittered across his mind's eye. Rachel's: "You mean blackmail? Papa? It's funny, I never thought of that before." Althea's: "Ronnie. My son, my little boy." Francie's: "Give me a good write-up in the paper. See that I get the credit, boy." And

Hugh's: "Two good friends I've had in my life. Nobody ever had better. Doc Buckmaster, and Francis Henshaw."

Dimly, he heard Myra begin a groping sentence. "Then Francie didn't—" She paused, and there came other sounds—a lightning-swift scuffling, a thud, a smothered cry from Rachel. Doc was too late this time. Too late by a full minute. By the time he got into action Hartley was picking himself up and Hugh was back in his chair. Again he was breathing a little heavily. And again the gun had changed hands.

"That's right, Myra," he said amiably. "Francie didn't. I did."

He's a murderer, Doc told himself. A murderer, and armed, and desperate for this letter. But it didn't seem like that. It still just seemed like Hugh Bovard (a good guy, Hugh, maybe a little quick-tempered, but a prince of a fellow) sitting there calmly, patting the gun that had belonged to his old friend.

"It was my idea," he was telling Rachel and Hartley. "Your father wouldn't listen to me at first. But he knew what Ronnie was doing to Althea and me. He knew she'd never consent to putting him in an institution. And Ronnie was one of the first to get the flu, there was a good chance he wasn't going to pull through anyway. Several people did die of it, that winter. Bix had just been born, and it seemed to me like the one chance, for Althea and me. . . ." He searched their faces anxiously, trying to explain. "It got so I couldn't think of anything else. I begged your father. I kept at him and at him, and after a while it began to seem right to him, too. The way it did to me. So right. So merciful and right. It still does. Only—"

Only, thought Doc, what seemed so right had gone so wrong. Althea must have been beyond help, even then. And somehow— a drink too many, probably, an unguarded word or two—somehow Mrs. Henshaw had found it out.

"She went to work on your father first," said Hugh. "Then

when he died it was my turn. I guess I—misled you a little, Doc, about the time she came to see Althea, three years ago."

"Just a little," said Doc.

"I had to." Again the effort to explain, the somehow pathetic wish to be understood. "I had to keep Althea out of it. That was where Mrs. Henshaw had me, of course. She'd send me the letters, whenever she figured another payment was due. Just to remind me. . . . About that night, three years ago. I didn't really know how much Bix heard. Enough to scare the bejesus out of her, I guess."

He looked inquiringly toward Hartley, who gulped a little, and, after a moment, spoke. "She wasn't sure. But you yelled at her, and *you* were scared of Mrs. Henshaw. That's what really got her. She couldn't imagine anything terrible enough to scare you. Then, the other night when you grabbed her in the alley—"

"But she thinks it was Francie! She couldn't possibly have seen me, she doesn't know it was me!"

"She—smelled you." Hartley brought it out miserably, and Hugh looked so stricken that for a moment Doc considered making another rush for the gun. The impulse died a-borning. He barely moved, and Hugh was once more alert and unobtrusively threatening. "You've got a special smell, she says," Hartley went on. "So then she was really scared."

But still loyal, thought Doc, after her own fashion. Her own confused, stubborn, forlorn fashion. The candlestick rubbed against her jacket, for instance, in case of tell-tale fingerprints. The almost unintelligible words whispered to him in the alley: "I—fell—." And the final, inspired switching of the spotlight of her fear from Hugh to Althea.

"We got our signals all mixed, Francie and I," said Hugh. "I guess we weren't very expert. I never dreamed he'd keep the candlestick. I went straight to his place that afternoon—afterwards. He said he'd get rid of it for me. He must have had some notion about this phoney confession of his, even that far back. We figured the rock through the window would clear Hartley. Only Francie must have collapsed in the alley on his way home—"

"My land," put in Myra, "think of that poor old man laying there all that time."

"I thought he was safely home in bed, of course." Hugh sighed. "Otherwise I never would have grabbed Bix. By that time I was good and worried about the candlestick and wasn't making much sense. I followed the three of you, after I heard Bix creeping down the back stairs, so I knew you'd found it. But I thought, they can't pin this on Francie because he's home in bed, and they won't suspect me, because I'm her father. . . . I didn't choke her, you know. All I did was throw my muffler over her eyes and give her a little shove."

"I know," said Doc. "She made that up, when we did pin it on Francie, after all."

"And Francie," ventured Myra. "He made it up, didn't he, about going to see Mrs. Henshaw all these years?"

Hugh smiled. "Of course. He'd never have gotten past you and the rest of Coreyville that many times. I was lucky to get away with it once. It's funny—" He shook his head in a bewildered way. "I can't remember, now, what made me push her. I didn't plan it. I knew I was going to have to pay her, the way I always had. It wasn't any different from the other times. But then, all at once—It's just kind of a red blur."

There was a silence before he spoke again.

"That brings us right back to the letter." He looked deathly tired. "Doesn't it?"

The letter. And the gun. "We all know now," said Doc. "You can't—dispose of all four of us."

"I wouldn't want to," said Hugh gently. "No, I wouldn't want to do that. On the other hand, I am not going to have Althea see the letter." His eyes made what seemed like a pilgrimage, a brief, hungry search of each of their faces. Myra's. Rachel's. Doc's. They fastened on Hartley's. "That's assuming, of course, that Rachel's right and the gun is loaded. Really and truly loaded. I still have my doubts. We could check, I suppose, but that seems pretty tame. I'm a betting man, myself." A ghost of the old humorous quirk passed across his face; with a playful air he aimed the gun at his own temple. "Any takers?"

He paid no attention to Rachel's half-choked protest, or the gesture Myra made, stirring around like a flustered hen. His offer, his challenge, whatever it was, was for Hartley alone; the others no longer counted. He had chosen Hartley. The one that Bix loved.

The boy stood with his head slightly lifted, as if he were listening. The deadpan look was still there; no telling what went on behind the high forehead and hazel eyes that were so like Rachel's. He swallowed once or twice, as if his throat were dry.

"You can depend on me." Hugh's voice was low but very clear. "Can I depend on you?"

Suddenly, under the pressure of that intense gaze of Hugh's, Hartley's face came alive, burst into a very blaze of affirmation and decision. "Yes. Yes. I'll bet you—" In a flash of movement that was like lightning he snatched the letter from Doc's hand and thrust it into the fire.

Smiling faintly, Hugh pressed the trigger.

It seemed to Doc that the report rocked the library, filled the whole world with a thunder of sound that, instead of fading, simply changed into other sounds. Queenie's voice, raised in frenzied barking. The drum of bare feet on the stairs, and Bix's screams.

"Daddy! Daddy!"

She stopped dead in the doorway, gawky and trembling. In the abrupt stillness the four of them looked away from her and at each other. It was like a pact. Their eyes met in unanimous, steadfast agreement.

Myra was their spokesman. And what she said held, for all of them, a strange quality of echo-in-reverse: here was what they would be saying from now on, as long as anybody asked.

"Bix honey," said Myra, as she put out her arms and drew the shocked child-face to her shoulder, "Bix honey, there's been an accident. Your Daddy was fooling with Doc Buckmaster's gun. . . ."